M000045763

CALIFORNIA SCREAMIN'

CALIFORNIA
SCREAMIN'

EDITED BY

DANIELLE KAHEAKU

California Screamin' Copyright © 2017 Danielle Kaheaku

Included stories copyright © 2017 by the individual authors

All rights reserved.

Published by Barking Deer Press.

No part of this book may be reproduced, scanned, or distributed in any printed or electronic form without permission. Please support the authors and do not take part in the piracy of copyrighted materials.

This is a work of fiction. All characters, names, and events in this book are fictitious. Any resemblance to persons living or dead is purely coincidental.

ISBN 978-0-9994495-0-9

Edited by Danielle Kaheaku
Cover Art by Ben Baldwin
Cover layout by Danielle Kaheaku
Interior Design by beapurplepenguin.com

www.barkingdeerpress.com

C✹NTENTS

CONTENTS CONT.

BETWEEN THE DREAMS AND SCREAMS

LORI R. LOPEZ

Some of Lori's books include The Dark Mister Snark, The Strange Tail of Oddzilla, Poetic Reflections: The Queen of Hats, Odds and Ends: A Dark Collection, and Chocolate-Covered Eyes. Lori's work has appeared on Hellnotes, Servante of Darkness, and Halloween Forevermore; in The Horror Zine, Weirdbook, The Sirens Call, Bewildering Stories, as well as numerous anthologies such as the H.W.A. Poetry Showcase, Terror Train, and Journals of Horror: Found Fiction.

California, they say, attracts all kinds. Including
a lot of weirdos. I guess that's why I'm here.
Somewhere between the dreams and the screams
I belong. In this gaudy, glorious, glittering
rain-gutter along an ocean; as far west as the road
will take you, they cluster — like twigs and leaves
and tumbled weeds. Odd riffraff. Cast offs or outs.
Lost marbles; found socks that fail to match.
Wealth-seekers, immigrants, innovators, actors and
presidents. A mouse or two. Stray cats and dogs.

Undiscovered talent. The musically-inclined or challenged.
Speculative writers, bizarre poets, idiosyncratic artists,
auteurs and epicureans of diet. Roamers, beachcombers,
escaped coconuts, the hopeful and forlorn . . .
Vanguards of Tomorrow who refuse to settle for less.
Gathering like crows.

Rickety edges of palisades, cliff-lines chewed by
nervous tides, flayed raw or chiseled by Trade Winds,
harbor the secrets behind Eternal Summer:
the glitter and gleam, the sunshiny allure of a golden state
that everyone seeks yet none can own. Free,
independent of spirit. Protected by shark-infested water,
Grizzly Bears, tall dark woods, sawtooth ranges,
myriad hills, lethal valleys, murderous flowering desert.
A contrast of glamor and sandy bare feet. Rich with potential,
ripe for opportunity, majestic and horrific of past.
No barrier could lock away its Hollywood scenery, its magic
and promise. The split-personality up-and-down qualms;
the unconformist, eclectic, nonconventional qualities
bundled in a single land of endless possibility. California,
I've heard, is full of crackpots. I guess I'm one. But I say . . .
you'd have to be crazy *not* to go there. At least to visit.
Strait-jackets optional.

AN INTRODUCTION

JONATHAN MABERRY

Jonathan Maberry is a New York Times bestselling author, 5-time Bram Stoker Award-winner, and comic book writer. He writes in multiple genres including suspense, thriller, horror, science fiction, fantasy, and action; and he writes for adults, teens and middle grade. His works include the Joe Ledger thrillers, Glimpse, the Rot & Ruin series, the Dead of Night series, The Wolfman, X-Files Origins: Devil's Advocate, Mars One, and many others. Several of his works are in development for film and TV. He is the editor of high-profile anthologies including The X-Files, V-Wars, Aliens: Bug Hunt, Out of Tune, Kingdoms Fall, Baker Street Irregulars, Nights of the Living Dead, and others. He lives in Del Mar, California. Find him online at www.jonathanmaberry.com

WHEN I WAS TEN, my brother handed me an old comic and said, "Here. You'll probably like this. You're weird."

Fair enough.

It was the summer of 1968 and the comic was seventeen years old. But it looked almost new. It had lingered at the bottom of a stack of superhero comics he collected.

"What's it about?" I asked.

He shrugged. "Horror stuff."

And he made a face when he said it. He wasn't into horror. He didn't even like horror movies.

I took the comic.

He was right. I probably would like it. I was, in fact, weird.

I think I fell in love with that book because of the cover. Or, at least, that's where the infatuation ignited.

It was a great cover.

Close-up of a man in a trench coat staring at his hands, which have sprouted wiry animal hair and long nails. He's not yet aware that his face has also changed and he cries out: "Good lord...what's happening to my hands? They're changing! They look...like an animal's!"

Yeah, that was love at first sight.

It was my first taste of horror.

Oh, sure, there had been movies on TV, but any tension they might have had was constantly interrupted by commercials. Late night commercials, too. Hair Club for Men. Bail bondsmen. Cheap used cars. Like that. Perhaps enlightening as to the human condition, or as a sad commentary on the low-income inner city where I lived, but they did nothing to allow me to suspend disbelief and feel any real horror.

That comic, though...yeah, that was different. I spent time alone in my room, late at night, reading those stories. Each tale was short, ugly, horrific, disturbing, disgusting, and thoroughly wonderful.

Roll forward to October of that same year. A friend of mine, a kid name Jamie, talked me into sneaking into the Midway Theater to see a horror flick. We were ten, remember, and no way should we have gone to see this particular flick. It was a black and white shocker called *Night of the Living Dead*. There's a chance you've heard of it. Jamie bailed out halfway through and had emotional issues well into his thirties. Me? I stayed to see it twice. And snuck in every day for the rest of the week. Same planet, different worlds.

I guess it was then that I realized that my world was horror. It had shadows and screams, it had shudders and icy winds. It was scary, and unnerving and wonderful.

Two years later, at the start of seventh grade I had the incredible good fortune to meet, and be mentored by, Ray Bradbury and Richard Matheson. Yeah. Take that in for a minute. Poor kid from a dead-end neighborhood in Philadelphia meeting two giants like that. Over the course of the next three years, every time they were in New York, my middle school librarian took me to see them at these little get-togethers of writers.

By then I knew I wanted to be a writer, too. Kind of always had wanted that, but meeting them and hearing their stories about writing cemented that dream in place.

They not only talked about their books and the writing life at their rarified altitude—travel, movies, TV, fame— but they mostly talked about writing. The process. The birth and cultivation of ideas. The weird ways in which a writer's mind takes an ordinary thing and plays the 'what if' game. Changing it, turning it this way and that, looking at it in all the wrong ways. Seeing more than its obvious surface.

They talked about horror in its many forms. They introduced me to Shirley Jackson and pretty much demanded that I read *The Haunting of Hill House*. And to have opinions about it the next time I saw them. They gave me shopping bags full of paperbacks to read. For Christmas one year, Matheson gave me a signed 1954 first edition of *I Am Legend* and Bradbury gave me a signed first edition of *Something Wicked This Way Comes*. Technically, the former is a cross-genre blend of post-apocalyptic thriller, dystopian social commentary, dark satire, and pandemic science fiction, but it was told as a horror story. And the latter was a young adult coming of age dark fantasy that was also told as a horror story.

Both writers encouraged me to read more horror. And to read outside of my comfort zone. Not just other genres—mystery, science fiction, high fantasy, and so on—but to explore the many subgenre of horrors. Ghost stories, monster tales, blood-drenched tales of gore, subtle psychology tales, and on and on. And, they said, it was important to read old and new stories, and equally important to read stories by the biggest and most well-known authors as well as those by writers whose names I'd never heard of before.

That last bit surprised me. You see, even at twelve I was a typical literary snob. I assumed that only the stories by famous writers would be 'good' and that stories by writers I'd never heard of would necessarily be less good. Ah, assumptions.

Saying that earned me a lecture. Well, several lectures, or rather one lecture in installments. During one of those lectures Harlan Ellison chimed in. He, as you may have heard, is not well known for his tact. He told me that I had to get my head out of my ass. Words to that effect. Or maybe those exact words. He was yelling at the time and I was trying to crawl under the sofa.

The upshot was that I began to read deeply into the many genres that comprise horror. I found most of the newer voices in anthologies. Sure, anthos are often anchored by bigger names. That's a marketing thing and it's a sensible marketing thing. However almost every single anthology I read had stories by people I had never heard of.

But in a lot of cases they were people I *would* hear about.

As I grew into adulthood and kept reading, I'd discovered deliciously unnerving tales by 'new' writers. You'll likely recognize some of those names because what was new then has become classic now. Stories by newcomers like Graham Masterton, Gary Braunbeck, Robert McCammon, F. Paul Wilson, Joe R. Lansdale, Kathryn Ptacek, Chet Williamson,

Elizbeth Massie, Poppy Z. Brite, Karl Edward Wagner, Mary Gaitskill, Nancy Holder, Charles L. Grant, Nancy Kilpatrick, Jack Ketchum and…

Well, you get the idea.

Everyone starts somewhere.

Everyone has a first short story. Or an early story that catches attention.

Everyone.

Which brings me to this anthology.

I don't live in a Philly ghetto anymore. Now I live in a Del Mar condo and I'm an occasional NY Times bestseller and I have a shelf full of Bram Stoker Awards. I've somehow become—god help me—a 'seasoned pro'.

But I remember when I was starting out.

Hell, I remember showing Matheson and Bradbury a three-page short story I'd written in pencil on loose-leaf paper back in 1971. The story sucked, I have no doubt. It was full of too many adverbs and not enough of the right punctuation. What mattered, though, is that both of those literary giants stopped to read it. To consider it. To accept it as a real story. And to give me advice on how to revise it.

They, you see, took me seriously as a writer, and as a result I took my first real step toward the confidence and optimism that has carried me to where I am now. And which will carry me farther still along this road.

The stories in this book represent, for some of the contributors, their first published works. They are, without doubt or reservation, worlds better than my first story. I'm not talking about the three-page scribbled tale. There are stories here better than my first *published* story.

Yeah. How cool is that?

There are also stories here by more *seasoned* writers (it's so great to use that word on someone else!). Those stories kick ass, too.

Anthologies like this still serve the purpose Matheson and Bradbury assured me they would. There are names I know, which means I had built-in high expectations. There are names I don't *yet* know, which means I have a ticket to go for a ride in the strange and exotic landscapes of their inner lands.

Again... how cool is that?

The volume you hold in your hands contains terrific stories. And lots of monsters. Lots of shadows.

Lots of horror.

Sure, I was a weird kid. Still pretty weird, truth to tell. I write a lot of weird novels, short stories and comics.

My readers are weird, because—like me—they dig that kind of thing.

You're holding this book.

You're probably a little weird, too.

Nice. So are these writers. Weird, and delightfully, deliciously so.

You're among friends.

Enjoy!

THE DARK WATCHERS

E.S. MAGILL

E.S. Magill is the editor of The Haunted Mansion Project Year One, co-editor of Deep Cuts, the author of a number of short stories, and a member of the Horror Writers Association. In addition to writing, she is a middle school English teacher with an M.A. in English. Her husband Greg supports her obsession with Halloween and horror.

No one knew who the watchers were, nor where they lived, but it was better to ignore them and never to show interest in them. They did not bother one who stayed on the trail and minded his own business.

-John Steinbeck

THE SPANISH CALLED THEM *Los Vigilantes Oscuros*. The Chumash people used the term *nunasis* to include all the malevolent beings dwelling in the shadows of the forest. Up until two days ago Kimball didn't know either term.

When he stumbled out of the forest and onto Pacific Coast Highway 1 in the middle of the night, he was screaming the same two words over and over until he collapsed.

A passerby found him curled up in the breakdown of the two-lane road and despite limited reception managed to get through to 911. The sheriff car arrived first, followed soon after by an ambulance. When the deputy and two paramedics approached him, Kimball jumped to his feet, screaming for them not to touch him. He lurched about in the breakdown lane, and the emergency personnel tried to keep him from stumbling into oncoming traffic. The deputy finally coaxed him into sitting down on the bumper of the ambulance. One of the paramedics, Padilla, got close enough to see the man's eyes were all black pupil. She promised that if he lay down on the gurney they wouldn't touch him. The confusion on Kimball's face cleared for an instant, and he climbed onto the gurney. The paramedics loaded it into the ambulance, and Padilla settled in next to him. Out of habit she reached for his wrist.

Kimball flinched. "Don't touch me."

"Okay, I won't. You're safe here." Padilla spoke calmly, trying to put him at ease. She picked up a clipboard and pen. "Can you tell me your name?"

He blinked several times. Padilla began to write *unknown*.

"Harris Kimball."

Padilla glanced up, then smiled in encouragement. "Great."

The deputy poked his head in. "Do you need assistance in transporting?"

"No, he seems coherent," Padilla said. "Told me his name was Harris Kimball. So, we're good. Let me know what you find out. Thanks."

The deputy shut the ambulance doors. Padilla's partner, Ruiz, picked up his radio to call the base hospital.

Kimball closed his eyes and began mumbling. His words slurred one into the other, creating a soup of nonsense. Padilla leaned in. Kimball turned his head, looked Padilla in the eyes, and said two words.

She jerked back.

"You okay?" Ruiz asked.

"Did you just hear what he said?" Padilla asked.

"No, I was calling this in."

"So, you know I'm part Chumash," Padilla said.

Ruiz sat back in the seat, giving her his attention. "Yeah, we talked about it."

"Well, when I was a kid, the elders told stories about the *nunasis*, the monsters who haunt the Santa Lucia Mountain Range," she said. "And about something else."

Ruiz smirked. "Is that what he's doing, telling you a ghost story?"

"This man said *Dark Watchers*."

"You're freaking kidding me." Ruiz put the radio down and looked at the man on the gurney.

"He keeps repeating *Dark Watchers*." The words felt like dry leaves in her mouth.

Kimball suddenly sat up, making both medics jump. He looked past them with glazed eyes.

"Dark Watchers," Kimball said loudly. "I saw them."

"Hey, lie back down." Padilla placed her hands on his shoulders.

Kimball recoiled. "Don't touch me. Don't touch me. Don't touch me."

Both paramedics backed off.

"Sure, no problem," Padilla reassured him. "Can you tell us what happened out there?"

"They knew the Watchers were there," Kimball said. "You think I'm crazy."

"No, we're just here to help."

Ruiz looked at Padilla "He said *us*."

"Who's us?" Padilla asked. "There were others with you? What happened to them?"

"Dead."

"Did you kill them?" Ruiz asked.

"No." Kimball shook his head. "*They* did."

Ruiz made eye contact with Padilla. She nodded, and he exited the ambulance. "The Dark Watchers?"

"They killed them," Kimball barked.

"Okay. Let's lie back down," she said.

"You don't believe me. Look."

Kimball pushed up his shirt sleeves. Black splotches creeped up Kimball's forearms.

The ambulance doors opened, Ruiz stood outside with the deputy.

"What the hell is that?" he asked.

Padilla leaned in to take a closer look. "They're not bruises or burns."

"A rash?" Ruiz said.

"Looks like handprints to me," the deputy said.

Kimball pulled off his shirt, exposing his chest and back. Black handprints stood out against his pale skin.

"Holy shit," the deputy said.

Padilla extended her fingers. She hesitated, then lightly touched the stained skin. Her fingers sank into the blackness.

"They touched me," Kimball whimpered. "They touched me."

Padilla looked at the inky substance on her fingertips and screamed.

* * *

"There's the exit for State Route 1," Jones said. She turned off the phone and stowed it in her Black Diamond jacket pocket.

"Done navigating?" Kimball had smirked when the woman first took out the phone, a rooky move. Getting a signal along the coast was next to impossible. When she produced a waterproof map, Kimball stopped smirking.

Kimball stole a look in the rearview mirror at the two people in the backseat, a middle-aged man and woman. The man was the Smith he had spoken with on the phone, the woman beside him Miller. The younger woman beside him riding shotgun went by Jones. When he had met up with them at the airport, the first thing he noticed was that none of the three wore jeans and their boots showed wear. Signs they were legitimate mountaineers. Their names, on the other hand, made him nervous. Smith, Jones, and Miller— he would be damned if those were real. The idea that they might be journalists and this some unseemly exposé worried him. He knew he would have to watch himself.

They drove southward along Pacific Coast Highway, passing through urban centers with the same big-box stores and chain restaurants cloned across the country's strip malls. Kimball wrinkled his nose as if smelling something bad. But he was surprised at how quickly the Best Buys and Golden Arches dropped away as the Coast Highway opened up to mountains, valleys, and that famous line of Pacific Coast. Kimball gave California credit for doing the impossible. Even though it was the most populous state, activism and legislation protected a whole swath of coast between Monterey and Morro Bay. There wasn't a chain store or fast food restaurant for over one hundred miles. No development at all. Homes and businesses, the few there were, remained discreet, camouflaged by nature.

His current clients hadn't commented on the beauty of the California coast even once. Usually, they oohed and awed over every mountain peak and squirrel crossing the road. Beside him, Jones had propped her head against the window and closed her eyes. Smith and Miller in the backseat were reading some old books. Kimball ticked off another point in the suspicious column he was building in his mind.

Their silence was fine by Kimball. Left alone with his thoughts was just the way he liked things. He had plenty to think about. Two weeks earlier, he had been curled up on his living room couch trying to feel as little as possible. A bottle of whiskey and piles of clipped articles from mangled magazines and newspapers littered his coffee table. He had read and reread the articles until they resembled moths that had beaten themselves against light bulbs. Not a single article offered consolation, however, let alone redemption for the accident.

Over the last several years, he'd gotten more and more clients who believed because they recycled and drove a Prius they were nature experts. They treated mountain excursions like they were at luxury resorts, refusing to believe nature came with teeth and claws and no conscience. On that last trip, what should have been his last trip, his clients disobeyed almost every order he gave. They were slow to put up the tents, wanting to pass a flask around instead, and ended up soaked in a sudden thunderstorm. The eldest of them developed pneumonia and had to be airlifted out. Kimball told them not to feed the animals or trample vegetation, which they proceeded to do anyway. He especially warned them not to wander away from camp and to stay in the company of his experienced guides. They took off on their own. Red flashed in Kimball's mind. Those people had been his responsibility, even if they were dumbshits. The media lynched him, and Kimball let them. He packed away his equipment, took down his website, and hid from the world.

But here he was, doing it one more time. Smith's team said they wanted him, no one but him. They wanted to hike the Santa Lucia Range in California. Kimball said no, he didn't do California. Even though its coast and even the Sierras were beautiful, Kimball found California too touristy. Millions of people visited places like Yosemite and Big Sur making them no better than Bourbon Street or Times Square. For Kimball, nature was a personal experience, best done on an intimate level. Smith put a number to his offer. Dollar signs wrestled with his guilt. This could be his comeback, his redemption.

But if it happened again—Kimball let the two sides struggle. In the end, guilt took the beating, and Kimball said yes.

All those bodies though...

Don't start, Kimball. Just don't start with that. Put it aside. Be here right now.

He turned his attention to the ocean on his right. It appeared as a flat mass clear to the horizon. To his left mountains stood guard at the lip of the continent. The mountains were all deception, though, because they and a large chunk of Southern California were not part of the continental United States. Here the Pacific Plate and the North American Plate smashed together. The Pacific Plate's primary mass lay submerged beneath dark waters, a world separate from man. Those underwater mountains had pushed themselves out of their watery depths thousands of years earlier and transformed this coast, the same way the first aquatic creatures had done. The result was the Santa Lucia Mountain Range.

Then modern man came along and hewed a highway into those mountains, and in some spots, it was nothing more than a ledge on the rim of the world. PCH meandered from the coast, inland, back to the coast. It bisected valleys—green pastures stretching from the east up to the tree line and to the west where more pasture land lined the coast. Cows grazed contentedly on those cliff-hugging pastures. It was virginal land that made developers weep with envy—especially to think only dull-witted ungulates had access to all that expensive real estate.

"Do you think any cows have ever gone over the edge?" Smith asked.

The two women chuckled. The fucked up comment startled Kimball from his reverie. He said nothing, just made another tick on his mental chart.

Traffic turned bumper to bumper at the famed Bixby Bridge. Vehicles lined both sides of the road. Sightseers left their cars to snap pictures of the bridge, the mountains, and the waves crashing at the base of the cliffs. Kimball understood the emotions a place like this evoked, but all the damned people scampering across the road to pose at cliff's edge just cheapened the experience. Kimball accelerated once he cleared the bridge.

"Watch out."

Kimball braked hard, snapping everyone forward like rubber bands.

A man ran out in front of their SUV. He didn't even acknowledge the squeal of tires or the bumper inches from his thigh. He just kept heading for the other side of the road, his phone held out in front of him.

"Goddamn moron," Kimball muttered. He continued driving.

"It's going to rain," Miller said. "Then all these people will be gone."

"Yeah, doesn't help us now," Kimball grumbled. "So, December's supposed to be a good month to visit? Still looks like too many people to me."

"Rain keeps people away. And it's too cold for most campers. So we'll basically have the place to ourselves."

Kimball grunted. "Don't know about you guys but I'm hungry. We're some ten miles from the Big Sur River Inn. That okay with you, guys?"

His passengers agreed and went back to sleeping and reading. Kimball turned his thoughts to the road and lunch.

While the rest of the country lay in snow, December meant growth for most of California. At first, he thought the green cast to the ground was grass, but when he looked closer, he saw the mass of ferns spreading from the roadside up the sides of hills. The coast road curved inland. He followed it until the inn's gravel lot appeared on his right. Because of the light rain, finding a parking spot was easy. His clients collected their items and followed Kimball. The enclave consisted of the squat red building of the restaurant, the inn rooms beside it, a small store, and tucked behind trees off to one side a multistory building of artists' studios and even a tavern.

"Must disappoint tourists who think they can drive into Big Sur and find some cheap fast food for the kids," Kimball said.

Smith grunted. "Development density is restricted to one unit per acre in tourist areas."

"Most of the coastal region is owned by the government or private agencies that don't allow any development," Jones added.

Miller continued the Wikipedia commentary, "The Big Sur Local Coastal Program which preserves the region as open space, a small community, and ranching was approved in 1981. It's extremely restrictive."

Kimball's lips pursed and his eyebrows drew together. For people who barely looked out their windows, they were damn knowledgeable about government regulations. Kimball eliminated journalists from his suspicions but felt it best to keep his poker face on.

"Here we are folks." He held the restaurant door open. He forced a smile as they filed past him. Something wasn't right with his three charges.

After a lunch of burgers and steaks, they walked down to the river. A couple of Adirondack chairs had been plunked down in shallow water and were occupied by a family of three. The husband had his arms stretched out, trying to take a group selfie. Kimball offered to take the photo for them. Miller and Jones wandered downstream. Kimball took the photo and then handed the camera back. Out of the corner of his eye, he saw Miller take something from her pocket, crumple it, and toss it into the river.

Kimball frowned. Had she just purposely littered? Kimball looked past them at the current where a ball of white floated downstream. Maybe she accidentally dropped it. The two women turned and came back his way. Kimball averted his eyes, focusing on the pine trees on the opposite shore. He decided to give them the benefit of the doubt and say nothing.

"We should get going," Jones said.

Kimball followed them up the path. Smith appeared, folding a pocket knife.

"We're going," Jones said to Smith.

The three walked ahead. Kimball looked back. A tree sported two long gouges and something that resembled the letter z.

Kimball cleared his throat. "Hey, Smith."

The women kept going. Smith turned to look at Kimball.

"What's up with the knife?" Kimball asked.

"Nothing. Just a knife. Why do you ask?" Smith looked him in the eyes.

Kimball got the feeling he was being challenged. When he didn't answer, Smith went on to the car.

Kimball stared after the man. He didn't know if there was something wrong with Smith or him. Was he being overly sensitive? Maybe the accident had caused him to swing too much to one side. He thought of his initial conversation with Smith. The man had reassured Kimball that he could do this trip—even though the newspapers had said those horrible things about him. He remembered being holed up in his apartment for a month.

Stop punishing yourself. It had been an accident.

Kimball reached the car and got behind the wheel. They continued southward. Their silence appeared to be a reprimand, and he felt embarrassed.

"Hey, any of you want to stop at the bakery or the Henry Miller Library?" Kimball asked, trying to sound like a congenial tour guide. He glanced in the rearview mirror when no one answered him. "Okay, then we'll just check in at the ranger station."

The map said Big Sur, but now he understood the misconception people had thinking Big Sur a town when it was, in fact, more of a geographic region. A concentration of buildings along a several mile stretch of PCH delineated what people called Big Sur village: old school motor lodges, a general store, a post office, a couple of restaurants, a public library, and a smattering of other independent businesses. Concentration was a misnomer since most of the buildings sat isolated, nestled in groves of trees over a short stretch of road. The parking lot of the Big Sur Station contained few cars.

Before Kimball could ask them if they wanted to accompany him, the three scurried off. Most of his clients wanted to tag along, meet the rangers, or just buy souvenirs in the gift shop. Kimball continued on alone. Inside, a few tourists were taking in the educational nature exhibit. Kimball approached the counter.

"Hi there, checking in." He removed the passes from an envelope.

"Kimball, right?" the ranger asked. "We've been expecting you." She picked up a pass and examined it. "You know this area you're going to has been closed to hikers since the last fires. So, you must have some pretty important people with you to get these. When the trails are open, you don't even need a pass."

"Yeah, I've got some clients who got their hearts set on hiking in the middle of the rainy season."

The ranger chuckled. "Hope they enjoy it." He knew what she meant. Soggy boots and cold nights made for miserable conditions.

"Okay, Mr. Kimball, I don't need to give you the 'leave no trace' speech."

"Only footprints."

The ranger tapped the counter with both hands. "Well, you're all set then. I've got you registered and expect you back here in three days." She handed the envelope back to him. "You be careful out there." Kimball tried not to read too much into the warning. He nodded and headed out.

A quick scan of the gift shop portion of the station revealed that his three clients weren't around. A painting on the wall near the door caught his attention. He felt drawn to its subject: a forest cast in shadows, the sun blocked out by redwoods, green foliage smudging the foreground—and something else. Kimball took a step closer. A black figure stood in the background amongst the tree trunks. From his peripheral vision Kimball spotted another dark figure, but when he looked directly at it, the shape disappeared into the forest.

"Benjamin Brode."

Kimball jumped, startled by the ranger's unexpected appearance beside him. "What are they?" he asked.

Lines creased the woman's face, replacing her earlier cheerful ranger-smile. "You see them then?"

He pointed to the distinct figure. "And here." He gestured to the left side of the painting. "But I can't see this one head on."

"Local legend—the Dark Watchers. Wait." She went off to the gift shop and came back with a book. "The artist teamed up with John Steinbeck's son for this project." Kimball flipped through the book of prints the ranger handed him. Not in every one but in most, he caught glimpses of the dark, shadowy figures. The ranger continued, "Some believe they protect the Santa Lucia Mountains."

Kimball nodded. He was familiar with this type of lore— beings that kept the forests safe from interlopers. From Leshy in the Slavic Regions to the Kodama of Japan, nature always had to protect herself from man. "Have you seen them, the Dark Watchers?"

The ranger shook her head. "Want to but it's never happened to me. How about you? All those trips to remote places over the years."

So, she was familiar with him. He shook his head. "Me neither. Felt things. That sacred presence that embues all of nature." He didn't feel silly saying tree hugger crap to the ranger. "How come they seem to be wearing tall hats and capes?"

"My theory is that the *nunasis*, the local spirits, took on the shape of the Spanish explorers because they perceived the newcomers as a threat. The Spaniards called them *Los Vigilantes Oscuros,* the Dark Watchers. Hikers who come across them up here in the Santa Lucia Range say they look like giants holding staffs. If you aren't harming nature, they leave you alone. Or it could just be the Brocken spectre phenomenon," the ranger said, referring to the optical illusion.

Kimball handed the book back to the ranger. "I don't care if it's ghosts or someone just seeing their shadow. Whatever spooky story it takes to keep people from fucking up nature is fine by me," he said. He stuck his hand out and the ranger shook it. "Thanks for everything." He glanced over his shoulder as he left.

She was still standing there, book in hand, staring after him.

Back at the SUV, Kimball's clients weren't around. He worried about what they might be doing. In the backseat, one of their bags was unzipped and a book peeked out. Kimball looked about. He wanted to have his suspicions allayed. He opened the door and slid the book towards him. The cover was leather carved with symbols. He opened it, and the smell of old combined with something sour wafted up to his nostrils. The sepia-colored pages were thick but not brittle like he expected for an old book. The exterior symbols were repeated inside. As he leafed through the book, a page with slash marks stood out. He thought of the carving on the tree at the inn.

"Who the hell are these people?" The crunch of gravel alerted Kimball. He tried to shove the book into the bag, but it slid out, tumbling to the floor. The three ambled toward the car. Kimball scowled at the wayward book but eased the door shut. "We're all set," Kimball said overly cheerful.

The three climbed into the SUV without speaking to him. As he backed out of the space, Kimball heard the backpack being zipped closed.

* * *

"The turnoff isn't far," Jones said. "A left just after we pass Limekiln State Park."

"Limekiln?" Kimball asked. "Like actual kilns that produce lime?"

Miller snorted. "Not anymore. Late 1800's, the lime was used to make cement for places like San Francisco. Had all the resources right here to do it: limestone and plenty of wood from the trees for the kilns. They even rigged up a cable line right down to the cove at the shore to get the barrels down to the ships quickly. Genius."

"Let me guess," Kimball said, "they decimated the forest in a few short years."

"Yeah, put them out of business. Men lost their jobs," Smith said.

Kimball heard their tone and dropped out of the conversation. He kept an eye out for the left turn he needed to make.

The sign at the entrance to the Nacimiento-Fergusson Road read "Closed to through traffic." Kimball went around it. The road was the only one in the middle of the state connecting the California coast to California inland. The sign at the entrance and its reputation for being perilous kept most people out. But it was also the fastest and easiest way to access the heart of the Santa Lucia Mountains, a geologically young range where wind and water had yet to wear down her jagged peaks into rounded scoops of rock and turn steep canyons into salad bowl valleys. Instead, they would be hiking a rugged landscape Mother Nature had yet to temper.

The road spiraled upward, creating the illusion that it was winding up into the sky. The ocean and sky melded into one expanse of blue. "Wow, look at that view." His reaction was spontaneous. Over the course of his career as a guide nature's beauty still caught him off guard, as if his mind couldn't retain images of such magnificence and had to be constantly reminded. Or maybe that was nature's trick. If people became blasé about mountains and oceans and sunrises, then nature was doomed to mankind's number one disease—progress.

The road narrowed so only one car could take the corkscrew curves at a time. Kimball was glad the rain had stopped but he drove cautiously anyway around the bends on the lookout for oncoming cars. As they climbed in elevation coastal scrub gave way to fir trees. The inclement weather produced clouds floating amongst the trees, the effect spectral, a ghost mist floating at eye level. Kimball drove around a pile of rocks that had slid down from the mountain. Lights approached. Kimball slowed and moved to the far right, the tires riding the edge of the road and sky. Once safely past the oncoming car, he resumed the middle of the road. It would be the last car he saw on that road. The sun was setting, and an evening fog poured over the hills and into the valleys.

Kimball drove in silence, thinking about the books and the arcane marks. Nothing added up. Now his suspicions pointed toward environmental terrorists who went out into the field to scope out ways to end or curb protections on untouched lands. He had encountered these people many times in his career. But their behaviors and the book just didn't fit with that scenario. Nothing made sense.

Up ahead a figure stood next to a tree just off the road. Kimball knew hiking was being restricted. There were several small campgrounds, both closed because of the last round of fires. As the SUV rushed towards the spot, the figure came into view. This wasn't a hiker. Kimball put his foot down on the gas pedal. He kept his eyes on the road.

"What's going on?" Jones asked.

Kimball glanced at her then. The dark figure appeared at her window. Kimball saw it clearly as if he had stopped and pulled over to the side of the road. He reached for Jones to pull her toward him, away from the window, but the panic disappeared as soon as they passed the spot where the figure stood. He slowed and glanced over his shoulder. He blinked, trying to recall what had just happened. He couldn't remember why he had been so frightened—just shadows amongst the trees playing tricks on him.

"Hey, what happened?" Kimball heard stirrings from the back seat.

"Nothing," he said.

"Did you see something?" Smith asked.

Tell them no. Admit nothing. "Just a deer too close to the edge of the road." He felt Jones staring at him, the other two hovering at his shoulder.

Jones watched him with her dark eyes as if waiting for him to split open, truth spilling out of him like a sticky syrup she would lap up. After a minute she turned her attention back to the map. "The Coast Ridge Road is up ahead."

"Too bad you didn't hit it," Miller said. "Would have made a good dinner."

"Seriously?" Kimball looked at her in the rearview mirror. "Hitting a deer with a car is never a good thing—not for the deer or us."

Miller shrugged and looked away.

They found the dirt road dusty and bumpy, but well-maintained. The plan was to go to its end, park, and hike in. In the growing darkness, the trees seemed to edge closer to the sides of the road. Kimball watched the shadows. His passengers put away their distractions and moved closer to their windows. They craned their necks. They were watching the forest as closely as he was.

Five miles brought them to the trailhead parking. There were no other cars. Kimball set the brake and was about to review the route and lay out the rules, but the three were out of the vehicle and had the hatch open before Kimball could unbuckle his seatbelt. He slammed his door and went around back, fuming. His stance was wide legged, hands on his hips.

"Look, I don't know what's up with you guys. You obviously don't need me to lead you. You seem to have some alternative plan that I don't know about. So, what the hell am I doing here?"

The three looked at him.

"We needed a guide, Kimball," Smith said. "You're our guide. You're one of the world's best. The accident was going to take that away from you. We thought we'd give you your second chance. What more do you need to know?"

Kimball looked from one to the other. He saw three people who hired him to go hiking. In that instant, Kimball felt foolish. Those red flags just seemed to be his own insecurities waving about in his head. "Sorry. Guess I'm still a little touchy."

"No problem," Smith said.

"We should get going," Jones said.

"It'll be dark soon," Miller added.

* * *

They reached a clearing that faced the ocean and backed the forest. Kimball declared this was the spot to set up camp for the night. He assigned jobs. And everyone took to their task without complaint. The tents went up first. Then Jones took out the hatchet to chop up deadfall. When she returned with the wood, Miller built a fire. Smith started supper. Kimball felt better about everything. After they had eaten, they drank coffee and watched the flames— normal camping behavior. The day had been long and tiresome. Kimball closed his eyes.

When he opened them, only Smith sat on the other side of the fire. The women most likely had gone off together to tend to personal matters, and he decided to do likewise. He grabbed a shovel and toilet paper. With everyone doing what they were supposed to be doing and not acting weird, he found his mood improving.

Kimball walked far into the woods. Even though he tried to head in the opposite direction he thought Miller and Jones had gone, he heard the women talking. He changed course. Peculiar sounds stopped him, and he went back. He crept forward, fallen leaves mushed beneath his feet. The voices came from behind an outcropping of boulders. He squeezed through an opening in the rocks. As he worked his way deeper, the boulders arched over him, forming a rock shelter. When he spotted the women, he crouched out of sight.

Jones and Miller stood before a rock wall. Jones held a flashlight as she chanted in a guttural language he didn't recognize. Miller held a can of spray paint, a splash of red on the walls. When he saw the white handprints beneath the red, Kimball erupted. "Hey, goddamn it!"

The flashlight turned in his direction, blinding him.

"You can't do that!" he yelled. "What the fuck? Those are ancient Esselen handprints. Get out of here."

A light rushed toward him. Kimball backpedaled in surprise, stepped on a rock and went down hard. He looked up to see the flashlight beam sweep past him. He waited until the women were well ahead of him before he followed. A gust of air pressed at his back. Kimball stepped to the side, out of the way. He expected to find Smith coming up behind him. There was no one. As he approached the camp, the three stood around the fire. Kimball remained at the edge of darkness and firelight, too angry to get near them.

"I've had enough," he spat. "I gave you the benefit of the doubt. I believed your little story back there at the trailhead. But after what I just saw, what I've seen all day, I want to know what's going on." He clenched his fists and threw his shoulders back when they didn't answer him. "Fine. We're leaving now. I have to report the vandalism to the ranger. Jesus Christ."

"Look around, Mr. Kimball," Jones said quietly. "It's night, too dark to walk miles back to the car. Don't you think?"

"The darkness doesn't bother me," Kimball said.

"So, you would abandon us here? We can't find our way back in the dark," Smith added. "What would people say?"

"He can't seem to take care of his clients," Miller mocked. "Leaves them to die."

Heat shot up from Kimball's gut to his face. These three had come to destroy, and he was their alibi. Kimball was the incompetent, they the innocent clients. He scanned the area, looking from the tree line to the trail, and then his immediate area. The hatchet sat atop a stack of logs, but he was too far from it. There was only one real option. He ran for the trail. Jones cut him off and flipped him over her back. Kimball and the ground collided. Jones came down hard, digging a knee into his solar plexus, holding him in place. Smith and Miller came over. Black pit eyes and mouth slashes looked down at him. The distortion caused by firelight and his perspective made Kimball see demons, not humans.

"You're not working out for us," Smith said. "All you had to do was be our guide, and you can't even fill that role. So, I suggest you crawl into your tent and stay there for the rest of the night."

"The fuck I will." Kimball struggled against Jones, who pressed down harder.

Smith picked up the hatchet, smacking the flat side of the head against his palm. "Get inside your tent." Jones took her weight off Kimball, who rolled to his feet. "I'm a good aim with this. Do you want to try me?"

"Okay, I'm going." His knife and cell phone were back in the tent.

Miller held up the two objects. She went to the cliff's edge and threw both into the darkness. Kimball backed up into his tent. Miller yanked the zippers closed. He heard a snap, a padlock locking the sliders together.

"Just stay there, Mr. Kimball," Smith said.

They snuffed out the fire and darkness descended over the tent. Unable to see, Kimball strained to listen. Over the top of his pounding heat, he heard their footsteps moving away from the camp. When he was sure they were gone, he groped around the dark tent for something to defend himself. His clothes and sleeping bag were missing.

God, how could he be so fucking stupid?

He sat down on the tent floor, the cold seeping up from the ground stung his buttocks. They had taken everything to make him uncomfortable. He drew his knees up and rested his forehead against them. Shit, all the weird stuff he chose to overlook or excuse. He had accepted the job because he wanted to prove to himself that he could return to the field. He hadn't wanted to be afraid. He just wanted to be who he had been. He rocked back and forth to warm himself. Something in his pocket jabbed into his thigh. He patted the pocket and felt the bulk of car keys. He took them out.

Footsteps approached his tent.

He shoved the keys back into his pocket. "Who's there?" Kimball held still. "I'm not afraid of you."

The tent shook.

"Go away!" Kimball shouted.

Someone walked the perimeter of the tent. Then one side ripped open. A shape blotted out the stars. Kimball saw the outline of the tall hat and the drape of a cloak. It lifted an arm and pointed at the forest. Then it was gone.

Kimball crawled out of the tent. He stuck his hand into his pocket and pulled out the keys. The car wasn't far. A scream slammed through the forest, and Kimball spun around to face the trees. He squeezed the keys, and they reminded him that he should run. The scream ripped through the night once again. Kimball squeezed the keys again.

"Fuck."

He shoved them back into his pocket and set off into the forest, heading for the rock shelter Jones and Miller had desecrated. Dark figures appeared and ran alongside him. One of the Watchers brushed up against him, and his elbow burned like acid eating through his shirt. He shied away from them, but the fear he experienced earlier wasn't there. Ahead, an orange glow and that familiar chanting steered him to a clearing.

He saw the bear first, rear legs bound, hanging nose down from a tree branch. It thrashed about like a hooked fish. Kimball fell to his knees and covered his mouth with his hands to stop his own scream. Three small fires formed a triangle around the bear hanging at its center. Miller and Jones gyrated and shook as they danced around the fires and the bear. With the hatchet, Smith slashed the bear's hide. The animal roared but whipped a paw tipped with daggers at its torturer. Smith ducked and retreated.

A dark figure materialized at the center of the triangle. The bear's pain had summoned the Dark Watcher. The chanting grew louder and more forceful. Jones and Miller moved faster. The Dark Watcher tried reaching for the bear but its arms stayed pinned to its sides. Smith joined the two women in their attack. The Watcher shuddered. The faster the three danced and chanted, the more the Dark Watcher vibrated until it was just a blur. Then the Watcher exploded, sending sparks shooting toward the stars.

Smith sprinted back to the bear and cut it once again. The hatchet's blade dripped black. Another dark figure appeared and the whole process resumed until they destroyed that Dark Watcher.

A Watcher touched Kimball's back. He flinched but faced the entity. Black eyes stared into him. Kimball whimpered. The keys were still in his pocket. It wasn't too late.

But he had been the one who had brought these three to this place.

"Hey, over here!" he yelled, waving his arms.

Miller turned and directed the chanting at him, throwing out a hand in his direction.

Kimball's head whipped back as if hit with a hammer. But he righted himself and charged Miller. She extended an arm to stop him. Kimball grabbed her hand and yanked her from the circle. The current Dark Watcher in the grip of the three broke free. Kimball pushed the woman to the Watcher. It swept her up in the folds of its cloak. When its cloak fell open, Miller was gone.

Smith howled and rushed Kimball, hatchet held above his head. Kimball knew he couldn't fight Smith. He turned and ran. The SUV was too far. He knew from the maps that Limekiln Park was below him and then the highway. Kimball plunged down the side of the mountain. He crabbed his way down, digging his boots into the hillside struggling for traction. When he stumbled, the Watchers were there to lift him up, their touch burning into his flesh.

Jones screamed. Kimball stopped to see her tumble past him. Her momentum was too great, and she flew into a tree. Her back broke like a tree limb snapped in half. Kimball kept going.

He almost ran off the side of the cliff himself. The Watchers stopped his fall. Before him loomed four dark giants against the night sky, the lime kilns. He came upon a footpath on the side of the hill and worked his way down to their base. A cramp thrust daggers of pain into his side. He had to stop, but Smith wasn't far behind. The Watchers encircled him and guided him to one of the kilns, pushing him into an opening whose jagged and broken bricks looked like a mouth filled with fangs waiting to swallow him whole. The woods snapped and rustled. Kimball curled up inside the kiln.

"Where are you, Kimball?" Smith yelled. "Let's talk."

Kimball massaged his side and tried to relax. He had to be ready to make a break for it.

"The world's changing, Kimball. Humans rule it. Not Mother Nature or dead ancestors or forest spirits. Humans have a right to this world. We have to let those old gods know that it's our time."

Smith was wrong. Kimball had spent his whole life amongst the mountains and forests. He thought of the mornings he had woken under the naked sky, the morning air biting, dew on everything, and having that first cup of hot coffee fresh out of a pot bubbling on the grate of a fire, a hawk circling above his head. The forest was his temple, the mountains his spiritual guide. Now, Smith was telling him those things no longer mattered. Kimball had led Her disciples. They followed him onto mountain peaks and across vast lakes. They witnessed fish leaping into the air as if they were trying to join the birds winging across the skies, and birds plummeting into watery depths, staying submerged for so long Kimball thought they had turned into fish themselves. Humans finding the numinous in nature mattered. When it stopped mattering, then humanity would be damned. And here in these California mountains, the Dark Watchers stood strong for hundreds of years against the encroachment of humans. Kimball crawled out of the kiln.

A club came down on Kimball's back, sending him sprawling onto the ground. Smith raised the log over his head. Kimball kicked at the man's knees. Smith buckled. Kimball rolled to his feet and stood over Smith. An incantation erupted from Smith's mouth, knocking Kimball off his feet.

Like some monster, Smith crawled toward Kimball. Each sound out of Smith felt like a noose. Kimball clawed at his neck, but the noose got tighter and tighter until his vision disappeared at the edges. Smith was killing him. Kimball kicked out, catching Smith in the mouth. The man screamed but stopped chanting. Free from his bonds Kimball struggled to his feet. He ran until he collapsed on the side of the Pacific Coast Highway.

* * *

In the back of the ambulance, Kimball watched as the blackness spread across his body, soon his body would be consumed in the totality of it. The paramedics and deputy backed away from Kimball.

He understood now.

He got out of the ambulance. Smith was still out there, and others like him would follow.

Kimball knew where he was needed and what he needed to do.

The Dark Watchers were waiting for him.

AGENCY COST

AARON C. SMITH

Aaron Smith is a family law attorney practicing in San Diego, CA where he lives with my wife, son, and two pitbulls. He has previously been published in Microhorror. com, Liberty Island and PJ Lifestyles. His short story, "The Cure," will be featured in the forthcoming anthology Trump Utopia and Dystopia.

"THIS PLACE ISN'T WHAT I thought it would be."

Mike laughed. "What were you expecting? A dungeon? Pits of fire?" he asked. "It's the 21st century. This is Hell's L.A. branch office. There are OSHA rules. They've got a fucking HR department here. *That's* Hell, man."

"I guess so." All I knew was that after stepping out at high noon on an L.A. heatwave, the air-conditioning in here felt amazing. "I mean, this is just an office building."

"I told you. It's a branch office. You really want to see the corporate headquarters?"

"Okay. Good point."

"Hey, you got one soul to sell, kid, so we've got to make this count. But remember Rule Number One: you can always walk away."

That attitude made Mike Kincaid Hollywood's top agent. His heart pumped perfectly chilled vodka through his veins. He'd negotiated one of his biggest deals on a cell phone at his mother's funeral. I'd seen him schmooze guys from the Chinese Ministry of Culture in fluent Mandarin, and then turn around without taking a breath and promise to help Richard Gere free Tibet.

Mike imparted his wisdom as we emptied our pockets and walked through the metal detector. The security station separated the Intercontinental Building— a towering glass middle finger to Heaven— from the rest of the world.

Shuffling through the checkpoint, I looked down at the mirror polished black marble floor and didn't recognize the face staring back.

What the hell was I doing?

An alarm screeched. A guard raised one hand, his other hand on a semiautomatic pistol. He smiled but his voice was firm. "Sir, please step over here."

I obeyed and he ran a wand over me. The wand squealed over my chest.

"Sir?" The smile in his eyes died a little.

I lifted a simple silver cross and matching chain from around my neck. The only other jewelry I wore wouldn't have triggered the alarm.

"Graduation present from my folks." I shrugged. "Sorry."

The guard's hand swallowed the cross as I passed it to him. A second sweep of the wand cleared me. I nodded and started walking away.

"Sir, you don't want to forget this." The guard held out my cross.

"Of course not." I half expected it to burn as he handed it back. Instead, it sat cold and dead in the palm of my hand. I slipped it over my head.

I took a couple of hurried steps to catch up to Mike.

"Put your game face on, kid. Price's a tough bastard. Gonna wrestle you like that one guy did the angel. Whatever the hell his name was… But I'm not letting him pop your leg out."

Gotta love Mike. He'd studied up on the Bible to try and talk my language when we first met; completely not him but the small-town boy in me liked it.

The air got colder as we walked towards my future.

Mike's voice got a little louder, pulling me out of my thoughts.

"Can't ever get enough of this," Mike said. He led us with a group of tourists to a pool in the middle of the lobby. People gathered around, watching massive koi swim under a spattering of lily pads. A three-story waterfall fed the artificial pond.

The people around me felt too close but they watched the water, not me.

Until they didn't.

"Oh my God, I think that's Elias Gage. You know, from *Hero's Heart!*" Two girls, one with blue eyes and the other green. They stood right next to the rail protecting the pond and had looked back at just the wrong time.

Meeting fans used to get me pumped. Not so much today. I wanted to be nobody.

"Go talk to him," the green-eyed girl said.

"Let's go," I said.

"Cost of doing business." Mike's lips didn't move and he put a hand on my shoulder.

That gave the girls just enough time to gather their courage and approach me. Except for their eyes, the tall, sun kissed beauties could've been twins.

"I need you to settle a bet," Blue Eyes said.

I said nothing.

"It's your job," Mike insisted. He squeezed my shoulder and stepped back, giving me room.

I sighed and centered myself for the role: movie star.

"Okay, ladies, so what's the bet?"

"You're Elias Gage, right?"

"I am," I admitted, turning on the million-dollar-smile that had just helped me sign a ten-million-dollar-contract. I leaned closer and whispered, "Don't tell anyone else though."

"See, I was right!" Blue Eyes said. "But if you don't give us an autograph, we're going to scream your name."

I laughed. "Ladies, this is my agent. You may have heard of him. Mike Kincaid. He's a big deal. Just ask him. But could you give him some negotiating tips?"

Mike handed them a pair of business cards. "Call my office. I can always use interns."

"Thanks," Blue Eyes became Wide Eyes. "And the autograph?"

"Amanda!" her friend screeched.

"No," I said. "She won, fair and square. You have a pen? Something to sign?"

The pair immediately tore apart their purses. They found makeup, breath mints, some tissues and even a parking ticket.

Like magic, Mike produced notebook and pen.

The girls told me their names and I signed.

Or tried to.

My name ended up looking like shaky Chinese. Nothing like the mass-produced autographs on my headshots and posters. I shoved my rebellious hand in a pocket before anyone could see it shaking.

The girls tried not to frown at the chicken scratch.

I forced a smile. "Handwriting like a doctor."

"No, it's great," Amanda said. Her friend nodded hesitantly.

My stomach turned and I shot a glance at Mike. Why'd he forced this?

I thought for a moment and pulled off my cross, handing it to Amanda. "Here. For winning the bet."

She protested but I turned and walked away.

Whispers of "drunk" and "drugs" followed me.

Jimmy Fallon had made fun of me last week because my fiancé and I refused to live together. If he'd realized we were high school sweethearts saving ourselves for marriage, his head would've exploded.

We're not saints. Sunday school taught us that. But we tried our best; didn't do drugs or drink too much. Sara and I spent three months living in our cars looking for the right church. Then we found apartments.

What we laid out for two places would pay a mortgage on a house. With a yard. And a pool.

We couldn't do that though. Neither of us could live with the temptation. We couldn't live together.

It wasn't something Conan or most others in this town would understand. But my life in L.A. had been a blur. I'd been struck by lightning twice: I'd found my big break in Hollywood and got diagnosed with youth onset Parkinson's.

Hero's Heart had been a surprise blockbuster and Mike landed me an audition for another superhero flick with zombies. I'd be a fire breathing version of Superman.

Leading up to the audition, I had worked out more but felt weaker. I blamed it on not getting enough sleep. And the shakes? Too much coffee and stress.

I'd made it to the audition and ended up on the floor outside the suite, unable to walk, but had managed to crawl into a bathroom and called Mike.

He'd smoothed things over, having the snake's tongue he did, and sent a driver to hustle me out and arranged another call time. When my doctor pronounced the death sentence, Mike made more calls and got me in to see Dr. Nils Pering, the top neurologist in the state. Pering confirmed the diagnosis.

My body was betraying me. I was going to die.

So, I was here to sell my soul.

Mike led me to an elevator guarded by velvet rope and large men. After we passed the goons, we pressed our fingerprints on touch ID pads before the doors opened.

The elevator allowed two stops. The twenty-fifth-floor housed management and fluff.

We chose the eighteenth, where real deals happened.

18.

6+6+6.

Cute.

The doors opened and a woman stepped forward.

"Mr. Gage, Mr. Kincaid? I'm Salome Davison. Mr. Price sent me to greet you." Her soft voice carried a faint accent, Australian or South African. One of those places that just minted darn sexy voices.

And, looking at Salome, darn sexy gals as well. She was about five-five, a foot shorter than me, with auburn rings that hung down to her shoulders and wore a skirt and blouse that barely rated as office safe. I'd have to flip a coin to tell which sparkled more, her blazing white smile or emerald eyes.

"Where's Price?" Mike demanded.

"Gerard is waiting for us," she replied and began walking.

Several men and women in suits passed us through the hallway, in their own worlds. They talked on cell phones or to their coworkers but got out of the shapely Ms. Davison's way as she led us to a pair of French doors. Blackout shades hid the room from prying eyes.

It seemed like overkill for my signing a contract.

"This way, gentlemen," Salome said. Her wide smile made me think of my mom's cat when it found a mouse.

The door opened, and the smell from the room hit me like a linebacker.

"No way," I muttered. "No frigging way."

I pushed past Mike. Forget playing it cool. This could not wait.

They had Ray's Barbecue. A mountain of beef ribs, each as long and thick as my forearm, dripped Ray's thick molasses sauce. Tri-tip hissed, the fat still sizzling and mixing with the juices. I didn't need to cut into the meat to know its center would be darn near raw.

Back home, my family went to Ray's every Sunday after church. That was my childhood on the table.

Salome sat on a corner of the table. She crossed her legs and plucked a rib from the pile. She smiled and tore into the meat.

"We thought some lunch might be appropriate," an old money, JFK-Boston accented voice informed us from somewhere to the left.

I paused and looked up. The food had kept me from noticing the man standing at the end of the table. In his early fifties, the guy stood ramrod straight, with a gym toned body and tanning booth glow. His suit probably cost more than my folks' first place.

Mike cleared his throat. "Food's not gonna make me forget about the fact that this was supposed to be a principals' only meeting, Gerry." He pointed at Salome. "A sweet rack isn't the price of admission."

I focused on a different rack and grabbed a rib.

"Uhmmmmgsssh." Grease dribbled down my chin but I didn't care.

Then the tremor hit. The rib slipped from my hand but I had enough control to catch it.

If anyone saw the slip they didn't show it. I wrapped the bone in a napkin out of habit, even though my dogs had stayed back in Topeka.

I swallowed. "How'd you get Ray's out here?"

Price smiled the same way I had at the meat on the table. "If you choose to enter into a partnership with us, Mr. Rockwell will be relocating to Los Angeles. He is currently looking at space as we speak."

Only years of improv classes gave me the skills to keep from dropping my rib again. "You're serious?"

Price nodded. "Of course. We would have preferred it had your favorite food been Arby's but we must do what we must."

My leg twitched. Was it shock or the Parkinson's? I rested against the table, just in case. "You're setting him up here?"

I'd come here to sell my soul.

My actual, immortal soul. But flying a seventy-year-old pitman from Kansas to Los Angeles was the most surreal thing I'd heard so far.

"Mr. Gage, I do not know what Michael has told you, but my firm is quite serious in its desire to partner with you. Barbecue is the least of what our resources can provide." Price motioned for us to sit.

"Don't want to interrupt," Mike said. "But this ain't Salome's place. Eli's not getting taken in by tits and ass." He shoveled a mound of meat onto his plate and pointed at Salome with the serving fork. "He's going to be a star. Pussy comes with the territory."

"I'm more than tits and ass," Salome said, sliding off the table and holding up a hand when Price opened his mouth to defend her. "I'm your liaison, Elias. What you need, I secure."

"Plenty of dealers in town," I said. "Besides, I don't use."

Salome smiled. "If you think this is about me scoring you a speedball, move on. Now, if you kill a whore with your speedball, then call me. However, my true job is to help you if you decide not to piss your potential away on such distractions. I received my MBA at Wharton. Do you know where Arnold Schwarzenegger made his fortune?"

I shrugged. "The *Terminator* movies?"

She smiled and shook her head, like one of my teachers back home when I blew an easy question. "He invested wisely. We value you more than just for your movie career. I will make sure that you meet the men and women who will give you a legacy. Elias, with Kincaid here, roles and money will come your way. I'm offering you more than connections. I will help make you a legend."

"What're you saying?" I asked.

Mike waved his hand in a move-it-along gesture. "He knows what you want, Salome. We're here to see what your boss'll give for it."

Price smiled. "Churchill once told me about a conversation he had. He offered a woman five million pounds to sleep with him. She said yes. Then he offered five pounds. She protested, asking what he thought she was. He pointed out that when she accepted his first offer, they learned what she was. At that point, it was simply just a matter of dickering over price."

My brain calculated how old meeting Churchill made Price.

Then the meaning of the words hit me. "You're calling me a whore," I said. I wanted to pound the table but would my hands obey?

"I am simply stating that we should not get bogged down in details," Price said. "But as Michael indicated, there are forms to observe. Are you ready to review the contract?"

I nodded.

"Is that a 'yes,' son?" Price asked. "You must say it and then sign the paperwork. There are formalities which we must honor."

My jaw tightened and wouldn't open. I simply nodded again.

"Come on, Gerry, that's good enough," Mike said. "There's no need to be a prick."

Price took off his glasses, rubbing his eyes and cleaning the lenses.

"I suppose we can consider an energetic nod as assent. There is precedent. After all, mutes can covenant."

Price opened his briefcase and withdrew the contract, placing it in front of me.

The stack slammed in front of me like a brick. I reached out to grasp the papers with a shaking hand.

That wasn't the Parkinson's.

I couldn't touch it.

This started as a joke over expensive Scotch in Mike's office. Touching the contract would make this real. My soul, reduced to 8.5" x 11" sheets of paper. From the looks of it there weren't even enough pages to make a proper script.

I jerked at Mike's hand on my shoulder. He let off.

"Nerves are okay, kid," he said. "This is kind of a big deal."

The agreement just sat there. It taunted me, challenging me to pick it up.

That would literally be a damning admission.

I'd sinned by entertaining Mike's suggestion in the first place. Each step into this building meant another step towards Hell.

"The terms are simple, Elias," Price said. "If you sign the contract, your health will be restored. You will be the most talked about action star of your generation."

"Not just action," Mike cut in. "He's not pigeonholing himself. Will Smith does drama. Bradley Cooper, too, from the *A-Team* to four Oscar nominations."

Salome stepped forward, raising her hands. "Kincaid, Elias will have his pick of roles. My connections–"

"You bang studio heads, hon, but by the time they see something, it's stomped on. Worthless. Eli wants to explore his art. Right?"

I nodded, still not trusting myself to talk.

Salome's eyes glittered like the diamond studs in her delicate earlobes. "I know about the best material in this town before the writers finish typing it out. The question for you, Elias, is whether you are willing to do this. You can only answer that question by looking at the agreement."

I turned over the papers and began reading. It looked like most other contracts.

Until the seventh clause. It was a gut punch.

They couldn't be serious.

Mike turned to me. "Well, what do you think, kid?"

My mouth opened and closed. I took a deep breath and managed to speak.

"I need to use the toilet."

*　*　*

Everyone was eating Ray's when I walked back into the conference room.

I'd been puking my guts out. The barbecue hadn't tasted near as good coming back out.

Still, I had an image to maintain, so I packed another plate and hoped it would stay down.

Salome smiled at me. "Elias, we were talking about you while you were gone."

"Not surprising," I said, picking at the meat.

"Your thoughts," she said.

I wiggled my fingers at her. The barbecue sauce coating them looked darn close to drying blood. "A little help?"

"Here," she said, passing me a steaming towel. Salome's eyes shifted but her face didn't move an inch.

I cleaned my fingers and picked up the contract.

"Paragraph 7?" I said. "No. That's non-negotiable. If you need it, I'm sorry for wasting your time."

Price nodded. "Are you certain?"

I looked at the paper. The words blurred but that one clause stood out.

Sara. They wanted me to stay with her, act like my life was normal.

I'd thought about this already. It wouldn't happen. The note she'd find taped to her door would explain it all.

"I'm positive," I replied, my voice low.

Price raised his hands. "I can understand your position, Mr. Gage." He reached out to shake my hand.

The earthquake hit from my shoulder to my fingers. My quivering hand hung in the air.

Price didn't even look at me with disgust.

He pitied me.

I wanted to tell him to fuck off.

Mike grabbed my arm. "Eli, stop and think, man. They're giving you what you need. We can work with their terms."

"No. I… There are just some things I can't do."

My agent opened his mouth but Price waved a hand.

"He is young and passionate, Mr. Kincaid. I can almost remember that point in my life."

"I… I have to leave," I said. The words scraped in my throat like sandpaper. I walked toward the open door.

Price and Mike asked me to sit but it was too late.

"Elias!" Salome called from behind me.

"Yes?" I answered more out of manners than wanting to hear anything more.

"You need us."

I did, if I wanted my life to be something other than extended torture.

"Not for this price."

"Why is this so important to you?"

"Sara is everything to me."

"Then why fight to throw her away?"

"Because *you* want me to keep her."

I reached under my shirt. The cross was gone but I had kept something else close to my heart. "Mike, did I ever tell you about this?"

"No," he answered, looking at a small ring of grass on a string. "I figured it was some hippy shit."

I rubbed the ring's smooth surface. "Sara gave this to me. She went with me for the second opinion. I tried to do the right thing and break it off there. I told her that she deserved a man. Someone she could have kids with, grow old with. You know what she did?"

No one answered.

"She pulled this out. Our first date, we ended up on the football field, looking at the stars. I made this ring for her. She took it home that night, put it in nail polish to preserve it because she knew I'd be hers. So that day when you set me up with Dr. Pering, Sara came with me and heard the news. She put it on my pinky and proposed, said she'd stay through that hell with me."

Mike shook his head. "Eli, Sara obviously loves you. And you love her. Why give that up?"

"Because she would want to stay with me, save me from what I'm going to become. I'd drag her along with me. And that's what they want, right? A two for one deal." I couldn't stop the bitterness dripping from my voice.

Again, no one said a word.

I turned to leave.

Mike's pained look told me that today he didn't really believe in his first rule of negotiating. He wasn't willing to just walk away from this deal.

"Mr. Gage," Price said. "Please wait another moment?"

Maybe I didn't believe in Mike's first rule either because I stopped.

"Have you considered what the commerce we are engaging means?"

"Sure."

"I do not know that you have. You understand what we give you but not what we gain in return."

"You get my soul. I understand that plenty."

"Yes, but why do we want it?"

I hadn't thought about that, not really. I mean, it seemed obvious. It was a soul.

Price nodded as if he read my mind. "The human soul is an exquisite creation. Billions are born throughout history but each unique. Priceless. There are countless interested parties out there seeking them. They get minted Up There but then it's anybody's guess who ends up with the finished product."

Price took a step towards me, his hands spread wide.

"I'll admit my organization gets more than its fair share. But we have competitors. Buddha. Allah. These upstart Wiccans. We are all hungry for each, infinitely valuable soul that we can get our hands on. You're virgin territory for us. Invaluable."

The flattery was nice but I was still ready to walk.

"Elias, have you considered what happens if you walk away and damn yourself?" Salome said. "You certainly won't get these terms. You might get nothing. But if you sign with us, you become something more than a commodity. You are a partner."

I shook my head. "What does that even mean?"

"We protect our partners. Consider this: According to my contacts, a cell of ISIS terrorists plans to kidnap an A-list celebrity, torture this victim on a live web feed before cutting his head off. That will be a mercy."

My stomach tightened. I'd seen ISIS videos.

"What's this have to do with me? You turning me over to them if I walk?"

"Of course not," she replied. "I am your liaison, your protector. I can make it known to my contacts that you are not to be touched. Not now. Not ever."

"You didn't answer my question."

"No, Elias, we will not hand you over to them. But if you walk out of here, you will not have our protection."

"And they'd listen to you?"

"We are rather adept at making our point," Price answered.

Mike opened his mouth, closed it and opened it again. "Got a question for you, kid."

"What's that?"

"The guy who's got your pink slip now, what's he done for you? What will he do for you? I mean, look at Job, a true believer. And He let the Devil kill his family, his pets and damn near kill him while his wife and his friends made fun of him."

God bless Mike and the *Bible for Dummies* he read.

"Job got repaid," I said. "More than repaid."

"You think new kids make up for dead ones?" Mike asked, his voice hard. "Sara dies today, are you ahead of the game if you get the Double Mint twins from downstairs?"

"Of course not!"

"Think about this, Eli. How do you know down the road, you're not going to cross the line and give the milk away for free? At least here, you know the terms."

Now it was my turn to shut up. Mike had a point. I could fall on my own, without a safety net. Price guaranteed my treatment in the afterlife. No lake of fire. No torture.

"Speaking of family, there's something else you haven't considered. Your family. You die, who takes care of them?"

"I have money." It even sounded weak to me.

Mike wasn't buying it. "You got a couple mil for *Hero's Heart*. Taxes ate half that. The houses you bought for you, your folks and your kid sister and my commission, took up most of what was left."

"But I got signed to *Ex-Heroes*! That was ten million!"

"Again, taxes. Commission. And Eli, if you get to a point where you can't continue shooting, they'll fire you and want that money back. Plus, you think your buddy Ray's gonna get his franchises if you don't sign? People depend on you, Eli."

"And your cut, right Mike?"

He nodded without any hesitation. "Of course, I'm considering my bottom line too, kid. But I'm also thinking of you ending up a vegetable. I like you, Eli. Your checks are great. But I've gone to church with you. I wouldn't do that for most anyone."

That stopped me. Could there be some blood in his vodka stream after all?

Yeah, he was acting from naked self-interest. He admitted it. But I didn't walk away.

Was I being selfish, trying to cover it up by playing the hero? I bit my lip, not wanting to talk but needing to. "Mr. Price?"

"Yes, Mr. Gage?"

"Sara and the church. Are they deal points for you or not?"

I wanted him to say no, but what if he said yes?

Price's face tightened and his eyes grew cold. "You are an influencer. A brand. Elias Gage, the young man from Middle America who has not been seduced by the city. That is part of what we want."

Salome bit her lower lip. "Gerard, can we talk?"

The older man nodded, his jaw tight.

"Take your time," Mike said.

As they stepped away to talk, Mike moved closer to me.

"Don't," I warned. So we waited in silence.

It wasn't a long wait. Salome and Price walked in.

"Your conditions are acceptable. You may leave Sara and your faith," Price said. "However, we shall pick replacements."

"You mean an arranged marriage? You pick my religion?"

This wasn't real. It couldn't be.

"No one said that marriage was required. Think of it this way. You wish to be Hollywood royalty? Well this is the life of actual royalty for most of human history. Companionship and faith were currency. Gerard and I believe there is an up-and-coming guru who can use his own Tom Cruise. There will be benefits for being an early adopter."

I closed my eyes and saw Sara.

Then I saw myself, in a hospital bed wishing for death.

I picked up the pen and signed.

* * *

Price and Kincaid clinked their glasses in a toast. No one heard them in the private dining room in Musso and Frank's.

"Another success," Kincaid said, sipping his drink. "God, they make the best martinis. Just the thing for a celebration."

"I was here when Frank Toulet opened the doors in 1919, Michael. The quality of their martini has never wavered. Even during those unfortunate years of Prohibition, a person with enough charm and remuneration could slake his thirst here."

The agent nodded. "Well after a day like today, we deserve a good meal."

"Quite. I thought we might lose the boy but you certainly steered him in the right direction."

"He needed his hand held, that's all. Had to admire his gumption, though."

"Your speech regarding children was quite compelling. I take it you had personal experience with losing a child?"

"Hell no. But you don't hang around actors without learning things. He needed, what's it the artist types say? Inspiration."

"You're nearly reaching your quota, Michael. How many more souls do you owe us?"

"Two. Then we're square. But then again, after seeing that Salome gal again, I might put Gage on the books for trade. Your guys good with that?"

"Of course," Price said, pleased.

Kincaid's debt would never be paid. When he sought his first deal, Price demurred. Kincaid gave away his soul some time ago. His offer to bring fresh offerings to the table proved more interesting. As of today, Kincaid had fed Price fifteen of his clients. But he never climbed out of his hole. Salome would do her part to keep it that way.

"Extraordinarily lucky of you, finding someone in such dire straits."

Kincaid smiled. "Winners make their own luck. Gage was fine. His trainer gave him some supplements I supplied."

"But his second opinion?"

"Dr. Pering's not a neurologist. He's a GP that pushes to most of my clients. He doesn't know neurons from Netflix. He didn't even want cash from me. He just needs the referrals. You think Gage will ever get it, the loophole?"

"Forgiveness and grace?" Price asked, chuckling. "Before he could seek that, he must forgive himself. I do not see that happening. He is already doing our work for us. Fiancé and church gone? He intended it as a sacrifice but it simply leaves him more isolated. Soon, he won't be able to forgive himself and won't consider that the other side will forgive him."

"Yeah, but if he does?"

"If we think we risk losing our investment, I initiate the contingency plan."

Kincaid waved his hand, inviting Price to elaborate.

"If we sense he is reneging, Mr. Gage will be involved in what appears to be a particularly brutal murder-suicide. He will not escape and his name will become synonymous with savagery."

"The most talked about action star of his generation," Kincaid muttered.

"Quite," Price said. "We made an agreement and we always keep our promises."

THE MOUNT OF DEATH

KEVIN DAVID ANDERSON

Kevin David Anderson's debut novel, Night of the Living Trekkies (Quirk Books) earned positive reviews in the L.A. Times, the Washington Post, Fangoria, and Publishers Weekly. He has published more than 60 short stories and was included in the Bram Stoker nominated anthology, The Beauty of Death (Independent Legions Publishing). Recent releases include the YA novel Night of the ZomBEEs and Night Sounds, a collection of stories heard on award winning podcasts like Pseudopod, The Drabblecast, The Dunesteef, and The Simply Scary Podcast.

"BEER-ME!"

Collin took a hand off the steering wheel, the one not holding his smartphone, and thrust it back toward Aaron.

Aaron shifted uncomfortably in the SUV's rear compartment, wedged between a cooler and sleeping bags. It was the only spot left since Collin and his girlfriend occupied the front, and Max and Carol took up the entire backseat. "Not gonna happen. You're driving... and texting."

And a colossal douche, he wanted to add. Collin's sober driving on the heavily forested, treacherous highway 39 through the San Gabriele Mountains was scary enough. There wasn't a chance in hell Aaron would allow alcohol into the mix.

"Hey, I'm not going to spend the weekend in the woods with you people, sober," Collin said. "Now, beer-me."

Max leaned forward on the back of the driver's seat and slapped Collin's shoulder. "Love you too, buddy."

Collin stretched his neck "I didn't mean it like..., for the love of—Aaron, will you please just get me a damn beer."

Collin's new girlfriend, Aaron couldn't remember her name—Debbie, Donna... something—turned from the passenger seat window and smiled at Aaron. "I'll take a Coke." Aaron narrowed his gaze at the young woman he felt answered the age old question *what would a Wookie look like if it lost all its hair*, then started looking for a Coke.

Max reached back and put his hand on the cooler lid. "Got a Red Bull back there?"

Aaron furrowed his brow. "When did I become the bartender?"

Collin drummed his fingers impatiently on the roof. "When you volunteered to sit in the ass-end of the car."

Volunteered?

Everyone had simply beaten him to the car. Aaron sighed. But whom was he kidding? It made sense that he be tucked in with the luggage. He was the fifth wheel, Max's best friend. Collin had Debbie or Donna or whatever the hell Wookie-face's name was, and Max had Carole.

God, Carole was amazing.

Beautiful, strong, intelligent. She had the brains of Dana Scully, the eyes of Deana Troy, and the tenacity of Katniss Everdeen. Her hair rested over the backseat right in front of Aaron, and he delighted in every breath he took filling his nostrils with her fragrance clean, fresh, a hint of strawberry. He was well aware of how creepy it was, but it wasn't like he could move, or find some other air to breathe.

"Hey, you awake?" Collin shouted. "Look, I'm putting my phone down. Now, beer-me."

Max slapped Collin's hand down off the roof. "Crystal Lake Campgrounds is less than an hour away. Just wait."

Collin put his hand back up, wrist wresting against the soft top and fingers shaped as if cradling a beer. "I want to be well into my first buzz by then. Now tell ComicCon back there to get me a beer."

"Collin!" Aaron sat up. "You vomit-spackled ninja-fart, I'm not getting you a beer. You can barely drive sober in the light of day, let alone in the dark. Jesus, man, its pitch-black out."

Collin made a wide sweeping gesture over the dashboard. "Aaron, my little nerdy friend, there is nothing out there in the dark that ain't there in the daytime."

"That's some real brilliant fortune cookie wisdom there, Buddha," Aaron shouted.

Max turned around. "Dude, that sounded kind of racist."

"What? No, that's not—"

"I could use a 7-up, or something like that," Carole said, turning around, temporarily paralyzing Aaron with the full power of her deep brown Diana Troy eyes.

"Yeah, I'll see what I can...uh..." Aaron looked away, and plunged his attention into the cooler.

When he looked back up, Max was staring at him, uneasy. He seemed to be reading something on Aaron's face. Something Aaron had been trying to bury for months. Although he hadn't done anything disloyal to his friend, Aaron knew it was more from a lack of opportunity than an unwillingness to do so.

Max brought his arm up and slid it around Carole's shoulder, pulling her close.

Shit.

Aaron turned away and continued rummaging through the cold cans. The weight of the guilt for something he hadn't even done yet crushed him. He and Max had been close since third grade, ever since they discovered their mutual interest in all things geeky, especially Science Fiction. Truth be known, Max was a little more Star Wars than Star Trek, but Aaron felt that when it came to best friends certain things can be forgiven. They cosplayed at conventions together, they joined a quidditch league together in college, they even shared a limo on prom night.

They were tight. At least until Max started playing lacrosse and began hanging out with troglodytes like Collin and his Wookie-faced girlfriend. Aaron felt them drift over the past year, and now he was falling for Max's girlfriend, a circumstance guaranteed not to improve the situation.

Collin turned down the rap music he'd insisted on tormenting his passengers with since San Bernardino, and then cleared his throat, clearly wanting everyone's attention. "Allow me to demonstrate," Collin said.

There was a soft click and the car plunged into darkness.

"What the...?" Aaron let the cooler lid fall and turned forward, unable to see the curvy road or the surrounding trees. In the driver's seat Collin's hands, illuminated by the faint glow of dashboard lights, waved in the air like someone reaching the big drop on a roller coaster.

Max slapped Collin in the back of the head. "Turn the headlights back on, asshole!"

Collin's hands lowered. There was a click and the lights came back on.

Aaron's hands were shaking. "Seriously! Is there any part of you that's not stupid?"

Collin's grin reflected in the windshield. "Just conducting a little science experiment about the dark."

"Well congratulations," Aaron said. "You proved you're a moron."

Collin raised his hand, once again thrusting it back toward Aaron, fingers cradling an invisible beer can. "I told ya' there ain't nothing there in the dark that isn't there in the daylight. Now stop being a beer-nazi or I'll conduct another experiment."

Collin's girlfriend turned around. "Yeah, stop being a beer-nazi."

Aaron pointed a finger. "Nobody is talking to you, Donna."

"My name is, Dedee, you skid-mark."

"Whatever," Aaron said. "Collin, when we get to Crystal Lake you can drink yourself into a coma. But let's get there alive." Aaron raised his right hand. "All in favor?"

Carole and Max raised their hands.

Collin shook his head. "Well this isn't a democracy."

Soft click.

Darkness swallowed the landscape and Aaron's entire body began to tremble. "Shit-head."

In a casual tone Collin said, "Beer-me."

"Alright," Aaron said. "Just turn them on."

"Another successful experiment." Collin flicked the headlights back on.

White light illuminated something in the road. Aaron only caught a glimpse. It stood on four legs with metallic eye-shine the shade of gunmetal. In a horrifying instant Aaron realized they were going to hit it. The full weight of Thor's hammer seemed to crash down on the hood. Everything rushed forward to the sounds of breaking glass, skidding tires, deploying airbags, and screaming. Ice from the cooler rose up, hung in the air then showered down like Texas hail. Aaron tumbled over the backseat, unable to give any resistance, as cold cans of soda and beer pummeled his back.

He careened into an un-seat-belted Max and they both slid to the floor in a tangle of limbs. Collin's rap music sadistically rose in volume like background music to a bad horror film as Aaron struggled to right himself in the dark. With arms and legs flailing all around him, he grasped something soft. Realizing it was some part of Carole he quickly let go as the SUV slid sideways. He braced for another impact with either a huge hundred year old pine tree or one of the colossal boulders that dotted the roadside. But it didn't come.

The sound of sliding tires suddenly silenced as the vehicle jolted to a stop. One or more doors had buckled enough to turn the interior lights on and Aaron looked down and saw his feet floating in the air. His blood felt as if it were flowing in the wrong direction, then he realized he wasn't looking down. He was looking up.

"Carole," Max said. "You all right?"

"Yeah, I think."

"Aaron, you alive?" Max said.

Aaron thought about that for a second. The cold rubber of the floor mat pressing on his face seemed to indicate that he was. "Guess so."

"Then how about getting your ass-cheeks out of my face?" Max said.

Aaron felt Max's hands clasp his belt, lifting him like a crane. He flopped back into the rear compartment. He then tried to look outside but most of the view through the front windshield was blacked by deployed airbags. The view on either side of Max and Carol was also obstructed by airbags.

A head rose up from the front seat, hair in disarray. Collin's girlfriend moaned, touching a finger to her bruised forehead.

"Debbie, are you okay," Aaron said, bringing out a pocketknife.

She moaned again. "My name is Dedee, ass-wipe."

Aaron sighed. "She's fine." He flipped open the blade and handed the knife up to Max. "Hey, Collin?"

There was no movement from the driver's seat.

Max plunged the blade into the backseat airbag to his side; a soft whistling sound filled the car. He reached out and put a hand on Collin's shoulder. "Hey, man."

Collin made a grunting sound like a gorilla fighting to wake from a nap. His head flopped to one side. "Feels like there is something sitting on me," Collin said. "Can't feel my legs."

Everyone sat still for a few moments. Collin's heavy breathing was the only opposition to silence.

Aaron glanced over at Max who seemed to take a deep breath, then said, "Okay, let's stay calm. Carole, call 911."

"I'm on it." Carole began digging for her phone.

Max handed Aaron back his knife, then opened his door.

Aaron grabbed Max's shoulder. "Where're you going?"

"I'm gonna check out the car. You stay here with Dedee and see what you can do for Collin." Max stepped out.

Aaron lowered his voice. "Why me?"

Max stuck his head back in, extending a hand toward Carole. "Cuz, you're studying to be a doctor."

"I want to be a biologist."

Max cocked his head. "What's the difference?"

Carole slid across the backseat to follow. Before she stepped out she whispered to Aaron, "I know the difference."

Aaron took a moment to watch her leave, then hopped into the backseat to take a look at Collin, while his girlfriend pushed on the steering wheel.

"Donna, what're you doing?"

She stopped, glancing over at Aaron. "It's De—oh, never mind. Just help me."

"Let's get this out of the way first," Aaron said, then stabbed the muffin top-shaped airbag that had deployed from the steering wheel. As the bag deflated, Aaron leaned into the front seat, looking into Collin's lap. The entire steering column had been bent downward to press into Collin's stomach. "Aaron," Collin said. "Can you see my legs? I think I'm stuck."

Aaron put a hand on Collin's shoulder, peering down. "Everything's gonna be okay. Help is coming. Just hang—"

"I can't move, man?"

Below Collin's knees Aaron couldn't see anything. The area around the pedals was completely caved in. Whatever they had struck must have been solid, heavy. "You're pinned in real good. I don't think you're getting out without help."

"Jeez, my head hurts." Collin touched a golf ball-sized welt on his forehead.

"Are you dizzy, tired, nauseated?" Aaron said, trying to muster up some genuine concern for a guy he couldn't stand, the same guy whose dumbass antics had caused this mess.

"Yes, yes, and yes."

The door of the rear compartment swung open. Aaron jerked around, seeing Max riffling through the luggage. "What's going on?"

Max held up a finger. "Not now." He pulled out a flashlight and shut the door.

What the hell? What could be so damn important that Max didn't have time to answer? *And why the hell am I in here taking care of his idiotic friend?*

Collin's girlfriend raised a hand, pushing the front passenger side airbag off of her face.

Aaron leaned forward with his pocketknife up. "Let me get that."

"No, I got it," she said before he could approach. She pulled a nail file out of her purse and stabbed the bag. It deflated in a few seconds.

Aaron looked at Collin, noticing his usually smug expression was slightly less smug. "Aaron," Max's voice sounded from outside. "Get out here."

"You need to stay awake." Collin let his head flop back onto the headrest. "Just a little nap."

Max's voice came from right behind him, "Aaron, I really need you to see this."

Aaron turned and looked at Max. "What?"

Max made an insistent gesture with the flashlight then stepped away.

Aaron turned forward and met Dedee's eyes. "Look, keep him awake and I'll be right…" His words faded as he glimpsed the windshield. A spider web of white cracks filled the glass, but not enough to obscure his vision. Something else lying on the hood was doing that.

Is that hair, Aaron thought? *And that looks like a...a saddle.*

"I'm gonna step out for a minute," Aaron said. "I'll be back."

Aaron hopped out, following the line of Max's flashlight illuminating Carole standing a good distance down the road, her smartphone pressed to her ear.

"What's she doing way over there?" Aaron asked.

Max turned around, his face lit eerily by the vehicle's only working headlight. "That's as close as she wants to get to this thing." He waved at Carole and she returned with a nod, then Max aimed the flashlight at the hood.

Aaron's mouth dropped open and he instinctively stepped away from the car. In a kind of perplexed daze he joined Max standing just a few feet in front of the bumper.

"What the hell is that?"

"You tell me," Max said.

"Is..." Aaron stepped forward, fascination beginning to override his initial horror. "Is it a horse?"

Max moved the light down toward the bumper, illuminating the thing's feet. "Do horses have toes?"

"Not lately," Aaron said. "Shine the light up on its back."

The beam drifted up the creature's alien, dark exterior. Its underbelly was gaunt, leathery and disturbingly unfamiliar. And then Aaron saw something that was at least a little familiar. "That looks like a saddle."

Max's head tilted a bit. "Are you sure that's a saddle, city-boy?"

"According to all the John Wayne movies I've seen, that's a saddle." Aaron held out his hand. "Give me that."

Max handed him the flashlight and Aaron brought it up over his head, aiming the beam down, illuminating the creature's entire form. "Jesus," Aaron breathed.

"What the hell is this?" Max said.

Aaron shook his head, taking in the enigma sprawled out on the hood. Its form resembled a horse, but that is where the comparison ended. Instead of hooves, the thing had three-toed muscular feet, each toe encased in a predator's claw, wide and jagged, stained in an array of colors from bone white to deep crimson. Short hair covered the equine frame that glistened in the flashlight beam like rows of staples. A tail dangled off the hood by the front tire, comprised of hundreds of thick, rust-colored and somewhat familiar strands. Aaron stepped closer, wanting to touch the tail and confirm the image his mind must have been imagining.

At the last moment he thought better of it and settled for shining the light on it and gazing at the strands.

Is…is the tail made of barbed wire?

"Damn," Max said. "Shine the light over here. Look at these teeth."

Aaron redirected the beam to the creature's head which lay on the roof; its lips receded along the protracted snout in an unsettling death grin. The light bounced off and through the teeth giving Aaron the impression that the fangs were icicles, frozen to its black gums. But as he moved the light back and forth he realized that the long spike shaped teeth were transparent, as if made from glass or crystal.

"What the fu…." Max said, moving away from beast's head. "This can't be real. Right?"

Aaron was about to answer but he'd moved the light down the thing's neck and his words caught in his throat. Growing from the spot a normal horse would have a mane of hair, protruded thick slimy follicles, with ungodly ridges spiraling around each strand. They too had an unnerving ring of familiarity. The beast's mane seemed made of a thousand oversized dead earthworms.

"I don't know what is creeping me out more," Max said. "The fact that I'm really looking at this… or that someone actually rides this thing."

"Could be pre-historic," Aaron said, moving around to its head.

Carole's soft voice cut through the dark. "You mean like a dinosaur?"

Aaron aimed the light at Carole, standing behind Max. "Not exactly." He gestured to her phone. "What'd they say?"

She rolled her brown eyes. "Assholes. No one can get here for at least a half-hour, maybe longer. And my battery just died."

"Jeez," Aaron said.

Max pointed to the front seat. "How is Collin?"

"He has a slight concussion; I'm guessing not his first. He's dizzy and stuck under the steering column. This thing caved in the area around his legs. He's pinned tight, and he isn't getting free until they can get here and cut him out."

"But he'll be alright?" Max said.

"Yeah. I mean, he'll still be Collin, but aside from that, as long as what's her face keeps him awake, he'll be fine."

"Is there anything we could do to help him while we wait?" Carol said.

Aaron shrugged. "I guess we could get this thing off him. Max, get its tail."

"You nuts? I ain't touching this thing."

Aaron shined the light on his friend. "It's dead."

"How do you know?" Max said.

"We just hit it with a two-ton car." Aaron turned the beam on the creature's defined ribcage, visible under hair-covered flesh. "It isn't breathing."

Max walked toward the creature's tail. "We don't even know if it needs to breathe. It might be from outer space, or another time. Or, a robot even."

Aaron shined the light on Max's face. "Dude, no more Syfy channel for you?"

Max gazed down, clearly fascinated. "But really just look at this thing."

Aaron turned his attention to the creature's head. Its face seemed too long for a horse, almost a foot too long, and its snout seemed to be designed for tearing meat from bone rather than grassing in a field. He found the thing's closed eyes and placed a thumb across one eyelid. Through the thin layer of skin he could feel that the eye underneath was ridged, not spherical or smooth. He pushed the lid up. There was a suction sound like someone pulling a shoe out of the mud.

The flashlight illuminated a small human skull cast from grey metal, like the kind of ring decoration found on the finger of a Hell's Angel. "Ah, crap-weasel," Aaron said stepping back, breathing fast.

"What is it?" Max said, his voice noticeably elevated.

Aaron staggered further away, the flashlight still aimed at the thing's face. He took a breath. "Just reconsidering your alien, time traveling, robot theory." He looked up at Max. "I don't think we should move it."

Collin's girlfriend stuck her head out the window, placing a hand on the creature's rump. "Hey, what is this?"

Max stepped forward and removed her hand. "Be careful."

She recoiled. "Okay."

"How's Collin?" Max asked, standing just behind the thing's back legs.

She sighed. "He keeps trying to nod off."

"Well, help is on the way," Aaron said. "So keep his eyes open."

She delivered a salute, "Yes, Sir," and disappeared back into the car.

Max glanced down at the creature, stepping in closer, holding his hands above the thing as if it were a warm fire. "Hey, Aaron."

"What?"

"Do you think it's worth something?"

Aaron furrowed his brow.

"I mean it's gotta be one of a kind, right?" Max sounded excited. "Couple of months back, there was this three-headed dog that went for ten-thousand on ebay. Hell, this thing could beat that, easy."

Aaron rolled his eyes.

"I'm talking even split," Max said. "You, me, Carole, Collin and even what's-her-name." Max grinned. "So?"

"So, what?" Aaron said.

"What do you think we could get for it?"

Aaron sighed. "I don't know, Max. My market knowledge of pre-historic alien time traveling robot horses is a bit limited. Besides, I think you're forgetting one minor detail."

"What's that?"

Carole pointed to the creature's back. "The saddle."

"Exactly," Aaron said. "Someone, or *something* owns this... whatever it is. And I'm not particularly interested in meet—"

Aaron stopped. His blood turned cold and his eyes went so wide they felt as if they would pop from their sockets. His mouth moved twice before his voice managed to come out as a hushed whisper, "Max!"

"What?"

"Get away from it."

"Why?"

"Now." Aaron took a step back, his gaze locked on the creature's face.

The skull eyes were wide open.

Aaron heard several soft pings, like metal moving through air. He glanced down. Steak knife-sized claws extended from the creature's hind legs like rear hallux talons on a bird of prey.

"Max, get back," Aaron shouted. "It's not dead."

Max took a step, but it wasn't big enough. All four of the thing's legs kicked out as it tried to get up. The back leg talons slashed across Max's mid-section and he went down.

Aaron rushed around the car, meeting Carole at Max's side. Max tried to sit up, his hands clasped around his abdomen. Aaron aimed the flashlight at his midsection. Blood poured between Max's fingers.

Max glanced down, then back up at Aaron. "It really hurts, man."

Aaron handed Carole the flashlight and grabbed Max under the armpit.

"It's just a scratch," Carole said, taking Max's other side. "Stop acting like a girl."

Max smiled for a second.

They lifted Max to his feet and held him up. Max kept one hand fixed on his abdomen as if struggling to keep things inside.

They dragged Max to the side of the road, Aaron fighting the urge to look back even as he heard Collin and Dedee begin to scream. Max pushed Carole ahead toward the forest and said, "Run."

Carole hesitated, looking back at the boys, but then she glanced over their shoulders and clearly saw something horrible. Her mouth fell open, her eyes bulged and even in the thin moonlight Aaron could see her tremble. "Just go," Max said. "Run!"

Carole spun on a heel and darted into the forest.

The sound of bone and talons scraping on metal echoed behind them and Aaron and Max paused to look back.

The horse-creature had righted itself, now standing on the hood. The SUV's back wheels were several inches off the ground, teetering like a seesaw on the front axle.

Collin's girlfriend screamed, looking up through the windshield, hands clamped tight on the dashboard for support. Her terrified shrills seemed to be aggravating the creature.

The angular snout arched upward, and each hair in its mane moved under its own momentum like the venomous strands on Medusa's head.

Aaron took a step toward the car, but felt Max's hand around his shoulder holding him.

With mouth open and transparent teeth glistening in the moonlight, the creature's head darted forward into the windshield like a predator bird diving into the water.

Glass shattered and the whole car shook.

Dedee's screams stopped.

The creature pulled its head back out, something round and fleshy stuck in its teeth. Snapping its jaw shut the thing began to swallow. Aaron saw the outline of the girl's head moving down a long, gaunt throat.

"I told her I'd be right back," Aaron said.

"You lied, man," Max said. "Let's go."

Using the bouncing light from Carole's flashlight as a beacon, they pursued her into the forest. They hobbled in a clumsy entanglement of limbs, but even terribly wounded Max seemed the more coordinated of the two.

Before they lost site of the road, Aaron looked back to see if the horror was following. It wasn't. The beast stood on the hood, slowly sinking into the engine as unimaginable weight pulled it toward the ground.

Instead of getting down, the creature stood up on its hind legs, and reared a monstrous head way back. The chest looked to be expanding, as if taking in an enormous breath like a mythical dragon preparing to breathe—

Fire erupted from the beast's mouth as the creature thrust forward. The car's interior was engulfed in flame, smoke and ash exploded through the rear window.

"What was that?" Max said.

Aaron jerked him forward. "Keep going!"

A tree limb smacked Aaron in the face as they crashed through the brush. Carole's bouncing light receded further away.

Max moaned, and his head slumped forward. Aaron felt the pull of his friend's full weight and they both tumbled to the ground. Aaron landed on top of his friend, their lips close to touching.

Max pushed Aaron off. "Not even if you were pretty and rich." He grimaced, shutting his eyes.

Aaron got to his knees. "Don't flatter yourself." He grabbed Max's arm. "Now walk it off, you big pie-hole."

Max pulled his arm away, falling flat on the ground. "I appreciate the words of encouragement, but I don't think..." He pulled his hand away from his stomach briefly. Aaron tried to mask his horror. "I think I'm done."

Both of them sat still, breathing heavy. Aaron looked away.

Max lifted his head. "I'm slowing you down."

Aaron felt it before he heard it: a rhythmic vibration stemming from the ground, coursing through his body like precision lighting, striking his flesh first then going deeper to rattle his bones. A thunderous echo was just a step behind the vibrations, galloping through the trees. Getting closer. Coming fast.

"What is that?" Aaron said.

"You know what it is," Max said, softly. "Aaron, go. Catch Carole."

"Knock the hero shit off," Aaron said, pulling at Max's arm.

Max yanked his arm away, sitting up. "I'll slow it down best I can."

"Max."

"Just go," Max said, reaching for a broken tree limb.

Aaron stood up. "Max, I—"

"Please don't say anything weird, man. Just go." Max's eyes locked on Aaron's. "Keep her safe or so help me, I'll find a way back and kick your ass."

Aaron turned away from his friend, and ran after Carole. The beam from the flashlight was at least a hundred yards deeper into the forest, blinking as it passed behind trees and bushes, fading from view. He was in danger of losing sight of her. He pushed himself harder. His chest pounded, sweat flowed, his lungs ached, and his legs screamed *no more*. He really wished at some point in his life he'd taken up running, or jogging, or any kind of exercise whatsoever. Tree branches slapped at Aaron's body as he ran faster than he knew how. The smell of pine filled his nose and he could feel his face beginning to rub raw from the scrape of needles. A pinecone hit him square in the forehead and he slowed to shake it off. He blinked his eyes a few times, then the sound of a bonfire being ignited with far too much accelerant boomed behind him. He looked back just in time to see a fireball in the distance ascend into the underside of the forest canopy.

Max screamed.

Aaron started running again. The bouncing light ahead was less than a hundred feet away, and he was closing the gap. When he could see her thin silhouette he called out.

Carole stopped, aimed the beam back at him.

Aaron held up a hand to block the light. "Turn that off."

"Why."

"You're like a freakin' lighthouse."

"Where's Max?"

"He... he went a different way."

"He did what?"

"He's trying to keep it off our tail." Aaron pushed her forward. "Go, go."

She turned toward him, defiant. "How is he going to keep it..."

Her words faded and sadness flickered in her eyes as understanding washed over her features. Aaron shook his head. "There's no time for this."

He grabbed her wrist and pulled as he started to move. She resisted for only a moment. Then they ran in the dark, stumbling every few yards. Aaron fell twice and Carol stopped each time, pulling him to his feet. After several more minutes, Carol smacked into a tree, tumbling backward. Aaron hit the same damn tree and fell across her legs.

Crap. Aaron rolled off her, feeling the damp needle-covered ground beneath him. "You okay?"

"Yeah. Need to rest."

"Just for a few..." Aaron breathed deeply lying flat on the ground.

Fear induced adrenaline flowed through him but he could do nothing with it. It was fuel for a machine that was grossly out of shape and all it did was cause his head to pound, his limbs to shake, and a displaced nausea that moved into parts of his body he wasn't aware could even feel nausea. A part of him wanted this over. To just let it end. But another part, the part that was focusing on the distant vibrations in the earth bearing down on them like a herd of buffalo had another idea.

Embrace the adrenaline.

Aaron sprang to his feet. "Break's over."

"Just a few more—" Carole began to say, but stopped as a distant galloping began to resonate through the trees. "I'm ready." Carole jumped up and took off running leaving Aaron standing still.

Soon Aaron was on her heels again, the galloping growing louder behind them. Aaron knew it was his imagination, but he swore he felt the thing breathing on his collar. He slapped at the rising hairs on the back of his neck, dirt and sweat running down his shirt.

The galloping was so close now; it couldn't be more than ten or twenty yards behind them–thunderous, pounding. Carole turned hard to the right and ducked at the base of a wide tree. Aaron joined her, tucking in behind, and they cowered at the tree's base, one of many that lined a small oval-shaped clearing where only moss-covered boulders and dead pine needles littered the ground.

The galloping stopped. The forest went still for a moment, nothing moved, nothing breathed. Carole put her hand over her mouth, trembling. Something moved by fast, forest debris caught in the enormous wake showered down in a rain of dirt, bark and pine needles.

As the debris settled, Carole and Aaron stood up slowly, each having a tight grip on the other.

"Where'd it go?" Carole whispered.

High above, a tree branch snapped in the distance. Then another. Then a symphony of breaking limbs sounded. Aaron looked up, but couldn't accept what he saw. The creature was above them, moving within the forest canopy like a snake through grass, defying gravity, reason, and sanity. Branches and pinecones hit the forest floor with echoing thuds forcing Aaron to believe.

Then the trees went quiet, needles continuing to float down in the silence.

They looked at each other, Aaron's nose inches from Carole's. "I think it's gone," he said.

Carole breathed deep. "What the hell is that—"

The ground shook, sending a tremor through Aaron's body.

The beast straightened up ten feet in front of them. Enormous, leathery, black wings slowly folded to its side, tucking just beneath the saddle. The creature blinked and jostled a fire breathing head. The hairs on an animated mane floated all around as if submerged underwater, giving life to each individual tendril. Teeth bared, the thing reared up on hind legs and the already wide chest expanded to the sound of air inhaled down the gullet.

"What's it doing?" Carole said, her nails digging into Aaron's back.

Aaron put a hand on her chin pulling her face toward him. "Don't look." He closed his eyes, resolute that after a few painful moments it would all be over. "Sorry Max."

A wave of cold rushed by, icy, biting.

Aaron opened his eyes.

A towering figure stood with its back to them, a dark cloak shrouding it from head to foot.

"Take it easy, my friend," the cloaked figure said in a deep and hollow voice.

In one hand the figure held a macabre looking bridle. Aaron narrowed his eyes. There was something wrong with its hands. They were extremely bony. No, not bony. They were bone.

Aaron's mouth went dry.

"Please excuse my pet," the newcomer said, sliding the bridle around the creature's snout. "He's naturally very curious about your world." The skeleton hand reached into its cloak, and pulled out a pile of something worm-like, fleshy, and placed it under the creature's mouth. "He wanders off whenever he gets the chance. Don't you boy?"

Aaron watched as the creature began to feed on the pile of night crawlers and maggots being offered. He loosened his grip on Carol. "That thing killed our friends."

"Yes, I suppose. Would it help you to know that it was their time?"

"What?"

The cloaked form turned around to face them. Aaron and Carole recoiled, bumping into the tree behind them. There was no flesh on the man's face, only a skull, with dark eye sockets cast down. He pulled a long scythe out of the night air and pointed it at Aaron.

"When it is your time," Death said, "the circumstances are irrelevant."

Aaron pushed away from the tree. "My friends aren't irrelevant."

Death shook his head. "You don't understand." He turned away and swiftly swung himself into the saddle. "You will." He gripped the reigns and turned his mount.

From under the saddle the bat-like wings uncoiled and began to flap. Death and his mount rose off the ground, the forest floor swirling beneath them.

Aaron and Carole stood still in the center of the clearing and watched Death ascend, then disappear in an ocean of stars.

In the thin moonlight, Aaron and Carole stared at one another. Carole grabbed his hand and they started walking back to the road. They stumbled in the dark neither of them completely sure if they were heading in the right direction, twigs and debris they couldn't see snapping under their steps. Aaron searched for a tree that was smoldering, the tree Max had been sitting under, not because he wanted to gaze upon his friend's remains but because it would mean they were near the road. When he spotted it he planned to veer away, go around. Carol didn't need to see that. He didn't need to see that. But he never got the chance.

Like waking from a nightmare, they stepped from the woods onto asphalt. The trees fell away and they were again under stars. Aaron took a deep breath, smelling pine with a hint of ash as he looked up into the night sky.

"Look," Carol said, pointing to their right.

Less than a hundred yards down the road from where they had emerged, flashing blue and red lights lit up the scene. A dozen silhouettes moved about the emergency vehicles, and before too long one noticed Aaron and Carol standing in the road.

A flashlight was aimed their way, and then another. Aaron looked at Carol not knowing what to feel. Her exhausted and spent features seemed to express the same feeling. They gazed forward, and then stepped toward the light.

* * *

"I'm just trying to get this straight. In your 911 call, you said that only one in your party was injured," the highway patrol officer recounted. "Can you tell me why three of your friends are now deceased and appeared to have expired on impact?"

Carole brought a hand to her brow. "I must have hit my head harder than I thought. I mean, I swear they were alive and talking after the crash. I guess that was just wishful thinking."

The officer flipped the page in his notebook. "Uh, huh."

Aaron could see disbelief in the officer's eyes. "Yeah, she ran off into the woods, talking like someone was with her. I went after her and I guess we got a little...lost."

Aaron swallowed hard. Lying was not really a part of his skill set.

The officer didn't write anything down, just stared.

"Hey, Mitch." A voice yelled from somewhere behind them. "Smoking gun."

Aaron and Carole turned around, looking back at the SUV, that was no longer in the middle of the road but wrapped around an enormous pine tree. Aaron could just see the top of Max's head slumped in the backseat, a piece of torn airbag lying in his lap.

A fireman stood next to Collin's crushed body in the driver's seat, his girlfriend, head and all, in the passenger seat next to him. The fireman held up an empty beer can.

"There's more than one," he yelled.

"Yep, that's a shocker," the officer said. He looked down at Aaron and Carole, clearly not trying to hide his distain. "You kids care to tell me how much the driver had to drink?"

Aaron met Carole's gaze. Carole's lips quivered but her eyes were dead still. He couldn't tell if she was putting it together or not, but Aaron could feel the cold touch of understanding slowly washing over him.

"Yeah, he had a couple of drinks." Aaron looked up at the officer. "More than a couple."

THE PERFECT PLAYGROUND

CHAD STROUP

Chad Stroup received his MFA in Fiction from San Diego State University. His short stories have been featured in anthologies such as Splatterlands and the San Diego Horror Professionals series, and his dark poetry has appeared in all four volumes of the HWA Poetry Showcase. Secrets of the Weird, Stroup's debut novel, is available from Grey Matter Press. Follow him at www.subvertbia.blogspot.com and www.facebook.com/ChadStroupWriter.

HEADLIGHTS GLARING ON A Cimmerian midnight, tires grinding the asphalt of a lonely urban road in Chula Vista, in a part of town where rural illusions sometimes still exist. A lone driver at her most vulnerable. Eyes heavy after a wild hangout session at her girlfriend's pony keg party in Eastlake. The mostly-finished bottle of her fifth strawberry daiquiri wine cooler rolling back and forth on the passenger floorboard like a man trying to put out a fire on his own body. Misty mouth that would undoubtedly fail the Breathalyzer test. Thinking about that moderately cute boy with the sideburns that she *almost* kissed. The stereo blares. Her off-key voice wailing alongside Smashing Pumpkins, too buzzed to care about the occasional sound of reflector bumps beneath her wheels.

Until—

A form sprints across the street. Not something as easily explainable as a clustered clowder of feral cats, or— as some have argued their eyes have tricked them into seeing—a naked man seeking suicidal freedom from the hardships of modern life.

Tall as a street lamp. Androgynous features. Thin as a mantis. Arms and legs like broken yardsticks. Sheer skin like laurel vellum.

It dashes in front of the quick-moving turquoise VW Jetta, a flash that the driver's eye only thinks it sees between the soft cracks of the frosty mist that decorates the windshield. On a night more fortunate than this, she might have encountered this shape elsewhere in the city, witnessing it in her rearview mirror while the vehicle was stationary and relatively safe in Terra Nova Plaza, waiting in the drive-thru of Jack in the Box for her two-for-a-dollar taco special. A brief encounter, before the form lunged into the bushes. Into the hills.

But that option never did and never will exist for Heather Chapman. She will never finish her unfocused Associate's Degree at Southwestern College. She will never lose her virginity to that Dylan McKay wannabe in the bed of his truck pulled off to the side of the road in Proctor Valley. She will never hit twenty.

A pair of middle-aged women wearing neon blue jumpsuits, out for their weekly power walking session, will discover Heather's husk the following morning. One will be yammering about her "*husband that absolutely must attend every Padres game.*" The other will turn to the side of the road and scream *OhmyGODthere'sabodydownthere,* then vomit up her good-for-your-heart Wheaties. She cannot stand the sight of blood. The women will both head quickly back to the comfort of their nearby tract homes located somewhere along the not-so-seamless border of Bonita and Chula Vista proper, gaining more exercise than they initially bargained for. The woman with the stronger stomach will phone the authorities. Police vehicles emblazoned with the City of Chula Vista logo—a sun rising above a mountain and rippling water—will surround the accident-gone-crime scene. The blood will only be a figment of the vomiting woman's imagination. The paramedics will later determine that all traces of sanguine fluids were somehow removed from the body. Forensic experts will comb the cracked, dying grass for hours, never finding a speck of evidence. This information will be intentionally omitted from any and all news articles, so as not to disturb the safe sanctuary of suburbia.

No, Heather will certainly never live to recount the tale of the unnamable thing she somewhat saw. In a split-second decision, she swerves at the sight of the mad runner, loses control. Her car flips once, rolls down a steep hill next to the road, and lands in the vicinity of a soon-to-be-built storm drain. Seatbelt never clicked. Airbag never activated.

In the distance, the unknown creature dances a mirthful, epileptic jig, gyrating like a Sea-Monkey in heat. It tiptoes on bare, wiggly, bendy feet, closer and closer toward Heather's strained calls for help. Giggling, lip licking, it inhales air through its toothless, tubular mouth hole. Humming with an insatiable hunger.

* * *

"*Saved by the Bell* sucks ass, dudes. Turn that shit off. I'm bored. What else are we doing tonight?" The sense of mischief in Chase's voice was as infectious as an STD.

"Ah, you're just mad 'cause you got caught trying to egg Mario Lopez's house that one time." Gabriel knew how to make Chase shut up, at least temporarily. "I say we go spray paint some shit on the library at Hilltop."

"*Trying* to? What the fuck do you mean by that? I hit the door twi—"

"Hey, you guys!" Danny said, somehow managing to defeat Chase's decibel level. "I don't think I have any spray paint, but if no one else has any good ideas…I've got some of *these*."

He rummaged through his tornadoed closet. He whipped out a half-used bag of assorted water balloons, a seemingly innocent possession just bursting with teenage troublemaking potential.

"Sounds as good as anything else, I guess," Gabriel said. "We could cruise down Telegraph Canyon on our bikes and hit joggers or something."

Danny laughed and almost choked on his third dose of Jolt Cola. "Remember that time we shacked that old fart right in the nuts? Classic!"

Chase made a jerk-off motion with his right hand and rolled his eyes. Been there, done that.

"Okay, fine," Gabriel said. He gazed into space, like he was trying to guess if the answer to an algebra problem was "A" or "C." "How about we launch 'em at cars from the hills out on East H Street?"

"Yeah, yeah, let's do that," Danny said. He grinned. "Let's call up that lamefuck Mark Torson. He can drive us."

Chase protested with gestures that somehow managed to be even cruder than his earlier motions, then leaned back, his body now nearly immersed in Danny's waterbed.

"Screw that," he said. "Mark's about as fun as a full pineapple rotating in my ass."

"But he can totally borrow his mom's car," Danny said. "Who else—"

"On second thought," Chase said, sighing, "maybe we shouldn't do this tonight anyway. I just got off restriction after that stupid fight at school with Shaun Ramsey. If we get caught, my dad's going to beat my ass raw and take away my Game Boy again." He absently picked at the corner of Danny's Faith No More poster.

"Chase, can you stop fucking with that? My dad just bought—"

"You got any nudie mags, Danny?" Chase asked.

"Nah, my mom found the last stash and flipped her wig. I've got—"

"Aw, come on dudes," Gabriel said. "Let's get out of here. It's been forever since we've done something like this."

"Mark. Sucks. Hairy. Nuts." Chase was always quite clear about his sentiments. He raised his body up from the waterbed coffin, peeked through the blinds, looked out at Danny's detritus-infested swimming pool.

"Well, we don't really have any other options, do we?" Gabriel asked. "He's the only one with a license. I don't know about the rest of you jerks, but at this point, I don't feel like fucking walking *or* biking all the way out there tonight."

"Yeah, no way," Danny said. "Let's just call Mark. You *know* he's not going to be busy. That limp dick is probably just watching *Alf* reruns."

"Okay, okay," Chase said. "But if he gets even slightly annoying I'm going to smack him in the head so hard that when he wakes up he's going to think he's watching *Star Trek* instead."

"I like *Babylon 5* better," Danny said.

"Are you fucking crazy?" Chase's face looked primed to kill. "Dude, just shut up. That's not the point anyway."

* * *

Mark had promptly picked the rest of them up in his mother's car after informing her that he was "going to Ben Christian's house for a Biology study group," being the lameoid mama's boy that he was. The boys parked in a cul-de-sac on Camino La Paz to take the back route to their chosen spot. The streets were lined with respectably priced vehicles guarded by dim lighting.

"You think it's safe to park here, guys?" Mark asked. "My mom's gonna shit a pig if we get broken into or anything."

"I dunno, man," Chase said, waving him away. "I heard all the vatos from VCV live on this street."

"What? But I thought—"

"Don't listen to him, Mark," Gabriel said. "He's just fucking with you."

Mark looked like a shamed puppy.

"Gabe, you dick," Chase said, "you never let me have any fun, dude."

They got out and trudged through thick bushes and lemon trees, Gabriel leading the way with a yellow industrial flashlight. Mark and Danny shared the burden of a mid-sized Rubbermaid ice chest stuffed with a small arsenal of balloons that were filled with a mixture of water from Danny's backyard hose and half a carton of milk. The ground was lumpy, but bearable. They had only been walking for about a minute, but Mark was already huffing and wheezing.

"Guys, can we take a break?" he asked.

"Oh, come on. You've got to be kidding me," Chase whispered incredulously.

"Here, just let me carry the other side," Gabriel said, grabbing the Rubbermaid plastic handle from Mark's clammy hand. He grimaced and the sweat off on his pant leg. "Keep moving, though."

After a few more minutes, they reached the clearing that led them to a small hill that overlooked East H Street. They faced sporadic lights on the opposite side of the road that highlighted the future Rancho Del Rey shopping center. Not far off to the west, they could see the outline of the Brunswick Premier Lanes building and wondered if it was Cosmic Bowling night.

They briefly turned away from the lights and back toward the trees, only seeing varying shades of green patterned against the dark sky. A small lemon fell from the nearest tree and bounced off the top of Gabriel's head.

Their hiding spot was decent, but lacking a certain perfection. Not quite close enough to touch their targets, and the cover of night and surrounding foliage was barely sufficient to shroud the four of them. A large green generator decorated with the illegibly tagged signatures of *Dopey* and *El Shaggy* (the latter of which had *"FAG"* permanently carved next to it) sat silently and hid them mostly from view. Cars sped along the street at an average of forty miles an hour. The timing for a toss had to be impeccable, and was based more on sheer luck than any sort of precise mathematical calculation.

Target practice proved to be mostly uneventful. Only Chase had any natural physical abilities to speak of, so only his balloons ever managed to make a splash on any passing vehicles. Even those successes were rare— they typically hit the corner of the trunk or a tire, likely unnoticed by the driver. They did their best to keep their eyes peeled for familiar vehicles. The last time they tossed water balloons from this spot was a few months back, and they had the misfortune of nailing Gabriel's mother's car. Gabriel would never forget the guilt he felt the morning after that incident when his mother unwittingly said to him, "I'm so thankful I have a good son who doesn't do awful things like that."

"Hey, you guys want some Doritos?"

One other good thing about Mark: not only was he a convenient chauffeur, but he always had some salty snacks in his tattered backpack that he never left home without. There were certain fringe benefits to having an overweight, junk food-obsessed faux-friend.

"I got, like, two kinds. And a couple of Chocodiles, too. We can split those if you want 'em."

Danny was busy attempting a double-fisted toss of balloons and didn't bother responding, both of which came nowhere near the intended car.

"Do I?" Chase said. "Do I? Does a Mexican pick lettuce? Does a beaner shop at Pic N Save?"

"Hey, fuck you Chase." Gabriel shoved Chase away, gave his shoulder and his pride a quick massage. He knew his friend was just being a cretinous jerk as usual, acting out of insensitivity and ignorance rather than malice, but that didn't stop Gabriel from being at least a little crushed deep down, since he was half-Mexican and had already swallowed his share of racist jokes.

"Yeah, fuck you right back, Gabe. With a used dildo." Chase threw his next balloon. It exploded prematurely. "Gah!"

"Guys, we're running low on ammo already," Danny said. He looked worried. Then again, he always looked worried. "We'd better get a good toss in soon."

Chase made a farting sound with his mouth. "Wow. *Big* surprise this night's a total bust," he said.

"Oh...lemmedovisun," Mark mumbled, his mouth stuffed with Cool Ranch. The savory crumbs tumbled with each word from the corners of his pudgy mouth.

His eagerness was obvious to the other boys, and they all groaned. According to Chase—Mark "threw like an African whore." Chase was not the World's Greatest Scholar. In his mind "whore" was spelled "hoar," and he only marginally understood what the word meant (as in, "Your mama's a hoar walking on Broadway").

"Mark, you're just gonna waste the balloon," Gabriel said. "You haven't even made one to the bottom of the hill yet."

"Lass won," Mark said. His mouthful of chips had now formed a thick paste. "I pwomith."

Mark pulled a balloon out of the cooler and stood up, swaying with anticipation, waiting for another vehicle to pass by. His Metallica shirt was about a half-size too small. His marshmallow belly peeked out the bottom of the hemline.

Mark cradled and cupped the balloon tenderly like it was his first attempt at fondling a date's breast in a near-empty movie theater.

After the longest thirty seconds in the history of time, the engine of a car could be heard in the distance, the first signs of headlights inching their way around the slight curves of the road. Mark geared up for the throw, his tongue protruding from his mouth in intense concentration.

The balloon soared clumsily, like a Japanese beetle that had just woken from hibernation.

Mark didn't just have plain dumb luck with his throw— Mark was a bona fide leprechaun. The balloon smashed on the windshield. It looked like God had blown His load all over the glass. The boys' mouths went agape and Mark was officially, though temporarily, initiated to be One of Them. They were barely able to control their cheering, belly bursting, and high-fiving.

Then—a screeching halt.

"Oh, shit!" all the boys whispered in unison, though there were likely slight variations of the expletive.

The car erratically pulled over to the side of the road. A man stepped out of the driver's seat. Short, balding, disheveled looking. Wearing the defeated attire of an oversized gray pocket tee and green sweatpants. Despite his severe lack of intimidating qualities, his adult status was enough to make the boys darken their undies. His anger multiplied that power exponentially.

"You goddamn kids! I see you up there!" he hollered, shaking his pudgy fists in their general direction. He began to walk toward the hill. "When I get up there I'm going to teach you—"

The boys were about to attempt the arduous run back across the canyon to the car when a sudden strange burst of movement came from the center divider of the wide street. The angry man was tackled by what appeared to be another, considerably more svelte, man. Chase bleated out a half-laugh.

"What the hell? I didn't know it was football season," Danny said, a goofball chuckle slipping from his lips. "Go, team!"

The driver was pinned to the ground, but the boys had trouble viewing the second man. His movements were quick and jarring, disconnected and flashing like he was a living strobe light. Disorienting, pale green flashes from a twilight dream. A wind dancer from a car dealership on a "This Weekend Only" sale made bizarre, terrible flesh.

The motions gradually slowed, and the boys were only slightly able to process what was occurring from their vantage point. Gabriel turned on his flashlight and cast the light toward the street. The skinny being peeled back epidermal layers on each of its long pencil fingers—creating a flower bouquet effect on each hand—then moved them up near its mouth, facing the sinewy stubs outward with a taunting gesture.

Nanny nanny boo-boo, it may as well have been saying. *You ca-an't catch me.*

The wiggling digits coalesced into an unfathomable proboscis. Writhing and squirming like the foulest eels in the depths of undiscovered oceans.

"Um, guys...do you see—" Gabriel had always prided himself in the fact that he had been blessed with "five better than 20/20 vision."

Chase cut him off.

"Holy fuckwad. What the shit is that?"

"Guys," Mark said, his mouth now finally clear of all edible interferences, "we gotta help him!" He stumbled down the hill a bit.

"Mark, what the hell are you doing?" Gabriel yelled.

He tried to grab Mark's shirt as he followed him down. Mark's backpack tumbled down the hill, the contents littering the side of the road. The beam from Gabriel's flashlight cut through the night like searchlights advertising a stereo blowout sale.

The creature now straddled the driver. The newly formed tentacle tube penetrated the poor man's mouth like a freshly forged sword fitting into a virgin leather sheath, muffling the man's terrified screams. Crisp sounds of sucking, squishing, and flatulence drowned out the pleading noises of human struggle.

How many sucks does it take to get to the center of a full-grown man?

The answer is three.

The victim's name was Howard Denney. He will never finish reading *Gorky Park*. He will never turn in his most professional grant proposal to his superiors on Monday. He will never make it home to finally confess to his wife that he was having an affair with her less attractive cousin (though, truthfully, he never would have confessed anyway).

The flashlight illuminated the creature's face just as it finished its midnight snack. It stretched out a pocket of flesh on the side of its newly distended belly and squirted some indeterminate creamy pink bodily fluid into the pouch, as if it was saving something special for later.

Gabriel felt his bowels in danger of loosening when he finally caught a good glimpse of the finished man-smoothie and its deadly drinker. The freak creature honed in on Mark and Gabriel with a hawk's accuracy. They reacted like living Munch paintings, with added sound effects.

If H.R. Giger had been the chief art designer of a Saturday morning cartoon, he might have come up with a character that bore a slight resemblance to what was now effortlessly gliding along the endless rows of ice plants toward them.

"Jesus shit! Run!" Gabriel yelled.

"But...my backpack..." Mark obviously did not have his priorities straight.

"Fuck your backpack! Let's go!" Gabriel tugged at Mark, then dropped the flashlight and grabbed the car keys out of Mark's hands like an aggressive designated driver, intending to get the car started even though he'd only completed one driving lesson from his older brother two months ago.

Gabriel sprinted up the hill. His fearful eyes were enough to make Chase and Danny haul ass alongside him without further explanation. Mark's preference for snacks over life caused him to fall behind the other three.

The other boys soon heard his curdling screams. They chose not to look back.

The car was in sight, but not close enough to give them any relief. Their pace quickened. Branches and brambles whipped and sliced at their faces and any other exposed portions of their bodies. Fallen lemons exploded beneath their feet like overdue pimples. Gabriel tripped over a small rock or log or some other obstruction that could not be seen clearly in the dark. He dropped eight feet into the canyon, landed on his left arm, howled in unimaginable pain. Contrary to their own selfish interests, Danny and Chase doubled back to help him. He *did* have the car keys, after all.

Gabriel's adrenaline forced him off the ground, but his arm now hung horribly, like a Dali reject.

The three remaining boys ran on, the sound of a straw slurping the hard-to-reach remnants of a root beer float lurking closely behind them. Followed by silence, then crunching leaves, bestial grunts, and gleeful sing-song laughter.

Danny hopped bushes like an Olympic hurdler.

Chase muttered a botched version of the Lord's Prayer. "Our Father Art's up in Heaven. Hollow Bee's his name. When the kingdom comes, you will be done..."

Gabriel held back tears and did his best not to take quick glances at the half-inch of cracked bone protruding from his forearm, a glistening white in the moonlight. He turned around to see how close their pursuer was. A few feet behind Gabriel, the creature somersaulted like an amateur gymnast. It hopped back to its feet and skipped playfully in a zigzag motion, then suddenly sat in the grass in a pretzeled yoga position for a few moments—its head bobbing back and forth like it had "Kumbaya" stuck in its brain on a loop, picked up a handful of lemons and juggled them like a trained monkey, then stood again, performing a mock rain dance to unseen gods before jumping back to its feet and resuming its pursuit.

The boys were beyond exhausted by now. Despite the creature's initial speed, it had not caught up to them yet. Gabriel had collapsed out of shock and the others were dragging him as best they could. As it neared them, they could see Mark's blood painting its elongated face like badly applied clown makeup. The monster seemed to be taking a leisurely stroll now, toying with them. As the boys neared the car, the creature seemed to grow bored and barely slowed its pace, not really even following them anymore. It rubbed its belly and belched like an infant, then skipped off in the opposite direction.

The boys kept their pace.

The car alarm disarmed.

They drove off in terror, eventually ditching Mark's mother's car at the corner of Madrona and Del Mar, a block from the Torson residence.

They made a pact to never tell their parents where they really went that night and that Gabriel "broke his arm trying to clear a set of ten stairs with his bike."

Mark Torson will never get himself into acceptable shape via a half-assed attempt at a gym membership. He will never design a top-selling video game called *Heavy Metal Cyborg Zombie Soldiers from Hell*. He will never have a curt fling with an out-of-his-league woman who accidentally ends up carrying his sole heir.

Mark's face will eventually decorate a milk carton. His body will never be found.

* * *

Years, months, weeks later, the further expansion of Chula Vista births the wealthy exclusivity of Otay Ranch.

On an overcast day, in a section of nature yet-to-be-developed into another crispy clean shopping center, a group of innocent, unassuming children play Tunnel Tag. The fuzz of dead dandelions clings to their play clothes. A pig-tailed girl spies a distorted form twisted and tangled in the tall grasses a few feet away from her frozen spot and decides to break the rules. From where she stands, it resembles a faded chalk outline from a long-forgotten murder scene. As she inches closer, she discovers that the form has volume. Her curious fingers confirm it is tactile. It almost feels like false flesh, a rubber body suit left behind from an unfinished Roger Corman shoot. It glides along her fingers, the slick, pythonic texture almost moving of its own volition. Dancing. Green residue marks her fingers as she allows the shed skin to float to the ground.

Mesmerizing.

The safe confines of suburban retreat stifle imagination. The perfect playground for the unexpected.

Children are not the only creatures that enjoy games.

MANANANGGAL

BILLY SAN JUAN

Billy San Juan is a doctor of psychology and published author in the Psych Geeks series of books. He has spoken on various convention panels and enjoys playing casual Magic: The Gathering. He is a proud Filipino-American and lives in beautiful, sunny San Diego.

"Don't kill her!"

The machete froze in the air, the rusty steel stopping inches from the old lady's throat. Thin, grey strands of hair wisped down the woman's wrinkled cheeks, clinging to her tears as she inaudibly sobbed. The farmland, usually bustling with workers in the daytime, now drowned in an infinite cold and deafening quiet. A bead of dew slid down the blade's worn handle, dangling ominously before dripping onto the lady's forehead in a macabre baptismal.

Jojo towered above her like a sentinel, his lanky shadow melding with hers on the musky farm soil. His eyes did not bother to look for the source of the plea.

Instead, they locked onto the woman below him with an intense rage. His breathing was short. Ragged. A combination of exhaustion and ire.

A few inches.

A quick swipe.

That's all he would need.

The voice pled again.

"Don't kill her!"

He held his arm steady.

* * *

Bobet trudged toward his cousin, arms outstretched. His gait slowed with every step through the soft mud, a sickening mixture of soil, dew, and manure. His thighs, sore from hours of picking crops, pled for him to sit and rest. Yet still he strode forward in hopes of stopping the potential disaster. Jojo's figure was unmistakable despite the midnight mist enshrouding them. Bobet would often tease Jojo for his height, asking for a weather forecast because his head was so far up in the sky. The teasing was in good jest, and not without merit. He stood a full six inches above the other workers, an advantage he exploited when harvesting fruit from trees.

"Stay away!" Jojo's voice echoed, soused with fear.

Bobet paused. The cousins had been raised together in the Philippines. They immigrated to California side-by-side. Bobet knew every idiosyncrasy in Jojo's arsenal, and fear was an unknown entity for his lanky kin. Jojo's newfound emotion, in turn, stirred a newfound feeling in Bobet. A feeling he hadn't felt half an hour ago, while sitting in a truck destined for Delano. It was a feeling Bobet had never experienced. A feeling he hoped he would never feel again, because it stripped him of his manhood and left him exposed and vulnerable. He felt...

Helpless.

"It's a monster," Jojo screamed. "It attacked Maria!"

"She's sick. She needs help."

"She's a manananggal!!"

"You're scared, Jojo." A slight warble betrayed Bobet's calm facade. "The stories aren't true."

"Stay away, Bobet!"

Bobet forced himself to continue toward his cousin. It seemed as though with every agonizing step forward, the mist in the field thickened. Despite his sensibilities, Bobet began to pray to the God of his mother's bedtime stories... the God that would supposedly prevent such situations from happening. The God he rejected years ago. He began to recite the prayers his mother taught him. He prided himself in being a logical Filipino who eschewed generations of Catholic family values, yet in this time of duress his skepticism had betrayed him. This would be the moment for his faith to be tested. Were God to intervene, Bobet would repent. He would believe.

He strode forward.

"Jojo, I'm here. She wasn't trying to hurt Maria. She was confused. It's the rabies. She needs help."

"No!"

The blade swung down.

* * *

Two days ago.

Bobet wiped the sweat from his forehead.

"We can make history," he said, tossing a freshly picked bushel of grapes into his lug.

He and Jojo had been working the grape fields of a farm outside of Bakersfield. Workers scattered the vineyards, tenderly filling their wooden lugs with Merlot bushels. The lugs were made of heavy wood, and the hastily gouged handles dug into their fingers with every step. Bobet's hands were sore from the day's work, a combination of dried skin and splinters.

"I don't want to make history. I want to make money."
Jojo's lug was much lighter than Bobet's, if only because most
of the fruit he picked ended up in his mouth.

"What money? We're not making money. Look at us." Bobet
stood, his knees creaking audibly. "We work hard, and for
what? To live in a camp and serve as a meal for mosquitoes."

The mention of the mosquitoes caused him to itch a bite on
his neck.

"It's not that bad. A lot of people have it worse back home in
the Philippines." He tossed another into his mouth. It popped,
filling his mouth with a sweet succulence. "It's not glorious, but
we have a roof over our heads and a steady job. We're not rich,
but we're not poor. We have a good life here, Bobet. A good life,
and grapes." He held the bushel up and smiled. "Lots of grapes."

Bobet swiped the bushel away from Jojo's hand and knelt
next to his cousin. "We are poor, Jojo. Itilong wants to change
that." Bobet's head swept the immediate area, and then
lowered his voice to a whisper. "Look, Itliong, Vera Cruz, and
some of the other workers are planning to strike in Delano.
We're organizing throughout the camps."

"Strike? For more money?"

"For fair money."

"You'll only make the farmers angry. We might even lose
our work, all because you're coveting more than our lot." Jojo
retrieved the bushel his cousin had swiped and blew the dust
off. He picked off one of the fruits and threw it playfully at his
cousin. "Stop worrying about the entire situation, Bobet. God
will take care of us."

"God is moving too slow for me." Bobet grinned, relishing
at the momentary shock that swept over Jojo's face. "The
farmers need workers like us to harvest the land. We're not
asking for much, just what is owed to those with aching feet
and sore backs." Bobet's head swiveled, alert for prying ears.
He leaned forward and whispered, "It's a revolution."

Jojo lowered the grapes. His normally blithe face suddenly
turned solemn. "You sound like you're joining them."

Bobet said nothing.

Jojo sighed. "Be careful, okay? Don't get arrested. Or worse."

Bobet smiled. He retrieved his lug and walked to the next batch of grape vines. "Nothing they can do to me is worse than having to look at your ugly face."

The carefree smile returned to Jojo's face. He prepped for a response, but was unexpectedly shoved forward.

"Ay!" Jojo exclaimed in shock. He turned to face a woman covered nearly entirely by rags.

The woman's tattered, gray hair draped around her thin form like a withered cloak. The stench of rotted breath assaulted Jojo's nose, stinging his nostrils with every breath. Her skin was wrinkled, like dried leather. Its complexion was paler than the other Filipinos or Mexicanos that worked the fields, a type of gray he had only seen on overcooked pork. Her eyes, jaundiced yellow with slit-like pupils, darted between the two men.

She hissed, and scurried away.

* * *

Bobet rushed his cousin, tackling him into the mud.

"What have you done?" he screamed, pinning down Jojo's arms.

He expected a struggle, but Jojo simply lay on the ground looking at him. Or rather, past him.

Tik tik tik tik…

The faint sound of wings flapping caught Bobet's ears, and he turned.

The lady hissed at him.

She rose from the ground with thin, gnarled bat-like wings that sprouted from her back. They watched as her body stretched upwards, as though some ethereal being had grabbed her by both ends and pulled her apart. Her wings thrashed hypnotically, lifting her higher and higher while her talon-like feet gripped the soil below. Her fingers, long and wiry, ended in sharp claws which matched the fangs lining her maw. The skin of her abdomen continued to stretch until it tore, detaching her from her torso. The sound of the flesh tearing apart caused Bobet to wince with disgust. Her entrails hung from the upper half like some sort of crimson tail dripping blood like tears. The putrid odor of fresh blood violated their lungs with each terrified gasp. She rose, higher and higher still, until her disembodied torso blocked their view of the moon and stars, disappearing into a featureless silhouette that eclipsed the very heavens.

Bobet whispered her name in disbelief.

* * *

One day ago.

"Lilibeth."

Embers from the campfire flickered into the air. Bobet sat with some of the other workers while one of the Mexicanos gently picked at a guitar. Jojo sat across from him, a pregnant woman, Maria, leaning against his shoulder. The loose, yet somehow harmonious notes of the guitar soothed their aching joints and sunburned skin.

"We call her Lilibeth," Maria continued.

She had recently moved from one worker's camp to this one, motivated by one too many drunken lashings from her ex-boyfriend. Jojo took care of her, and eventually she moved to the camp to be with him. Whereas Julio became monstrous after a few beers, Jojo simply became overly affectionate with kisses.

"She doesn't talk to anyone," Maria continued. "We didn't see her leave her room except in the morning to go to the fields. She didn't bathe with us or eat with us."

"Maybe she's sick," Bobet offered.

He remembered the old woman's jaundiced eyes and furrowed flesh. Several workers had been stricken with rabies in the previous months, having been bitten in the fields and in their sleep by frenzied skunks or bats. Jojo had even killed a possum that wandered into the campground with foam at the mouth. None of the workers who had been bitten were around the campfire that night. None of them worked the fields that day.

"She's not sick," Maria countered. "She's weird though, been this way since she came to this area. Sometimes, we'll find animal bones near where she sleeps. We think she eats them." She instinctively completed a sign of the cross. "And when she put her arms out, I saw her fingers like this." She twisted his arm into a talon-like shape. "Maybe she's a devil or something."

Bobet shook his head. "You're messing with us, Maria. That, or the baby is making you crazy."

The Mexicano stopped plucking the taut strings and laughed. "She was crazy before getting pregnant. You'd have to be crazy to sleep with Julio."

The group laughed. Maria smiled and massaged her bulging belly. "It would have been crazier to stay with him." She leaned against Jojo and gave him a kiss on the cheek.

One of the workers lit a cigarette in the fire's embers. "Bobet, are you still planning to strike in Delano?"

Bobet nodded. "You should join us. All of you should. The more of us who stop working, the stronger our voice will be."

Jojo's arm wrapped around Maria. "You save the world your way, cousin. I'll save it my own."

Bobet grinned. Jojo's height, along with his calm demeanor, made him very attractive to the female workers. And yet, he chose the woman who was pregnant with someone else's child. It made sense, he supposed. Despite their radically different personalities, they were both two young men seeking to be heroes.

He motioned for a drag from the cigarette. "Four days until we head to Delano."

Maria looked up. "What's in Delano?"

"The strike. Many of us are joining. We'll only be gone a few days."

"Hopefully," the Mexicano said ominously. He looked down at his guitar. "Still, we deserve equal wages. We're not animals."

Maria turned to Jojo. "You're not going, are you?"

Tobacco smoke billowed from Bobet's mouth as he watched his cousin reassure Maria. "No, I have my own things to take care of here." He placed his hand gently on her stomach and smiled.

* * *

Bobet and Jojo ran.

"Why didn't you kill it?" Bobet screamed.

"I tried!" Jojo yelled.

Exhausted, Bobet slowed. He turned towards his cousin, who had also taken pause. The boys slumped in exhaustion, each breath of frigid aid burning their parched throats.

"If we can't outrun it, we'll fight it." He held out his hand, eyes fixated on the creature in the distance. "Give me the machete."

Nothing.

"Jojo, the machete!"

"I dropped it."

Bobet's eyes left the horizon and glared at his cousin. "You idiot!"

"You were the one who stopped me!"

Tik tik tik tik...

Bobet grabbed Jojo's arm and pulled. "Run!"

The cousins fled towards the campground. With each panicked stride, they frantically searched the farm for any sort of weapon. Their eyes scanned the empty field, its vast expanse offering no hope for shelter or refuge. Their feet sank into the mud with each frantic step, as though the earth itself was trying to hold them down as a sacrifice for the pursuing beast. The scarcity of options almost seemed intentional, as though the very earth had deemed the cousins as unworthy for combat.

There were no weapons. No options. Only the field. And the grapes. And the...

Bobet pivoted and grasped one of the wooden stakes that anchored the grape vines. He grunted in pain as he struggled to free it from the dirt.

Jojo joined him, and together they pried it free.

Silence.

"Wait," Bobet whispered. "I think it's gone."

They scanned the area behind them, but Lilibeth was not there. The night lay silent, void of the sickening *tik tik* of leathery flesh against the cold air.

The brothers stalled, bracing their stances back to back. Bobet held the wooden post high in the air, ready to swing. Jojo clenched his hands by his face, ready to launch a fist with his lanky arms. They scanned the skies.

"Why did you stop me back there?" Jojo accused

"I didn't know."

"I thought you were going to Delano."

"I was until…"

* * *

Two hours ago.

Maria ran to the truck as it drove from the camp. Inside, Bobet and the workers had been set for their road trip to Delano. The truck cabin held two, but the bed of the truck held a good eight more. The workers, who for too long had harvested for the farmers, would soon travel to reap the future.

"Bobet!" Maria cried. She stumbled towards the truck bed, her wavy hair clinging to her forehead with sweat. Her eyes pleaded for help as she told Bobet everything.

Bobet's throat tightened. "What happened to Jojo?"

"He's taken a machete," she sobbed. "He's chasing Lilibeth."

Bobet nodded to the others and leaped off the truck bed.

"Go on," he instructed. "I'll find a way there tomorrow."

"Do you need help?" the Mexicano asked.

"He's my cousin, I'll take care of it. Go, change our destinies."

The Mexicano nodded and the truck roared away.

Bobet turned towards Maria and softly grasped her shoulders. "What happened?"

Bobet was glad the other workers were not present to hear Maria's story:

She had woken up to Lilibeth standing in her and Jojo's room, the woman's jaundiced eyes eerily glowing as she approached Maria's womb. Her fingers, with claw-like nails, were outstretched and cupped like a child reaching for an apple. Her thin, cracked lips had drawn back to reveal thin, razor-like teeth that glimmered in the moonlight. The teeth at the very front of her mouth looked like sharpened fish bones, as though they were made for precise incisions. Lilibeth's foul breath, the same stench of rotted flesh which assaulted Bobet in the field, filled every crevice of the decrepit hut with the foul stench of decayed innards. The thin rags she normally wore lay piled at her feet, and in the moonlight filtering through the window Maria could see every wrinkle in her baggy skin. Maria watched helplessly until one of the fingers poked at her bulging stomach. She screamed, violently waking Jojo. Lilibeth glared up in the same way a snake darts its head towards a predator and quickly slithered out the open window.

Jojo, having gained his bearings, instructed Maria to find help. He reached towards the table, grabbed the machete he often used for clearing brush, and sprinted after the creature.

* * *

Jojo turned towards his cousin. "You should have gone to Delano. Then I would have killed the monster, and you'd be safe."

A rustle caused Jojo's head to swivel. A rabbit darted from its burrow, running from an unseen predator. He took a deep breath, and walked to one of the other wooden stakes to pry it from the ground.

Bobet lowered the post in his hands. "We need help. We should head back to the camp."

They vigilantly began walking back. Bobet's ears analyzed every sound in the night's silence, alert for the now-familiar *tik tik* noise. There was no clicking, only the sloshing of mud beneath their soles. The warbled screech of a lonely cricket. Jojo's soft recitation of the Hail Mary below his breath, each word in rhythm with his gait. Any other night, this would have been a pleasant walk.

They approached the spot where Bobet had tackled his cousin. The location looked like any other part of the fields, except for the grapevines that had toppled in their panicked escape. Jojo's attention was attracted by a glimmer. The machete, lying unceremoniously in the dirt but otherwise undamaged. He retrieved it and wiped the blade clean of debris. The pungent, metallic stench of blood turned his attention from the blade to a short, odd shape nearby.

He screamed.

Jojo looked down at the bottom half of the monster's abdomen that stood like a silent totem, the innards neatly pooled in the open cavity like a morbid bowl of bloody soup. The reptilian talon-like feet had anchored into the mud, each protrusion ending in a dirty, jagged claw. The body was still alive, flesh twitching, waiting for its upper half to return.

"No," whispered Bobet.

Jojo approached the torso. He had suspected, but it was fantastic to believe.

"Manananggal."

* * *

One hour ago.

"Manananggal?" Maria's confusion betrayed her attempt at bravery. She and Bobet had arrived at the edge of the grape field, the direction she had last seen Jojo heading towards.

"Yes, Manananggal. In the Philippines, it's a type of... like, a vampire. It detaches right here," he motioned to his naval, "and flies on demon-like wings at night to look for prey. Jojo's mother

would tell him all sorts of stories about them, because she thinks she heard one when she was a child. She was in the forest, and she heard an old lady begging for help in the forest. She didn't go, because she had been warned never to go into the forest alone. But she believed it was a Manananggal trying to lure her as food."

"So, it eats people?"

"It feeds on people, but it mostly eats..." Bobet stopped. He couldn't believe he was harboring this thought.

Maria questioned him, her curiosity challenging his discretion. "Mostly eats what?"

"Nothing." Bobet involuntarily glanced towards Maria's pregnant womb before he motioned towards the camp. "It's impossible. Manananngal is a myth from where we come from. Listen, Lilibeth is sick. She probably has rabies. If she bites Jojo, he'll get it too. We know it's been going around. Go back to the camp and get help. I'm going out there to stop him."

Maria watched Bobet run into the grape field before she turned towards the camp.

* * *

The men paused, torn between fear and disbelief. They stared at the upright abdomen, its entrails pulsating to an unseen heartbeat.

Bobet broke the silence. "How does a Manananggal even show up here? We're in America, not Visayas."

"I don't know," Jojo replied. "Maybe it stowed away on a shipment."

Bobet shook his head, his eyes fixated on the gory half-figure in front of him. It was real.

Was it real?

If a manananggal existed, then so did the other monsters of his childhood fairytales. So did the God that his mother swore would protect him. The God that had subjected him to poverty, a life of toiling in the fields for ungrateful farmers who...Skepticism took hold.

"Of course," Bobet said to himself.

"Of course, what?"

"It's the farmers. They're trying to scare us. They heard about the strike and they're trying to spook us."

Jojo shook his head, "That doesn't look fake to me." Bobet rubbed his head. It didn't look fake to him either. But it had to be. This was impossible. "Then it must be a type of rabies," he justified. "A type we haven't seen."

"Have you ever seen rabies do that?" Jojo's lanky hand pointed in the direction of the dismembered torso. "Okay," Bobet relinquished. "Maybe not. Either way, we should get back to the camp."

Jojo nodded. "Just, one thing first." He approached the torso. "If we kill this, the creature can't rejoin it. And it will die when the sun comes up."

The logic by which he lived his life had suddenly collapsed. The fairy tales of his youth had come true, a situation he was not equipped to accept.

Rabies.

Rabies doesn't make you grow wings.

Rabies doesn't chase you down a field, screeching like a demon.

Bobet surrendered. "Sure. Let's destroy it."

The cousins raised their weapons.

A sharp screech and the flap of wings bellowed behind them.

* * *

Maria returned to camp, gasping for air and protectively cradling her belly. She gathered the workers and explained what had happened. They gathered their tools, their machetes and axes and shovels. Armed, they ran into the field. A young woman, whose name Maria did not know, led her back to her bed for rest. Maria's descent into sleep came swiftly due to exhaustion. The young woman then grabbed her Bible and rosary and ran to join the others.

After all, machetes and axes were inferior to the Word of God.

The workers split into groups of two, each pair walking through a row in the vineyard. Within the hour, a whistle pierced the stillness. Everyone converged to a horrific sight. The two young cousins lay in the mud. The lanky one was covered in slices, their origin no mystery due to the nearby machete. The other, identified by the guitar-plucking Mexicano as Bobet, was missing a chunk of flesh from his neck.

The workers lowered their weapons. Murmurs speculating the gruesome scene began to grow, with a consensus quickly reached. Jojo, infected with rabies, had chased Lilibeth into the field. Bobet attempted to rescue her, but Jojo had tragically succumbed to the disease. Bobet must have fended off Jojo's attacks with the machete, but not before he had suffered a deadly bite to the neck.

The workers shivered and cried. One vomited. The young woman, who had escorted Maria to bed, read aloud from her Bible. She did not notice that her feet were standing an inch below everyone else's, resting in the imprint of two suspiciously large claw-like indentations. The workers then carried the bodies back to camp for a proper burial, saying silent prayers to their respective gods.

The burial was silent. Solemn. Tragedy was not unknown amongst the workers. After their prayers, they would rest. They would pray. And they would rise the next morning to work the grape field.

All except Maria.

Because as they stood in the night, digging the graves for the two young men, they did not notice the open window leading to Maria's bed. Nor did they notice the old woman kneeling at the foot of Maria's bed.

Nor did they hear the old woman feed.

FEED YOUR MUSE

R.W. GOLDSMITH

R.W. Goldsmith writes science-fiction, fantasy, and horror. For a decade and a half he was the scriptwriter for The Fallbrook Outlaws, a top Southern California wild-west stunt troupe in which he also directed and performed. He currently lives in San Diego county.

AT LONG LAST, PREPARATIONS were complete; fame was within my grasp. Table, brushes, oil paints, stretched canvases, the largest easel my inheritance could buy, each was in its proper place. Except for a full-length mirror, the studio walls were bare, awaiting the inevitable prestigious awards my art would bring. Wouldn't be long before I'd need more wall space. A bigger house, however, would have to wait until the money started flowing my way— shouldn't take but a week or two. My wife, Darcey, was happy enough living here in Burbank with all the other philistines, but I was destined for a more prestigious, cultured style of life—a home in Beverly Hills, perhaps.

All that was needed was for me to paint a masterpiece or two and reveal my genius to the world.

Leonard J. Filster, what an excellent name I had. Leonard J. Filster: artist extraordinaire. Leonard J. Filster: father of the renowned Filster Movement. Leonard J. Filster: benevolent—

The studio door cracked open. "Leo, are you in there?" Darcey poked her head in. "Christ, Leo, I asked you an hour ago to change Kittykins' litter box. It's stinking up my kitchen."

The woman was obsessed with interrupting my work. "I'm busy."

"Doing what? I still don't see any paint on the canvas."

"If you're going to be like that, you can change the litter box yourself."

"That's not my job. Neither is waiting for you to do what you say you'll do." She entered my sanctum and crossed her arms. "This is the last time I let you throw our money away on one of your half-baked dreams. We've got a garage full of *Filster for Mayor* signs, a piano neither of us can play, and a dozen other useless things taking up space, all because you want to be famous without ever actually doing anything. Well this is it. I've had it. I'm through with you wasting our money on pipe dreams. You either learn how to paint, or you can get off your butt and get a job like normal people do."

"Talented people don't need to learn. I have a gift for art. I can feel it."

"Yeah, yeah. Like I haven't heard that one before. I'm giving you one week, and that's it. You either show me this talent of yours, or I'm turning your studio back into the guest bedroom and inviting my mother to visit."

"A week? But I need inspiration to paint. It's not something one just pulls out of thin air."

Darcey walked to the mirror, turned her back to me, and fussed with her hair. "Find your muse. Isn't that what you artist types call it—the thing that inspires you to create?"

As she was likely spying on me in the mirror, I kept my expression neutral. "Yes, dear, but muse is just a figure of speech. Real inspiration comes from one's soul, that and suffering; suffering's also supposed to be good for inspiration."

With a toss of her hair, she turned and faced me with a sly smile. "Well, there you go, cleaning the litter box should provide you with all the inspiration you need. And while you're at it, take out the trash."

"I should say no."

"Just get it done. I've got clients interested in the Parkview house. I won't be back until late if they make an offer."

Not even a 'please' from the woman. How was I to work in such a hostile environment?

With a white-plastic trash bag in one hand and a reeking litter box in the other, I made my way out the back door to the trashcans lining the backyard privacy fence. Summer in Southern California, the worst of times when my terrycloth robe soaks up the mid-morning sun as quickly as it does the sweat of my toil. Once the money poured in, I would hire someone to take out the trash and clean the damn litter box.

Curled up on the cushion of a green-plastic lawn chair, Kittykins stretched and yawned. The useless animal only came indoors when it wanted to crap, piss, and eat. Darcey's real-estate clients often relayed stories of the cats they'd lost to coyotes. No such luck with Kittykins.

I flipped open the trash-bin lid. The ghosts of kitty-litters past assaulted my nose. So unfair I should have to endure such unpleasantness. A senseless waste of my talents dumping garbage when I could be painting.

The stench of next-door-neighbor Aaron Mildue's cologne preceded him as he creaked open my backyard gate, the deep-woods scent so strong it might have been distilled from lumberjack sweat. "Hey there, buddy. Hope you don't mind. Beemer's on red. I need to borrow some gas."

"Sorry," I said, though actually I wasn't. "I haven't refilled my gas can since the last time you borrowed it."

"Really? Shoot, how about I borrow your wife instead?"

As if I would ever agree to such a thing.

Aaron smiled. "Kidding, just kidding, okay?"

He headed back for the gate. "You should keep your gas can filled. You never know when you might need it."

Aaron let the gate slam behind him as he left. I wished for the hundredth time that Darcey would pick up a padlock for the gate like I'd asked her to do.

I paused before closing the trash-bin lid and stared at the sight of a full-color flyer atop the kitty-litter-garnished bags of garbage. The flyer featured a full-page color copy of Van Gogh's bandaged self-portrait with an advertisement printed in a bold font.

FEED YOUR MUSE
FREE YOUR INNER ARTIST
FULFILL YOUR DREAMS
NO EXPERIENCE NECESSARY
NO MONEY DOWN
MONEY-BACK GUARANTEE
WHAT HAVE YOU GOT TO LOSE?

"Fulfill my dreams? Oh, hell yeah. Sign me up."

The flyer was a prank rather than a scam, of course. Anyone with half a brain could see that. The leaflet contained neither a phone number nor an address of any kind—an impractical method of defrauding people, to say the least.

Earlier, Darcey had told me to find my muse. She'd also had me empty the trash. A set up for sure. She and Aaron were in this together. He'd distracted me while Darcey snuck in and placed the flyer on top of the trash bags within the bin. Hard to imagine them working together though. She claimed to dislike the man as much as I did. What could have possessed her to collaborate with him?

How about I borrow your wife?

No. It was a ludicrous idea. Darcey would never betray me like that.

No money down. Money-back guarantee. Had to be Aaron's doing. He was all about money. He'd pulled the prank on his own. Didn't surprise me in the least he was adept at sleight-of-hand.

With a final look at the flyer, I closed the trash-bin lid. Sad really. If only the advertisement were real.

* * *

Although a stack of inspirational books had sat atop the studio table for the better part of a week, inspiration eluded me. Having stared at the books for nearly half an hour, I was feeling a twinge of impatience when a loud shave-and-a-haircut knock came from the front door. Darcey was off doing whatever it was realtors did. Her friends knew better than to drop by unannounced. Had to be a salesperson, they always showed up at the most inopportune times. If I simply waited, they'd go away.

When I thought they'd left, a cop-knock rattled the door. "Open in the name of the law," boomed a megaphone voice. "We've got the house surrounded. Throw down your weapons and come out with your hands in the air."

The police—my God, what had I done? Was this about the marijuana cigarette Aaron forced on me a few months back? The unpaid parking ticket? Oh Lord, what if Darcey were involved in some nefarious realtor scam?

"Have it your way, tough guy. All right, men, break it down." A battering, splintering of wood shook the house.

"No, no, I'm coming out. Don't shoot." I raised my hands and moved from the studio to the living room with shaky steps.

"Come into the kitchen then and don't try anything funny. Snipers have you in their sights."

Snipers? Oh my God. I didn't see any red dots. Didn't mean there weren't any on my face or back. "I'm coming. Don't shoot."

"Keep your hands where we can see 'em if you don't want things to get ugly."

Slow, deep breaths. Don't look guilty. This was all a mistake. Everything would be fine.

I hurried from the living room to the kitchen. Condiment containers, bread and lunchmeat packages lay strewn about the kitchen countertop upon which sat a man chowing down on a sandwich. He swallowed and held the sandwich in one hand like a fat cigar.

"There you are," the man said in the booming voice, then shifted to a far less boisterous tone. "Did you know you're out of horseradish?"

Instead of the police, there was a lunatic in my home. Dressed in flowered surfer shorts and a red t-shirt with *The Devil's in the Details* emblazoned on the front, he grinned at me as though awaiting a friendly retort.

"You're not the police. Get out of my house." It was all the friendly he deserved.

"Hold on there, bucko. I didn't call you. You called me."

"You're crazy. You broke down my door. Get out, now." I could be quite firm when angered.

"Don't get your ascot in a knot, Dolittle. Your door's fine. Give us a sec while I checks me records."

"That's the worst Cockney impression I've ever heard, and—oh my God, what are you doing?"

The lunatic had shoved his half-eaten sandwich into his shorts and was visibly moving his hand about beneath the fabric. A demented smile lit his face, and he pulled out a standard-size clipboard. He ran a finger down an attached sheet of paper. "Is this 2323 South Who-cares Street, et cetera, et cetera?"

Dismayed as I was by the fate of the missing sandwich, I answered. "That's certainly not how it's pronounced, but yes, it is."

"Check. And are you or are you not Leonard J. Filster?"

"Yes, I am, but I don't understand. How—"

"And did you not ask that your inner artist be freed so as to fulfill your dreams?"

"Yes—no, I mean I did, but I thought it was a joke. It's not?"

The man hopped off the counter and bowed with a highly exaggerated flurry of arms. "Please allow me to introduce myself. Manny Niflheim, at your service. Key Master, big-shot CEO, and Chief Provocateur for Feed Your Muse Enterprises."

Manny snapped his fingers and produced an archaic writing quill, then offered me it along with the clipboard. "Sign on the bottom line, and we can begin."

"I'm not signing anything."

Manny shoved the clipboard and quill into his shorts, tore the paper into tiny pieces, and tossed the confetti into the air. "That's okay. What's a contract among friends? So, what do you say we get started? Follow me."

If this was a con job, the man had picked the wrong mark. I'd spent the last of my inheritance on setting up my studio. As I'd nothing to lose should he turn out to be a swindler, I followed him to the back door.

Manny paused with his hand on the doorknob. "Every artist requires a medium. Allow me to present you with yours." With that, he opened the door.

To say I was dumbfounded would be an understatement. Where, a half-hour before, the backyard had been a jungle of crabgrass, weeds, and plastic lawn furniture, a paved patio now lay within the confines of the fence, the concrete set and dry as though poured the week before.

With a sweep of his arm, Manny ushered me outside. "Bet you weren't expecting this, eh bucko?"

I rubbed my eyes and looked again. The patio was still there. "How's this even possible?"

"Art isn't about the possible. It's about the impossible."

I stepped from the doorstep. No illusion, the concrete was solid beneath my feet. "I don't have the money for this. Try your scam on someone else."

"Money," Manny said, "'tis such a trivial thing. What we're talking about here is assigning you a muse and unleashing your inner artist. This has nothing to do with something so mundane as money."

"You're serious?"

"Deadly serious."

"But why a patio?"

"This is no patio, bucko. This is a canvas."

"What, you expect me to paint on concrete?"

"What else would a sidewalk artist paint on?"

"But I bought an easel."

"And a damned fine easel it is, I'm sure." Manny handed me a Twinkie-size stick of white chalk pulled from his shorts. "This is yours."

Before I could grasp the chalk, he snatched it away. "Silly me, I almost forgot. Before I assign you a muse, it's paramount you agree to certain stipulations. A muse is not to be summoned lightly. As you know, they're quite rare."

This was it, the crux of Manny's scam. He thought me gullible enough to buy a mythological muse as if they existed. "Is this the part where I sign away my first born?"

"No, this is the part where you swear the tiniest of oaths. No oath, no muse. Shall we proceed?"

Like the flyer said, what did I have to lose? An oral agreement without witnesses would hardly stand up in a court of law. Besides, curiosity demanded I discover what this insufferable oddball was up to. "I suppose."

"That's the spirit." Manny again reached into his shorts and pulled forth a beat-up Spiderman comic book on which he had me place my left hand while raising my right. "Do you, Leonard J. Filster, swear to feed your muse three squares a day, plus an occasional late-night snack?"

Feed the muse? What did muses eat—fairy-dust-frosted unicorn flakes? "Sure, why not?"

"You have to say, 'I do.'"

"I do."

"Here you go then. She's all yours."

Manny handed me the chalk and returned the comic book to his shorts. Retracting his hand, he flicked his wrist and unfolded the blade of a shiny red-handled straight razor.

"Here now, pay attention," he continued. "This is the traditional way to feed a muse."

Placing the blade to his palm, he drew a crimson line, then held out his arm, made a fist, and squeezed. Blood streamed from his clenched fingers, splashing on the concrete below.

"Fuck!" I leaped back, lest the lunatic's blood land on me. "Okay, that's it. You need to leave. Get out of here before I call the real police."

"No need. I leave you with this." He pressed the back of his forearm to his brow and looked skyward with a tragic gaze. "No life without suffering, no art without life." He lowered his arm and grinned his lunatic grin. "Don't you just love those Hallmark sayings? They've got one for every occasion, you know."

Manny handed me the razor. I declined the offer, and he set it on the door step. "I'll check back with you later, see how you're doing."

He paused at the side gate and turned. "And Leo, no excuses—feed your muse."

The gate clicked closed behind him.

I glared at the gate until my anger vanished with the sudden realization that this entire episode had been staged by Darcey and some TV prank show. I'd been set up from the moment she gave me the deadline to find my muse. They'd had their fun. It was time I called them out and showed the world what a good sport I was.

"All right, you got me." I crossed my arms and peered around the yard, expecting the host of the show to make his appearance. Several seconds passed, and I set my foot tapping upon my beautiful new patio. "You can show yourselves now."

A half-dozen sparrows flew overhead and perched on the fence. Other than that, no one came forth.

So, what now? Did they expect me to make a fool of myself in front of their hidden cameras by actually trying to paint something on the patio with a white stick of chalk?

"Come on, Darcey, I know you're there."

Still no one. Being the artist I was, I had my limits. I stomped my foot. They were carrying the prank much too far.

Then again, they'd obviously invested a lot of effort and resources into this production—couldn't blame them if they wanted the prank to end with a bang. Well, nobody could say I wasn't a good sport. I would let them have their final laugh. Then I could get back to the work of waiting for my inspiration.

I knelt on the concrete near Manny's blood: it was fake, of course, and no longer of concern. To speed along the process, I held the chalk like a scrub brush and made long sweeping arcs, covering a wide swipe of concrete.

My plan had been to feign dismay and say, "Oh no, I have been tricked. I am glad no one is around to see how foolish I am." Only I didn't do that. Instead, I knelt there staring at what I'd created with that piece of white chalk, a swath of colorful wild flowers so real as to trick my eyes into believing they could be picked.

This was no special-effects illusion. No parlor trick. My talent was real. Just as I knew it would be. Just as Darcey would soon admit. She'd given me a week to find my muse. I'd found it in under an hour. There was nothing I couldn't do once I set my mind. I took in the breadth and width of the patio, three-hundred square feet at most. Good. No challenge was too big for a man like me. I would finish painting the entire patio before she returned home. She'd never doubt me again.

Kittykins appeared from whatever hole he'd been sleeping away the day in. He rubbed against my leg and meowed, probably upset at the changes to his backyard hunting grounds.

"Go away. Scat." I gave him a firm yet humane kick on the rump. "I'll let you in the house when I'm done."

The cat dashed off, and I set to work. I had a lot of canvas to cover before Darcey returned home.

The day moved on. Dedicated to my art as I was I persevered beneath the merciless California sun. It was hot as hell. Inconsiderate of Manny that he'd not included an awning in the deal.

By the time I'd covered a third of the patio, my arm shook with exertion. My back ached. My knees had grown numb.

I took a break and stood. Oddly enough, the chalk remained the same size as before. Some sort of space-age material, no doubt, though it was my genius alone which accounted for the field of wildflowers virtually growing in my backyard.

From every angle, the illusion stayed the same, a three-dimensional landscape of flowers, some so tall they rose above my head. But there was something else there, something I could not remember having created. A painted crack in the earth ran down the center of the work, a sheer-sided chasm dividing the heavenly field of flowers in two. Unable to stand on the painting without smudging the chalk, I leaned in as far as I could but could see no bottom to the pit, only rocky walls descending into darkness.

The fissure added a certain dark mystery to the work, a genius touch that would set me above the rest of the so-called sidewalk artists. Manny had called it right. Chalk really *was* my medium. Never would I be able to create such breathtaking art on anything that would fit on an easel. First thing tomorrow, I'd have Darcey register me for the next major chalk-artist exhibit in the area, preferably one to be held among the stars of Hollywood Boulevard. If the prize money were substantial enough, I might even consider traveling as far as one of the artsy beach communities to display my work.

The one drawback to chalk was it wouldn't last. Wind would scrub. Rain would wash. Not much to worry about there, even cloudy days in Southern California seldom brought rain. Of course, there was always the possibility of vandalism. No shortage of that. And there was—

"Kittykins, no! Get off." I rushed around the painting to where the damn cat was stomping across my masterpiece, marring the chalk with its paws. I inched as close as I could to the chalk, but it was impossible to reach the cat without damaging the painting.

"Scat!" I clapped my hands so hard they hurt.

Kittykins bolted.

And vanished with a wail shrinking to silence.

What had just happened? What I thought I'd seen—Kittykins dropping over the chasm rim, scrambling for purchase where there was none, falling from sight with a cry of terror. No, it wasn't possible. I was just fatigued from all my hard work. My eyes had played a trick on me was all. Perhaps they still were. I knelt for a better look. No paw prints marred the chalk. The painting was as pristine as the moment I'd applied the chalk.

Obviously, I'd imagined the entire thing. Kittykins had never walked across my work, never screamed in terror as it disappeared into the painted depths of the chasm. Kittykins was sleeping safe in a hidey-hole somewhere.

Manny should have warned me about the overactive imagination that came with freeing one's inner artist. Had I been anyone else, I might have thought I'd lost my mind. Thank God, I was me.

The hours slipped past in a haze of artistic bliss. Darcey was still not home. Her clients must have made an offer. If I kept on working, I'd finish before she returned, preferably before dark. Better to view my work in the glorious light of the sun than the dim-yellow glow of the back-porch light.

The pain in my back faded to memory. My arm grew stronger with each stroke of the chalk. The concrete cushioned me as through I were kneeling on a cloud. I was in my element.

The painting was three-quarters done. The chalk remained the same size as when Manny first placed it in my hand, a true marvel of our age.

The field of flowers stretched off into the distance. The chasm too had expanded, widening and cleaving the field like a rift in space and time. As proud as I was, I couldn't look at that crack in the Earth without thinking of the cat, of how he'd seemed to plunge from sight within the rift. Strange he hadn't shown up again. Stupid thing should've asked to be let into the house to poop or eat by now. Cats, what good were they?

The gate groaned open, and Aaron barged through, barraging my senses with the stink of his moss-riddled-forest cologne. "Outside again? Careful you don't OD on vitamin D there, buddy."

"What do you want, Aaron?"

"What, can't a neighbor drop by and say hi without wanting something?"

I moved in front of the intruder lest he step on my work. "As you can see, I'm rather busy."

"Helping the weeds grow, are we?"

Aaron was such an ass, dismissing my work as though it didn't exist. I wasn't about to give him the satisfaction of acting like I cared.

"Just mind your step, okay?"

Aaron frowned and, looking past my shoulder, scanned my work. "Say, while I'm here, you mind loaning me a can of Darcey's hairspray?"

"What on Earth for?"

"Best thing for getting lipstick out of clothes, if you know what I mean." He winked and poked me in the ribs.

I could never understand why women were attracted to someone as crass as Aaron. "I'm sure Darcey doesn't want you using her hairspray. Try soap."

"That's okay, and you know what? I get it. You're ticked at me because I'm always borrowing your stuff. And you're right. I've been kind of thoughtless. Tell you what, first thing tomorrow, I'm bringing over my lawnmower and straightening up your yard."

I cocked my head and gave him my best 'are you crazy?' look. "Are you crazy—can't you see what I'm doing here?"

"Not really, but look, even if *you* don't care about these weeds, I'm sure Darcey does." Aaron stepped around me and strode across the flowers, smudging the colors with his glossy patent-leather shoes. "A woman like her, she deserves better than—"

"Stop! Get off. You're ruining my work."

Aaron turned with a confused look. "You're joking, right?"

He shook his head and continued on across the field, destroying golden-orange poppies and yellow daisies, along with purple, red, and blue flowers whose names I didn't know. Hours of work ruined. On he walked, closing in on the fissure. For a moment, I wished the rift were real, that it would suck the bastard in and send him straight to hell.

I said nothing as he stepped over the chasm edge. Only as he fell screaming did I voice my shock.

Aaron was gone. Unlike the cat, there was no way he could have dashed off to hide without me seeing. The painting had swallowed him whole.

Round and around in circles I paced, chanting, "Oh my God," over and over and over.

Sooner or later the police would investigate Aaron's disappearance. The most damning evidence was the trail of shoe prints he'd left behind. Horrific as the prospect was, I needed to wash away the evidence with the garden hose. All my work had been for nothing, the hours of toil destined for the gutter. It wasn't fair. It wasn't right I'd have to start over because of one obnoxious neighbor.

Perhaps all was not lost. I'd mastered my craft with so little effort. How difficult would it be to paint over the evidence? Evidence which—

Hope beyond hope, I got down on my hands and knees and examined the area where Aaron had tread. The shoe prints were gone. The field of wildflowers was as it had been before, flawless, vibrant, and alive, as though Aaron had never set foot in my backyard.

Something else about the painting seemed different though I wasn't sure what. Not that it mattered, not as long as no telltale signs of Aaron's disappearance led to me.

"What are you doing out here?" came Darcey's accusatory voice from behind.

I stood. The late-day sun hovered just above the roofline. Shading my eyes, I gave her my disappointed look. "I was hoping to have it finished before you got home. What do you think?"

Darcey walked toward me, kicking Manny's straight razor off the step. It skidded to a stop at my feet.

"Think about what?" She planted herself a yard away and folded her arms across her breast. "I looked for you in your studio. Did you even *try* to paint while I was gone?"

I heard the words, but it was my wife's scent I focused on. A scent distilled from deep-mossy woods.

The fucking bitch. I'd done everything for her, and this was the way she repaid me, by screwing Aaron?

I couldn't look at her cheating eyes. The red-handled razor at my feet deserved my attention far more than my Jezebel wife.

Feed your muse.

Manny had given me the razor for that very purpose. Oh my God, I'd been such a fool. Manny hadn't been joking. The muse was real. I should have fed it as he'd said. It all made sense. Darcey and Aaron hadn't betrayed me of their own free will. They'd had no choice. The muse had made them do it. Kittykins, Aaron, both missing because I'd failed to feed my muse.

Darcey took a step back. Fear shone in her eyes. Fear and the guilt of her betrayal.

I picked up the razor and eased toward my wife. Never again would I fail to abide by my oath. Life would be wonderful. I could forgive Darcey. She wasn't to blame. Wealth and fame would make everything right. I'd need never again empty another trashcan or litter box as long as I lived.

I raised my hands in forgiveness. Darcey's eyes grew wide. She stumbled backward, scuffing my masterpiece with her cheating feet. I remained calm and invited her into my embrace with open arms. Then the unimaginable happened. What appeared to be several vines of ivy snaked out from the painting and coiled around Darcey's ankles. She screamed. The vines snapped taut, wrenching her from her feet. She landed on her back, cracking her head on the concrete. She ceased her struggles. Went silent. The ivy tugged and dragged her across the paint.

It was then I realized what was different about the painting, what I'd failed to notice before—the strands of ivy creeping up the chasm walls from the darkened depths, the very ivy now dragging my beloved toward the bottomless rift.

I scooped up the razor, threw myself on Darcey, and cut at the binding vines, cringing at the feel of the blade scraping uselessly across the concrete. On and on she slid, plowing through the flowers, the vines reeling her closer and closer to the precipice edge.

"Let her go. I'll give you what you want."

I grabbed Darcey's wrist and slashed her palm. Blood welled forth, streaming a crimson trail across the paint. But the vines did not relent. The chasm drew closer. Darcey's feet passed over the rim just as she opened her eyes. Over the edge she dropped, screaming as she plummeted into the dark below.

The sun dropped behind the roofline, casting the chasm in shadow. My heavy breathing, the only sound.

I picked myself up and washed the patio clean with the garden hose, then walked inside the house. I didn't care what happened to me. Life had struck me a tragic blow. My darling wife was gone. I needed time to mourn. I might never paint again.

* * *

I pleaded my innocence at my trial and spoke the truth of what happened. No one, including my lawyer, believed me. They exhibited photos of my excavated backyard, of the graves, the bodies of my wife and neighbor. Of poor Kittykins.

I was shipped to the Atascadero State Hospital, at least that's what I was told. As nobody believes me, why should I believe them?

My wardrobe consists of a pair of baby blue slippers, pajamas, and bathrobe. Not all that different from home, really. Stark white walls. Cold concrete floor. A small room, but very private. Better than home in some ways. No one asks me to take out the trash or clean the litter box here.

An orderly walked in, a tall bruiser of a woman who looked the very stereotype of a cuckoo's-nest heavy. In violation of the state's strict smoking ordinances, she gnawed on the butt of a fat cigar crammed in the corner of her thick-lipped mouth.

I rebuked her with an affected cough. "I'm certain this is a smoke-free facility."

Bruiser shoved a baseball-glove-sized hand deep inside her white orderly's slacks, pulled a clipboard out, jabbed a meaty finger at the attached paper, and peeked at me from beneath a suspicious brow. "Leonard J. Filster?"

This was all too familiar. All that I could think to say was, "What?"

"Get with the game, bucko. You're supposed to say something like, 'Leonard's not here right now.' I mean, when in Rome, do as the Romans do, right?"

"Manny?"

The bruiser stuffed the clipboard back in her pants and retracted her clenched fist. "Ah man, what gave me away? Was it my cologne? ... Too soon?"

"What are you doing here, and how do you look like this?"

Manny squatted and rubbed his hand over the floor and shifted the cigar to the other corner. "I told you I'd check back."

He straightened up, backed outside and said, "Tootles," and closed the door.

That was it? This was Manny's idea of checking up on me?

A mail-slot sized panel opened in the door.

"Hey Leo, I almost forgot."

A tray slipped through the opening. On the tray lay a Twinkie-size stick of white chalk and a straight razor with a shiny red handle.

BUMMING SMOKES

BRIAN ASMAN

Brian Asman writes stuff, mostly horror, but also whatever weirdness pops into his head. He loves a barrel-aged beer on a sunny Southern California day, punk rock blaring in the background, and his Staffordshire terrier, Emma. His stories have been featured in Double Feature magazine, Deciduous Tales and the anthology We've Been Trumped! Find him at americanphantom.com.

I NEED A SMOKE *I need a smoke oh Jesus Christ in a jetpack I need a smoke...*

I'm sniffing the air, looking around wildly for a telltale puff, anything to put me on the scent. But of course, there's nothing. I'm in the middle of a goddamn *farmer's market* for crying out loud. Walking past booth after booth, it's like a murder's row of shit I *don't* need in my life. Avocado paste and organic candles? Check. Artisanal peanut butter hand-ground with free range unicorn horns? You betcha. Fucking *kale?* They've got all that crap, but god forbid anybody actually has a cigarette like a normal human being and not some *Natural News* caricature, some walking approximation of a tuneless Phishy noodle-fest inelegantly strummed on a weathered guitar covered in faded Widespread Panic stickers that somebody traded for a ride to freaking Bellingham. Of all goddamn places.

I don't know why I'm here. At a La Jolla farmer's market, or in the Golden State in general. Nobody smokes, at least not tobacco. Pot, sure. I even saw a couple dreadlocked assholes pulling on those stupid boxy vape pens surrounded by clouds of cotton candy scented vapor. Some people like those things, say they've helped them quit smoking. I've never bothered— they won't work for me.

Sure, they've got nicotine.

Allegedly.

But I don't need the nicotine, I need that *sweet, sweet smoky sell your ass for one more drag of that shit, one more hit I don't give a fuck if that bloody-gummed hobo just lipped that filter give it the hell here* kind of goodness.

C'mon girl, think, I tell myself. But I can't think.

I need.

I need.

I NEED A CIGARETTE.

* * *

He sighs, shifting from one leg to the other behind his table covered in homemade candles. Scratches the back of an ear, just for something to do. The distraction's fleeting.

He could really go for a cigarette.

Especially after that last lady—typical entitled upper-middle class Whole Foods shopper. Some kind of Japanese or Chinese symbols inked up the inside of her arm, wearing a tank top covered in mandalas. Carrying a purse with a faux-Warhol photo print of Nelson *Mandelas*. The kind of chick who actually thinks the universe cares about her. Like Jupiter's trying to make sure all her stupid chakras are aligned or something.

Jupiter's busy trying to keep all those moons from flying off into space, lady, he thinks. *It doesn't have time for your bullshit.* He wishes she'd *actualize* herself a better attitude. The price is the price. The "no haggling" sign is the "no haggling" sign. He doesn't even set the prices. Corrine does. She makes the candles in her funky little granny flat right off Sunset Cliffs. Infuses them with all the crunchy earth-mama scents people like that last lady go gaga for. He's just there to man the cash register. For his trouble, he gets to take home fifteen percent of total sales.

It's not the best job he's ever had, but it's not the worst. And considering he spent way too many years as a roadie, leaving him with a head full of rock and roll memories, a bad back, and few appreciable skills, he counts his blessings more than his complaints.

But now he could really stand to burn one. He fingers the pack in his pocket, head ratcheting back and forth, looking for a place to go. The market's out in this parking lot behind a shopping center. The truck's out of the question—it's not his. He told Corrine he'd quit, but dealing with some of these people just makes him want a cig. She worries about him. Keeps slipping cannabis oil into his food, since it supposedly kills cancer cells. Mega-dosing him with vitamin C. He figures all that shit's probably just as poisonous. David Bowie died from cancer. If they were hiding the cure from the Thin White Duke, no way in hell some hippie chick's got it at the bottom of a hemp handbag.

The way the sun's tilted in the sky, or the earth's tilted in space, there's this burning hot sunray slicing down past the tent flap right onto his neck, so hot he can picture his grey hairs sizzling and turning black. He slaps at the back of his neck, as if he could bat away the sunlight. The heat keeps on coming, beads of sweat rising from his leathery skin in response, and those silky fingers tickling his lungs like Ray Manzarek's digits dancing across his keyboard just increase in tempo.

He's got to make a move. Soon.

Back behind the dumpster looks promising. There's a black-helmeted security guard rolling around the lot on one of those dumb-ass scooters, looking to all the world like a giant hard-on. Maybe he can wait till the guard zips over to inspect the other side of the parking lot. Then he can get the lady selling avocado paste to watch his table for a minute, make sure none of these hippies steal his stuff. That's one thing he's learned about these kinds of places: everything's a free sample if no one's manning the booth. If he were to just walk away, without enlisting a fellow vendor to watch his back, he'd likely come back to an empty tent.

Yeah, that's what he'll do. He fingers the pack in his pocket again, watching the security guard. Tries not to make eye contact with anyone walking by, he doesn't want anybody coming over right now to sniff the candles while they ask him the same two or three questions.

Are these organic? Do you make them yourself? Do you take credit cards?

When he sees the security guard zoom past the Petco loading dock and around the side of the building, he gestures at the avocado paste lady. She nods, and he's off.

* * *

I need a smoke I need a smoke oh Buddha in a biplane I need a smoke…

I don't know what I was thinking. What had I hoped to find at a farmer's market anyway? I just saw the flyer on the board at the coffee shop and figured *hey, what the hell else should I do for the next couple of hours?* Sampling ethically-sourced goat cheese seemed as good an idea as any I suppose, considering that I'm stuck doing activities of the non-physically taxing variety. My body's been falling apart on me lately. Nothing much else I *can* do but buy things and stick them in the back of the fridge till they go moldy. Forget hiking. Stand-up paddleboarding. Salsa dancing.

I feel like a three-hundred-year-old trapped in a thirty-two-year old's body, and that body isn't long for this world.

Most people are seventy percent water. I feel like I'm seventy percent tumors. Give or take a few percentage points, but frighteningly enough I'm probably not too far off. Boiling black masses line my insides. Leaking pustules cluster in my lungs. My uterus is full to bursting with cancer babies, crawling all over each other like they're playing in a fetid ball pit.

Yeah, you're welcome for that image. Fuck off, I'm the one that's got to live with it.

I shouldn't be alive. And I'm not, not really. You're probably wondering why I'm not in a hospital bed, IV going in, catheter going out. Surrounded by friends and loved ones and tastefully understated floral arrangements, all to a soundtrack of *whirs* and *pings* and ranting dementia patients.

That kind of thing just isn't my style.

What can I say, I've lived a hard life. Several hard lifetimes, it feels like, back to back. My current condition wasn't much of a surprise to me—the cancer started growing from the moment I opened my eyes. And even if I wanted to go stew in my own filth in a fucking hospice, there wouldn't be any teary-eyed relatives crowding around me. Just a bunch of orderlies getting paid fifteen bucks an hour to wipe my ass.

Which, as far as I'm concerned, isn't *nearly* enough.

I'm literally going to die if I don't get a cigarette. Sure, I could go to a liquor store, but I need one *now*. There's not enough time to haul this fleshy sack of tumors all the way to the car on the far side of the parking lot and then drive to a store, jangly nerves making me drum out a stuttering rhythm on the steering wheel, and then surrender the requisite arm and leg California voters have determined one needs to pay for a pack of smokes these days. *I need one now.*

I stalk the farmer's market, scanning every tanned and toned and Botoxed face for familiar tics. Search every smile for yellow and brown, my two favorite colors. Sniff the air every time someone walks past, hoping to catch a whiff of tobacco underneath all the organic perfume and fair-trade body wash.

No such luck.

A woman bumps into me and doesn't say anything, just keeps walking away, swinging a purse covered in Nelson Mandela's face. I open my mouth to say something, but don't have the energy. I can feel it. My freaking *prana* or whatever, seeping out of my pores. Fleeing my body, running as far the fuck away from me as it can get.

I'm going to die. In a fucking farmer's market, of all places.

This'll teach me. If I get out of this, I'm moving somewhere where everybody smokes. Like a casino. Or Eastern Europe.

* * *

He ducks down behind the dumpster, nose curling at the miasma of sour scents emanating from the trash bin, and pulls the pack from his pocket. American Spirits. He laughs at the outline of an Indian smoking a doobie on the box.

Maybe I'm not so different from all the rest of these hippies, he thinks. Then he realizes he only has three left, and figures he'll switch to Newports. Just to spite them.

His customers. Or Corrine's, to put a finer point on it.

His hands are shaking as he puts a butt in his mouth, so nervous he lips it filter-*out,* like he's a drunk college kid or something. Tastes grainy tobacco on his tongue. Reverses the smoke, sucks on the filter instinctively before he's got it lit. Flicks the wheel of his Zippo, feels the fire on his face as he brings it closer.

The cigarette ignites. He sucks in.

So fuckin' good.

It's like the best damned guitar solo he's ever heard. So good he wants to cry out in ecstasy. Do a little dance. Or maybe just sit here all day, lighting one cigarette off the next. Content in his cloud of cancer-causing chemicals.

But he's only got three left. And if he doesn't sell Corrine's candles, he doesn't get paid.

He squats behind the dumpster and sucks smoke into his lungs but he's nervous. Maybe the guard rolls by again. Maybe some yoga teacher spots him back here and makes a big deal out of it, face twisted in a mask of horror at the thought that someone would *smoke* in *public*. Even now, getting his fix, he's not in the mood to take any more guff off anybody. Not here. Part of the job when he's dealing with customers. But as long as he's got the card table covered in candles in front of him, he's good. He's got his barrier. His moat. Back here, without a big purple and red banner linking the overweight, road-gnarled ex-roadie with Corrine's Organic Candles, LLC?

He doesn't trust himself.

So he sits and smokes and hopes it doesn't come to that.

* * *

I need a smoke I need a smoke oh Ganesh in a gondola I need a...

Oh yes.

You ever see the Zapruder film? You got that grassy knoll. The puff of smoke. That's pretty much what I see.

Except it's not a grassy knoll. It's a dumpster.

And that puff doesn't equal Jack Kennedy's brains spattered all over Jackie's dress. That puff equals my salvation.

I'm positively giddy as I hot-foot it across the parking lot, dodging baby mamas pushing strollers, pony-tailed dudes with their *March Against Monsatan* t-shirts, the whole crowd sprayed down with a firehose gushing form-fitting Lululemon attire. There's a smoker here. Somewhere, in this godforsaken sea of superficial, health-conscious, nearly unconscious *assholes,* there's a smoker.

"Hey," someone says as I shove them aside. I'm running on vapors, but the sight of that cloud is all I need.

I will not die today.

I step behind the dumpster, and see a fat old guy sucking on a cigarette. My heart falls into my stomach. Why couldn't it have been someone younger? In better shape? He's got a massive gut, busted-up knuckles, fucking *jowls* for god's sake. I sniff the air and somewhere, underneath that sweet, sweet aroma of tobacco smoke, I can smell the rot. The decay. He's got cancer, too.

Only he doesn't know it yet.

I look at the guy and pull the biggest, best smile I can under the circumstances.

Beggars can't be choosers.

* * *

He recoils when he sees the woman round the dumpster, looks down at the burning cigarette in his hands like he's got no idea how it ended up there. Looks back at her. She's staring at him, the expression on her face hard to read. From the way she's dressed, crop top and tight jeans, she doesn't look that old. But her face is heavily lined. Loose skin droops down her cheekbones like she's melting. Her arms and legs are bundles of sticks, so fragile he thinks he could snap them over his knee, while her bare stomach bulges unnaturally. Like something inside's just waiting to tear its way out.

"Uh, hey," he says.

He's busted. He still doesn't take another drag, and he's not sure why. Like if she doesn't see him inhale, maybe it's not so bad. He grits his teeth. Readies himself for the abuse she's going to level at him. *Those things kill, you know. My kids are right there, asshole. Eww, disgusting.*

But she says none of those things.

Instead, she opens her mouth, and in a weak, reedy voice says, "You got another one of those?"

He gapes at her for a second. Surprised he'd run into a fellow smoker at a place like this. "I got you," he says, pulling his pack out and tapping the bottom. A single cigarette pokes out the box's mouth. He offers it to her.

She accepts.

She slides the smoke between her lips, hands shaking worse than his had been. Before he can ask if she wants a lighter she's got one fired up. The cigarette lights, molten cherry winking conspiratorially, and she takes a long pull. Longer than he's ever seen, really. Like she's trying to suck it all the way down to the filter in a single drag.

Which would be a neat trick. Like that one guy on Letterman, or Leno, blowing smoke out of his eye.

He takes another puff, while she's pulling. Then she opens her eyes wide and exhales her smoke right in his face, the cloud blacker than it should be, like he'd bent down in front of an oil-leaking car's exhaust pipe at just the wrong moment.

Greasy barbed fingers crawl down his throat, clawing their way through his trachea, burrowing inside his lungs. He's coughing, hacking. Fighting the invasion.

He can't breathe. He drops his cigarette to the ground. An exploratory hand goes to his throat, but he knows immediately that's not the problem. His airways are open for business. It's not that he can't get air *in*.

It's that he's filled up with something else entirely.

The smoke scrapes him from the inside out. Abrading epithelial cells. Scoring cilia. Fighting its way from bronchiole to bloodstream, where it runs rampant. White blood cells muster and quickly fall as the foreign substance divides and sub-divides, going wherever it will. Overrunning his immune system. Digging in for the long haul.

His whole damn body feels like it's on fire.

He wants to scream but his lips move soundlessly. His fingers rake his chest, tearing his flannel shirt open to scratch at the skin. Bloodying himself. As if he could dig through his chest, expose his lungs to the world, and get this noxious black cloud of *her* out.

But it's too late. It's inside him.

Or rather *she's* inside him.

Because she's not in front of him, anymore. Not in any way that matters. Her body is already crumpling to the ground, the cigarette he'd given her rolling out of her fingers and into a crack in the asphalt, filter-down like the very earth itself is taking a drag. The smoke curls up and up to the sky.

Inside his head, a voice tells him in no uncertain terms to *get the fuck out.*

And then he's gone.

* * *

I don't need a smoke. Mohamed on a Moped, Krishna in a Cadillac, Zeus in a Zeppelin, I don't need a smoke.

Not at the moment. I will, sooner or later. But now I've bought myself a little time, at least.

No more farmer's markets, that's for sure. No more California, if I know what's good for me. Seventy different cities have banned smoking, for god's sake. I can't risk getting stuck like that, a body suddenly giving up the ghost and not a smoker in sight. Maybe I'll head back east. Trade in the palm trees and ocean breeze for muggy summers and freezing winters and a more laissez faire attitude towards tobacco products. Something like one in four Kentuckians smokes. One in four! I'd have to be an idiot to stick around here, even though I'm definitely going to miss the fish tacos.

I'm fine for now, but this body's barely an improvement. You know when you move into a new apartment, and you keep noticing all the shit that's wrong with it? The water pressure sucks, the toilet keeps running, the linoleum under the sink's starting to peel? Exactly. I keep wondering how this guy fucked up his back so bad. There's a crick in the neck I can't get rid of, no matter which way I stretch it. Thanks to the arthritis I might as well be wearing oven mitts when I go to pick up a pencil. And then there's the cancer he already had. We're like a couple of dogs, sniffing asses on the sidewalk, trying to figure out whether we want to fuck or fight.

We're still undecided.

Still, I can't complain—this body's got a few more weeks, at least. Even with something like me in it. It'll last me till I can find something better, something more my style. Maybe I'll stalk the strip clubs. Find some twenty-something that still has some tread on her tires. A body they haven't worn out already themselves.

Because I live a hard life. Hell, if you brought a cigarette to a baby's lips and coochie-cooed until they inhaled, and I rode that shit into them, I'd still rot that baby body out from the inside in a couple years and any parent's going to notice something like that. Then they'll take them to the hospital, let the doctors stick them in a CAT scan machine and see if they can't figure out what's wrong with darling little whatever-their-name-is.

And that simply wouldn't do.

I've been doing this a long time. I plan on doing it for a long time to come.

No, right now I don't need a smoke.

But soon.

Soon.

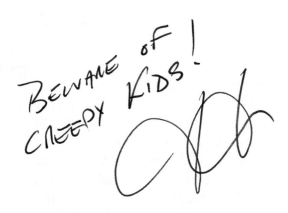

Beware of!
Creepy Kids!

KENNETH IS DROWNING

JAMES JENSEN

James Jensen has been selling other authors' books for over 25 years. "Drowning Kenneth" is his debut horror short story. While working on a novel about Edgar Allan Poe's, C. Auguste Dupin, he shares a book choked apartment with his patient wife and a hungry gecko named Freddie.

SLOW SINGLE NOTES ON a piano drew him closer to the darkened house. Finding his way to the Shasta Lake campground at this late hour was out of the question. A dim yellow lantern illuminated the window and cast a path through the heavy downpour. The song sounded familiar, but Jake couldn't quite place it.

He knocked on the door and the music paused. Quick steps echoed inside. The door opened and a small, pale face leaned out into the storm, looking left and right before settling on him.

Water dripped down her bangs, onto her eyelashes and down her cheeks. Had it not been like a monsoon outside, Jake could have mistaken them for tears framing her frown. Her oval face favored his niece a little. So, he reckoned that she must be about ten-years-old, maybe eleven.

Yet, her eyes told a much older story. She didn't fidget or look around nervously. Her sad unwavering stare caused Jake to shift his weight from one foot to another, a nervous shuffle that had dogged him since he was a child.

"Thanks for opening the door," Jake said. "Your house was the only one with a light on."

Although the girl only opened the door about two feet, a weak circle of yellow light illuminated an upright piano against the far wall inside. A wooden bench by it had a thick quilt, double-folded so that someone short could fully reach all of the ivory keys.

She turned to follow his line of sight.

"I play it so they can find their way back," she said.

Her voice sounded flat and emotionless as if delivering an often-repeated explanation. Yet, when she turned her face back to him, there was a flash of something behind those ancient looking eyes that made him step back just a little. It was gone in an instant.

"Help who find their way back?" he asked. He glanced around. "Your parents?"

She again stuck her head a few inches past the threshold, turned left and then right before replying. Heavy raindrops bounced off of her cheeks, yet she did not blink them away.

"They will be back for me soon," she said. "They told me to wait but they would come to get me before it came. Will you stay?"

Jake turned to look at the other buildings that lined the street. They sagged side by side like many of the dying California mining towns tucked away in the foothills just beyond the encroaching urban sprawl. Between a moonless night and the driving rain, the small town wavered on the edge of invisibility. Had it not been for the lamp in the window and tinkling piano, he would have kept stumbling all night through the stands of pine and cedar that populate the hollows and canyons around Shasta Lake.

"I had hoped to make it to the campground before dark but the rain got me all turned around," he said.

She said nothing.

"I was up by the dam most of the day and should have headed back sooner," he continued. "But the lakeshore is hard to navigate in this downpour."

She just stood in the doorway while her dress continued to drip onto the floor. Jake shifted his backpack off and set it on the wooden porch. Her lack of reaction to the rain tapping on her face gave him a shiver that wasn't entirely due to the cold.

Jake considered trying one of the other buildings. A thirty-year-old male stranger hanging out with a young girl was frowned upon in the best circumstances. Add to that a dark, stormy night and no parents around and he was a candidate for *Catch a Predator*. Still, that damn rain and he was cold as Hell.

"Do you mind if I come in and dry off a little bit?" he asked. "It looks like we both could use it."

She stood to the side and opened the door wider.

"They will be back for me soon," she repeated. "They told me to wait but they would come to get me before it came. Will you stay?"

"Sure," he said as he walked inside. "So, they were supposed to come for you before the storm came?"

Jake leaned his backpack against a scuffed wooden chair that sat next to a potbellied stove. The lamp on the wooden table by the single window cast wavering shadows around the small room. Both floor and walls were made of bare planks the color of driftwood. Only the dull reddish-brown piano provided a color break to the drab interior. It had the air of a movie set more than a home.

A few seconds of fumbling through the numerous pockets of the backpack produced the small plastic tube that held his waterproof matches. Although out of the rain, his exhales still produced puffs of condensation in the frigid room.

"I'm going to get a fire going so we can both dry out," he said as he bent down next to the stove.

A cabin that he had rented about 600 miles south of here in Big Bear last year had an old stove like this soot blackened hunk of iron. Its surface would get orange hot and singe anything that got too close. Yet, its heat barely radiated beyond a few feet. It was the last time he'd pay a ridiculous price for the charm of a "rustic cabin." A tent with a good sleeping bag was money better spent. Still, Jake would gladly deal with a little singed wrist hair if it would bring life back to his numbed fingers.

Even though the stove radiated no warmth, he instinctively tapped a finger on the coiled iron handle to test it before he grabbed a hold. The metal was even colder than the room. He twisted the handle and it creaked downwards a quarter of an inch.

"Damn," he cursed and stood up to get a better grip. "When is the last time someone used this thing?"

He leaned on the handle with all of his weight and it groaned downward. Out of its mouth rushed a stream of green-brown brackish water that was mixed with chunks of slimy coal. A smell of rotting fish and swamp weeds filled the small room.

"Jesus!" Jake shouted and jumped back.

"Kenneth is drowning," the girl said.

He turned to look at her. She stood in the glow of the lamp on the table, staring out of the window and oblivious to the mess on the floor.

"Who's Kenneth?" asked.

The girl turned and walked towards a door at the rear of the room. As she passed him, a scent similar to the stagnant stove water trailed behind her. Except it possessed a subtle edge of a sickly sweetness.

"Pa says that I have to be all packed for when they come back to get me," she said.

Without looking back, the girl opened the door and went into an unlit room. Jake started to walk towards her but stopped short as the door swung shut and the lamp went out.

"Son of a bitch," he said.

As if in sync with the sudden darkness, the storm outside died. Faint dripping from somewhere in the blackness kept time with Jake's racing heartbeat.

He reached into his pocket for the tube of waterproof matches. Jake tapped out one of them and struck it on the small pad of sandpaper. Its head caught and assaulted his nostrils with a quick puff of sulfur. The flame flared bright white and then dropped to a whisper of dull blue as if starved for oxygen. Jake cupped it in his hands and walked over to the lamp.

A crack of thunder shattered the new silence and he dropped the match to the floor in surprise. The feeble flame hissed out as it hit the puddle that extended from the stove.

"Oh, come on," he said.

Jake let out a frustrated sigh and shook out a second match from the tube. Another flash of yellow and whiff of sulfur allowed him to make it to the lamp on the table. He lifted the glass dome and lowered the flame to the wick. It too hissed out as it touched the cloth

"What the hell?" He squinted in the blackness and brought the charred stick close to his eyes.

It smelled brackish, as if it also had been in the belly of the stove. He threw the impotent twig to the floor and ground it with the toe of his boot. He'd paid extra cash for the damned things to be guaranteed waterproof and light in any conditions.

Jake reached into a lower pocket of his cargo pants and withdrew a four-inch sturdy flashlight. A quick twist of the metal head turned it on. A broad stream of brightness shot towards the floor. He twisted the handle a little more and narrowed the beam. Unlike the useless matches, the heavy military grade torch blazed as advertised. He swept it around the room in a test arc. Shadows leapt out of its way as it played over the sparse furniture.

He pointed it at the door where the girl had left and the light flickered. Jake tapped it on his palm and the beam steadied. As he watched in disbelief, the bright white rays slowly shifted to a yellowish green bile color as if some unseen hand had placed a filter over the LED lens. Twisting the handle did nothing to change the eerie hue.

"Yet another expensive piece of crap," he muttered.

Giving up on making it brighter, he pointed the flashlight towards the lamp and walked over to the table in search of the matches the girl must have used. Nothing. The lantern sat alone on the bare wood. Its glass well base was full. Jake removed the chimney and touched the wick. It was wet and slimy. He sniffed at his fingers. They did not smell like kerosene or lamp oil. Instead, they gave off the scent like an aquarium gone bad.

"This is getting ridiculous," he said

He picked up the lamp and swirled the liquid around as he shined the flashlight at the reservoir. Like a filthy snow globe, bits of small twigs and algae floated in the glass. It reminded him of a gift his girlfriend had given him last year. One of those enclosed glass bulbs that housed a small branch of an underwater plant and tiny shrimp-like creatures. It had been called an Ecosphere and was supposed to be fully self-contained. Everything in it died within a week.

A low gurgling sound interrupted Jake's lamp gazing. It started soft, like a coffee pot dripping to life. As he strained to listen, the water sounds grew louder and more urgent like a toilet about to breach the seat. He set the glass down and spun the beam of his flashlight around the room. Pointing it at the stove, he half expected a fresh flow of rainwater to be issuing from its gaping mouth. Yet, other than an occasional drip, its discharge had ceased.

It came from beyond the room.

Jake walked to a painting on the wall. Moses, with his staff in one hand and stone tablets in the other, stared down with righteous anger.

He leaned his ear closer to the wall below the picture frame. The sound of bubbling water came from behind the rough planks. Not a small trickle of leaking rainwater, this rising noise reminded him of a filling reservoir.

A door slammed in the next room.

"Christ!" Jake yelled as he jumped and turned in the direction of the sound.

It came from the room where the girl had disappeared. He kept the light pointed on the door as he slowly edged closer. He shivered as he drew near and saw his breath puff out a faint cloud as the temperature dropped a few degrees.

Jake reached out and his hand slipped on the cold, slick doorknob. He used the tail of his shirt to get a better grip and flung the door open. Sweeping his flashlight around the even smaller room revealed nothing. No small girl hid there. Not even a stick of furniture broke the weak beam of light coming from his hand. He saw no windows, just a closed door that led out of the back of the building.

"Where the hell did she go?" he asked the air.

Crossing the floor took only three full adult strides. He rested a hand against a panel on the door. On the other side, he could hear the unmistakable rush of turbulent water. Flash floods were common in the dry California hills. He got down and felt the floor at the base of the door. Although cold and clammy, no water seeped in around the edges.

Jake eased back onto his heels and opened the door. His flashlight revealed a churning, chocolate milk colored torrent that filled the narrow alleyway. Just an inch or two below the door jam, the flood careened against the steep slope that rose up behind the house and formed a ten-foot wide river.

"Oh God, she didn't have a chance," he said. He knelt and leaned out looking for any sign of her.

A thin hand reached out of the deluge at his feet and grabbed Jake by his collar. He fell head first into the water and began tumbling along with the waves. Flailing his arms to find a purchase, he glanced off of the dissolving hillside and felt fist sized rocks strike his shoulder. Someone still gripped tight to his jacket as he struggled to keep his head above the swirling surface. Each dip below the waterline caused him to swallow some of the cold, gritty water.

The hand jerked him sideways and he stared into a swollen death-gray face with milky white eyes.

Jake screamed.

The grotesque visage parted its bloated pale lips as if to scream back at him but only thick, dark mud oozed from its gaping mouth. Jake struck at the monstrous head with his flashlight. The metal scored the gray flesh on its forehead and revealed a flash of bloodless white skull beneath.

Jake screamed again and broke free of the grip. A sudden jolt knocked the wind out of him as he slammed sideways into a stout tree that divided the washout. He dug into the rough bark with his nails and then managed to grab hold of a thick branch that angled upwards. With a desperate heave, he pulled himself out of the flow. Above him, the broad limb reached out and draped over a two-story building to his right.

From below, he heard a groaning creak as the massive tree he was straddling twisted slightly and leaned a few degrees away from the building. Jake reached up and clawed his way over the limbs until he was level with the railing of the second floor. A quick swing of his legs and he dropped down onto the slick wood of the balcony. He stood as the tree groaned again and tipped over into the torrent below. The exposed roots made the washout explode in a burst of frothy rapids between the hillside and the structure. The soil on the hill crumbled away, gouging a new path for the water.

"Too close," he said and turned to take stock of where he landed.

From his narrow perch, he looked left and could see a long row of buildings that he had recently gone plunging past. Being at the rear, most of the structures did not have any porches or anything more than a back door. Jake had managed to scramble onto the only building with a second-floor balcony. As he looked to his right, he swallowed hard and felt the grit work down his throat. Beyond the haven he had attained, the confined river burst open and spread out into the darkness beyond. Had he missed this building, he would have joined the clutching corpse forever.

He turned and saw the dim outline of a door. Thank God it was unlocked and he stumbled inside. As he closed the door behind him, the din of the washout faded into the background. He looked down, surprised to see the flashlight still gripped tightly in his numb hand. Turning the handle brought it back to life with the same muted glow.

Something moved in the shadows to his right.

"Hello?" he called out and swung the light around, its beam shaking as it moved along the walls.

To his immediate right stood a twin bed, covered with a patchwork quilt. Beyond that, a simple wooden desk and chair rested against the wall. Something moved to his left, scratching its way just beyond the weak beam of light. It sounded like the shuffle of a raccoon, only slightly bigger.

"Hah!" he yelled and tried to sound bigger and fiercer than what he felt.

A shadowed creature cowered in the corner by the hallway door and shuddered as the beam of the flashlight fell upon its crouched form. Jake saw bony feet sticking out of a ragged pair of dungarees. An equally shabby flannel shirt hung loosely on an emaciated figure who held claw-like hands over its eyes. Dark strands of shoulder length hair hid the rest of the face and made it hard to tell if it was a man or woman, adult or child.

He took a step and a floorboard creaked in protest.

The figure whimpered.

"Hello?" Jake tried again. "Are you ok?"

"Is she still here?" a voice croaked from the huddled form.

"Who?" Jake asked. "The girl?"

"THE DEVIL!"

Jake stumbled back a step as the huddled form sprang up and turned to face him. Sagging bluish flesh on its face hid whatever gender the creature might have been. Dark hollows in the place of eyes stared out blindly and dark fluid gurgled over split lips and down a nightshirt.

"Holy Hell," he said.

The creature lunged at him and Jake threw up a protecting hand over his face and struck out with his flashlight. He felt it connect something that burst like a rotted melon. A wave of putrid wetness struck him hard and knocked him against the wall. Jake fell to his knees and groped for the light. His wrist knocked against metal and he heard the flashlight go skidding across the floor.

Jake stopped and listened for the next attack.

Silence.

A thin arc of light slowly rolled a few feet away from him. The beam stopped as the flashlight touched a puddle where the specter had been moments ago. Jake shuffled over on his knees and grabbed the light. It smelled of the now familiar brackish lake water. He wiped it on his shirt and stood up.

The room tilted and he stutter-stepped a few paces. Either the knock against the wall or standing up too quickly had turned his knees to jelly. He closed his eyes and took a deep breath.

From beyond the room, the sound of a door slamming broke the silence.

Jake ran to the opposite door and threw it open. His flashlight revealed a narrow set of stairs heading to an empty room below. Wet footprints led down the stairs and ended at the front door. Jake followed them and opened the door into the night.

Outside, the rain had stopped. In its place, a low mist rolled along the muddy path and began to expand between the darkened buildings. Glancing down the street, he saw the raging flood had slowed to chocolate colored rivulets that flowed around snags of twisted branches and upended scrub brush. Jake knew that California flash floods were like newlywed sex, full of sound and fury but short in duration.

"Where are you?" he shouted for the girl.

He moved out into the middle of the path and stared down the short row of buildings. Without a light in the window, Jake could not be sure which house she lived in. As he walked a few yards, movement in his peripheral vision made him swing the flashlight to his left. Although only a glimpse through a grime clouded window, he swore another grotesquely swollen face stared back at him. Only it seemed taller than the figure that had attacked him. He took a step towards the window but only the reflection of his light greeted him. If there had been something there, it did not want to be seen.

The scent of lake water and a chill on his knees made Jake glance down. The mist had grown thicker and swirled and ebbed around him with olive colored tendrils. The air grew heavy and he could hear the gurgling like that had been behind the walls of the girl's house. As he walked, his steps became sluggish and difficult, as if the fog held onto his legs while everything above the mist moved normally. It reminded Jake of wading through a lazy shallow pond.

Up ahead, a light came on in a window and the sound of a piano drifted over the top of the rising fog. Jake's pulse quickened.

"Hey!" he called out.

The notes from the piano hesitated for a breath and then started up again. As before, each note was a singular key, tapping out a careful tune. As he leaned towards the sound, the song came to mind, "Camptown Races." Played so slow, it sounded like a dirge more than a dance.

Jake struggled forward towards the light. His legs were numb and moved like they were fighting a growing undertow. Up to his waist in the mist, he crept closer to the house at an agonizingly slow pace. Grasping the post of the porch he pulled free of the fog. His legs made a slight sucking sound as they emerged from the vapor morass. The hole his absence created filled up and swirled away in a dark eddy.

Knocking did not seem necessary. She already knew him. He wasn't a stranger anymore. Had it been his niece, the very same age as this lost girl, he would have hoped someone would have swept her away to safety. Somehow, the fog exuded an air of danger, even death. He would take her to the campground office and she could call her parents. He could save her.

He opened the door and saw her sitting at the piano.

"We need to go."

She turned and cocked her head.

"They will be back soon," she said. "They told me to wait and they would come to get me before it came. Will you stay?"

Jake reached for his backpack that still leaned against the wall. He slung it on his back and cinched the straps.

"Nobody's coming in this mess," he said. "I'm going to take you where we can get some help reaching your parents."

She jumped off of the stool and ran to him. He stumbled back a little as she wrapped her arms around his waist. Reaching down, he tried to pry her loose. Instead, her grip tightened and she wrapped her legs around his knees.

"You have to stay here with me" she pressed her face against his chest, muffling her voice. "They will be back soon, they promised."

Jake tried again to push her away but her grip had grown stronger. Too strong. Her bony arms dug into his sides and chilled his skin through the jacket. She rocked and whimpered slightly as she wrapped herself around him.

He heard the gurgling behind the walls again. It grew louder as he struggled to break free of the girl. That is when he noticed the first tendrils of the mist. They rolled through the open door and began swirling around them, moving upwards. His legs grew numb again as the gray fingers rose and climbed with their embrace.

"Don't lie like the others," the girl said. "They promised to stay but they all left. Kenneth is drowning"

Jake stared down into her upturned face. The child's eyes blazed with anger and she gritted her teeth so hard that her jaws flexed in violent convulsions. Both repulsed and fascinated, he knew this thing clinging to him was nothing like his niece. Whatever she appeared to be, it had shed any pretense of being normal.

"Let go of me," he tried to push her away.

The fog crept further up their bodies, swallowing legs, torsos and arms. Everything the mist touched went numb. Finally, only the girl's head stayed above the swirl and Jake could not feel anything below his arms. Her long hair pooled around her head as if the mist held substance. Before the child's face disappeared, she started to laugh. Almost innocent and sad, the laughter choked off as the mist covered her face.

Jake's shrieks of fresh terror echoed off of the wooden walls.

Only his head stayed free of the rising tide. The rotten tangy scent of dead water assaulted his nostrils. Numbness invaded his core, paralyzed his muscles and made it difficult to breathe. He tilted his head back to keep his nose above the mist. It crept up his scalp and covered his ears, muffling the sounds around him. Icy fingers of fog closed over his lips and tickled the inside of his nose. He took a deep breath as it overcame and drew him down.

Blood pounded in his ears as his lungs cried out for air. When he felt his brain eating up the last of his oxygen, he finally dared to open his eyes. Far above, he saw a dim light floating on the surface of the grayness. He kicked his legs and reached up for salvation. His body strained with the effort and then suddenly snapped free of its bondage. Jake clawed upwards towards the light like a spirit seeking heaven.

Lack of air took its toll. His vision dimmed and he gave in to a growing sleepiness that tempted him to let go and give in to the blackness.

A dark shape loomed above and blotted out the light. Jake felt a strong hand grab his hair and the world went black.

"Hey buddy, breathe already," a voice called out of the faraway darkness.

"Christ, he's dead," another voice said.

"Shut up and keep pushing his chest," the first voice said.

Jake coughed and felt an impossible amount of water gush up his throat. Someone pushed him onto his side. He felt another convulsion in his gut and a sudden rush of bile-laced lake water projected out of him and onto the fiberglass deck.

Someone thumped his back.

"Shit, he's alive."

Icy cold air tore into Jake's lungs. Never had pain felt so good. Pain meant he was still alive. He tried to prop up on his elbows but fell cheek first into the mess he had made on the bottom of the boat.

"Take it easy pal," the first voice said.

Jake lay on his side and opened one eye a crack. The voice belonged to a chubby Santa Claus looking guy with ruddy cheeks. The man wiped his huge hands on his yellow waders and offered Jake a hand. Jake hesitated, gathered his strength, and then sat up and looked at the two men. The other guy wore matching waders and clenched a smoldering pipe in his brown stained teeth.

"What the hell were you doing floating around the lake at this time of morning?" Santa asked.

His partner took his pipe out and tapped it on the side of the boat.

"You're lucky that backpack kept you floating," he said.

Jake saw his soaking pack propped against a large tackle box. He was in a large bass fishing boat. The guy with the pipe sat down on a red cooler and stuffed the pipe into a bib pocket on his chest. Four tall fishing poles stuck out over the lake like insect antennas. Their tips would twitch every second or two.

Beyond the two guys staring down at him, he saw the morning horizon turning to pink above the looming walls of the dam.

"I was trying to save the girl," Jake managed.

Both fishermen looked to the water around the boat.

"What girl?" Pipe guy asked. "You're the only one out here."

"Not out here," Jake said and sat up straighter. "She's in the town. I must have been washed into the lake by the flood."

Santa looked to his friend and raised an eyebrow.

"The nearest town is miles away from the dam," he said.

"Yeah," his friend agreed. "And it rained a bit but not enough to do any real flooding."

"It was enough to drown some kid named Kenneth," Jake insisted.

Both of the fishermen visibly paled.

"What did you say?" Santa said.

Jake hesitated and looked from one man to the other.

"The little girl said that Kenneth was drowning," he said.

Both fishermen jumped up and quickly reeled in their lines. Pipe guy pulled on a blue and white nylon rope until a small anchor bounced onto the deck. Santa scrambled over to the boat's cockpit and started the engine.

"What's wrong?" Jake asked.

"There ain't no Kenneth," Pipe guy said.

"But she said," Jake began.

"There was a Kennett," Pipe guy interrupted. "It's a town at the bottom of Shasta Lake. Been there since the dam went in and covered it up."

Jake's mouth went dry and he heard a slight buzzing in his brain. Right before the fisherman revved the engine, he heard another sound coming from the water.

"Do you hear a piano?" he said.

"Hell no," Santa snapped back at Jake and stared off over the lake as the boat roared away from the dam.

FEAST OF THE GODDESSES

K.C. GRIFANT

A founding co-chair of the Horror Writers Association (HWA) San Diego chapter, K.C. Grifant is a New England-to-SoCal transplant who writes horror, fantasy, science fiction and weird west stories. Her nonfiction articles have appeared in hundreds of magazines and newspapers while her fiction stories have found homes in magazines, card games and anthologies, most recently the Lovecraft Ezine, Electric Spec magazine, and the Stoker Award-nominated "FRIGHTMARE: Women Who Write Horror." Visit www.SciFiWri.com to learn more.

BODIES WRITHED, CEREMONIALLY BATHED in the neon red of laser light. Tendrils of artificial fog diffused the glow as I snaked my way between dancers toward the back bar.

Gazes flitted toward me like moths batting against glass and, though this wasn't my scene and there was no one noteworthy to impress, I felt my usual strut come on. One guy actually stopped dancing with his lady friend to stare slack-jawed. Beach bum, guessing from his sun-bleached hair and deep tan.

"*Seriously?*" his lady friend snapped, slapping the well-sculpted muscles of his bicep.

"He can't help it, dearest," I murmured as I passed. I grinned as I heard the sharp inhale of his breath as he caught my scent. "It's not every day a guy like him sees a goddess."

"No doubt," the guy blurted.

I stepped away as his friend really went off on him, screeching like a banshee against his half-hearted protests.

I wasn't one of the goddesses. Not really. Though the goddess-imbued powers humming through my cells allowed certain…advantages.

I spotted my charge instantly as I reached the back. She was nervous, twisting a half empty beer in her hand and smoothing down her ponytail with the other, pheromones firing with an anxious energy that seeped from beneath her hoodie and biker shorts.

I fought the urge to roll my eyes. Why people thought it was okay to go out in sports clothes was beyond me.

I perched on a barstool next to her, the burrowing stares from other patrons against my skin intensifying. This was a more rundown spot in LA than most of the clubs I frequented. The patrons were covertly or openly scanning my figure, wondering what it was about me—the tussles of honey-kissed hair that looked like a Pantene commercial, my glowing, make-up free face, or maybe the figure-flattering Alexander Wang jeans, sheer polka-dotted Prada blouse and gold Jimmy Choo platform sandals. But it wasn't just the appearance of effortless beauty that gave me that *je ne sais quoi*—it was an animal charisma that no high-end cosmetic store could bottle, no surgeon could sculpt and no diet could bestow.

"Here for the Call?" I murmured.

The girl wiped perspiration from her lip and nodded, eagerly sticking out one unmanicured hand. I shook it, trying not to *tsk* at her overdeveloped forearms and unplucked eyebrows.

You were that nervous too once, I reminded myself. It felt like ages since I was first initiated, but it was only what, five years? And now my fashion career had taken off, I'd be planning my wedding next year, and requests for endorsements appeared more plentiful than the SoCal sunshine. *Praise the goddesses.*

I gave her a reassuring smile. "What's your name, darling?"

"Daphne," she said, nervousness making her voice go hoarse.

"Oh fantastic!" I clapped, Chanel cuffs clanking against my tanned wrist. That explained the sweatshirt and biker shorts. "Do you know how few Ds we get around here? With the proximity to LA it's almost all Vs for recruits."

First letters of names were a little signal from the goddesses in our modern times: by sheer coincidence or more mystical intervention, most initiates had names starting with "D" for Diana, goddess of brawn, "M" for Minerva, goddess of wisdom, or "V" for Venus, goddess of beauty. And it wasn't uncommon for eager recruits to change their names to appease the goddesses.

"And which are you?" Daphne took a hearty chug of her Pacifico.

"Can you guess?" I struck a pose for her. "Vanessa."

"Is it true Vs can fuck anyone they want?" she said and immediately blushed.

My lip curled at the word. So crude.

"It's more about charm," I said. "And intuition, sensing a person's deepest want. You, for example. Competition of some sort coming up, I take it?"

Daphne's mouth fell open and she caught herself, nodding. "Surfing. I want to go international."

I could see easily for her what surfing meant: winning. Probably compensating for some family-rooted insecurity. If I'd wanted to seduce Daphne, I'd go with a subtle "I'm so weak, you're so strong" tactic. While pinpointing the correct approach was step one to seduction, execution was everything. And mine was flawless. Vs were also great at social dominance: someone more uncouth than me could have easily used a cutting comment to push Daphne out of her comfort zone and into embarrassment, a step away from sheepish servitude. No need for that here.

"A lot of Ds want literal brawns, to be the best boxer or dancer or athlete," I said instead. "Others focus on political or executive power." The V ladies could get to powerful positions too, based on charisma alone—that was why I had always thought to myself Vs were the best, though naturally I'm a bit biased. I shifted; interview time was over.

"But you probably know all that from the manual." I gave her a stern look. "Did you finish the entire manual?"

"Um, mostly. It was pretty long."

"It's a beast, huh? Took me about three months. But you read the part about marking?"

She nodded and I grabbed her hand—clammy and unpleasant—and pointed to a scene presently taking place at the other end of the bar. "Good. It starts now. What do you see?"

I followed Daphne's eyes. Two women stood behind the counter: one was the stunning bartender, not so discreetly sniffing a bit of coke from her pinky nail during a lull. The other employee, older, sporting a red Express blazer and liquid black eyeliner, tapped a clipboard.

"Ciggie break?" the bartender asked, already pulling out a pack of Camel Lights. The one with the clipboard nodded with a roll of her eyes.

"Um…" Daphne stalled.

Ds often struggled longer with words and descriptions than the Ms and Vs. I had trained all three types, but by far fellow Vs were my main charge. Couldn't get too far in Hollywood without some beauty after all, where plenty of raw bodies were tucked up, painted on and decked out with as much money as possible. Nothing subtle to it, this regional fanning of radiant feathers and displaying of wings and virility, so it wasn't surprising that a lot of Vs popped up around these parts. That, coupled with the active fault lines that the goddesses needed to move around, made LA the perfect recruiting ground.

"Who in this scene might be a good choice for our prey?" I prompted.

"Bartender for being addicted?" Daphne ventured.

I shook my head. "The cokehead's a sweet little thing—gave a dollar to a homeless guy this morning. But see the manager? She's a real racist POS. Cyber-harrasses almost every night. Likes to urge people to kill themselves. Sick, isn't it? That's why you *have* to do your research beforehand."

"But how do you know?"

"You need to stalk the prey for a bit. Make sure they're someone who deserves it, someone that is unworthy. It's a boatload of responsibility, determining the fate of others." I gently touched her shoulder to calm her uncertain face. "Don't worry. You'll learn in time. Now all we have to do is mark her. Want to give it a try?"

I reached into my Louis Vuitton and passed her a stick of my favorite Korean lip gloss. "It has to be something meaningful to us. You, for example, could use surfboard wax or your sunscreen. A simple smudge is all you need—the goddesses will take care of the rest."

"What if I mess up?"

"Don't worry this time, the goddesses are benevolent. *However.*" I let a frown cross my face. "If you wrong them, there is a punishment. Consider it worse than death. For Ms, it's typically stripping away their minds to leave them blathering fools, their worst fears. For Ds, some brutal disease that robs you of all function. And for Vs, well." I tried not to think of a photo I had seen on our forums of a woman who, to put it nicely, made Phantom of the Opera look like a charmer. "Usually a horrible and disfiguring 'accident.' And that's just the start of it."

Daphne looked terrified.

I patted her arm. "You've *got* this," I said. "Breathe and let their wills flow through you."

Daphne uncapped the lip gloss with one hand and finished her beer with the other. She waited until the manager started walking toward the employee door in the back, then jumped off her stool and followed.

I watched as she intercepted the woman by the bathrooms, smearing glittering pink along the back of the prey's hand. Daphne mumbled something to her before disappearing into the women's room. She emerged a minute later, grinning at me as she plopped down.

"What a rush," she whispered. "Was that okay?"

I shrugged. "Not terribly subtle but it will do."

The ground gave a rumble beneath our feet, too slight for anyone but me to feel, in what would be recorded as a tiny tremor along the nearby San Gabriel fault line. Nothing out of the ordinary here in sunny SoCal.

"Just in time too." I winked at her. "The goddesses will take care of the rest—they have what some of the girls call hypnotic sway over marked minds. Ready for your first rite?"

"Hell yeah!" Daphne said, cheeks pink from the beer and her first marking.

I stood and pulled out my car keys. "Time to go."

* * *

The goddesses aren't what you'd expect. They're ancient, fickle, unknowable beasts. Somewhere along the line they became immortal and inhuman and moved across cultures and across continents. We—the goddess-imbued, the initiates—can never truly understand anything about them or their existence but we know three things for sure:

One: They always knew what was done on their behalf and their wills could not be refused, but for grave consequences. By trusting in the goddesses, we would always be taken care of.

Two: They summoned ones they deemed worthy by both name and the Call to engage in their rites, which were bound by the strictest secrecy.

Three: They could make the earth itself shake and appear in whatever region they pleased, with no apparent regard to time or distance. They heavily favored active fault lines, which is why so many initiates popped up around places like California, New Zealand, Tibet and Chile. It also explained why many of the goddess stories originated around ancient Greece's historically vigorous seismic activity.

There are plenty more rules documented in the manual and forums, slightly updated over the millennia but more or less the same. I went over the highlights with Daphne while we drove, crammed between a snaking line of cars under a haze of palm trees and concrete. Behind us, the sun was a glaring spot baked into my rearview mirror, inching lower as we wound out of the city.

A cop pulled up alongside of us at the next red light. Daphne seemed to shrink a little when he glanced over.

"The police don't have any idea do they?" she said after a moment, whispering as if he could hear her through the glass. "Of the divine powers. Has anyone been caught?"

I shook my head. "The goddesses will watch over you, in their mysterious ways. Rule one, remember?"

Our light turned green and I rolled forward, only to hit the breaks as a Ferrari whizzed across our path and peeled sharply through the intersection. The cop didn't seem to notice.

"What kind of luck is that?" Daphne said. "What an ass."

I grinned at her. "Mercury."

She looked at me in astonishment. "You mean...?"

"Good chance. Male Ms live fast and fun and get tons of lucky breaks. We can't know too much about the god initiates—we're not even supposed to interact with them all that much, according some decree from way back when."

I took the tone of tour guide as we turned toward the mountains. "Most concentrations of initiates are about where you'd expect them, some gorgeous city near a fault line: Los Angeles, Athens, Santiago, and so on. The goddesses flow to each and all."

"Each and all," Daphne murmured, looking dazed.

"Wait til you see this." I smiled as I took us toward the general direction of the San Gabriel fault zone east of L.A., my instinct guiding me in an increasing feeling of rightness with each turn. All of the faults connecting to the San Andreas were a complexly branching system that even today's geologists hadn't completely mapped out—and which provided the virtual underground highway for our goddesses.

I parked my Range Rover on a remote dirt trail on the foothills of the San Gabriel Mountains and marched us over a rocky path to the cave opening a few hundred feet away, not a hiker in sight. It was still hot, the long, lingering rays of the sun threatening to melt my foundation and casting oblong shadows along the rocks. The dry landscape looked almost alien, dotted with squat succulents that grew the occasional fuchsia or neon orange flowered offshoot. I nudged one of the lettuce-like plants with a red stalk sprouting determinedly from its center and wondered if the goddesses saw the same beauty of this world as we did.

"The handbook didn't mention what happens at the rites. Is it hard?" Daphne stood next to me, kicking the stones and starting to sweat again. "Vanessa, tell me the truth—is it an orgy?"

I burst out laughing. "No. Fun as that might be, this is equally delightful. It's something you will remember forever, I can promise you." I blinked away a bit of moisture, caught at how special this moment was. Even after countless initiatives, I still felt nostalgic at others' first time. Daphne solemnly trailed along, up and over the lip of a cave and I passed her a mini flashlight from my purse.

"What is this?"

"Shimmer Caves, we call them." I carefully picked my way down, mindful to not scuff my sandals. "They can be anywhere near the faults. I've never been to the same one twice, personally. The goddesses will guide you to them through your instinct."

This particular Shimmer Cave wasn't as dank as some of the other ones I had been too. Rather, it was dry and comfortably descending, a network of tunnels that faded to darkness in every direction. It grew wide enough for the two of us to walk side-by-side after ten minutes or so, the only sounds Daphne's heavy breathing and our footsteps, tiny and muffled in the still space.

A few moments later, the rock quartz walls of the tunnel begin to glisten, which I knew to be a foretelling of the goddesses' presence. I picked up our pace until the tunnel emptied into a large cavernous opening, the walls glittering as though coated in ice. It was cold and utterly devoid of vegetation or movement, as though no earthly creature had set foot in these caves in ages.

The manager, our prey, was laid out nearby, her liner-smudged eyes wide and blank from whatever mystical force the goddesses used to subdue her. Her red blazer seemed to glow beneath the Shimmer Cave's luminescent walls.

"How is she here?" Daphne sputtered. "We just left the bar."

"What is the third principle of the goddesses?" I pulled out one of those shrink-wrapped ponchos and a package of wet wipes from my purse.

"No regard to time or space," Daphne said numbly. "I just didn't think…"

"Never mind that, now comes the best part." I grinned like a magician about to reveal her best trick and knelt down to cradle the woman's torso. She still breathed slightly, but not for long. "I'll start."

I lifted her shirt and bra and used my fingernails to peel open the prey's skin as if I were ripping open layers of Tiffany tissue paper in a gift box. Dark blood gushed out, eager as a volcano, onto her equally red blazer. I shifted my elbows to move the poncho so it covered my clothes and began to dig.

A smell like raw bacon and high-end cured Italian meat permeated the air. Heady, delicious and completely intoxicating, the aroma curled about my cheeks and danced against the walls.

I set aside flaps of muscle and fat and began to expertly break the lower ribs like I'd cracked crab legs in Martha's Vineyard last month. Some girls went straight for the heart—they liked the symbolism—but the goddesses didn't seem to care, and I found the heart a little too chewy for my tastes. I preferred to reach into the upper abdomen area and grab whatever guts felt good in the moment. Variety is the spice of life, after all.

I tugged off a reddish-brown flap and slurped the spilling blood like an oyster, being careful not to drip on myself. Eating organs was as dangerous as eating spaghetti and required just as much finesse to not make a total mess. With each bite, my hair lengthened and shone, brushing against my scalp, and my lips grew heavier and more luscious. I glanced up to check on my charge.

"Daphne, dearest, if you're going to retch please do it behind that rock. I *really* don't want to have to clean puke off of my shoes."

Daphne responded with a dry heave.

I sighed. "I freaked out my first time too, but if you manage a bite, it's much better, I promise."

"But it's *horrible*. I didn't think it'd be this horrible." Daphne was nearly on the verge of tears, spittle hanging from her chin and her ponytail in a complete disarray. "*Horrible*," she repeated, reminding me of one of my sorority sisters in college when we first introduced her to Jagermeister.

"Human sacrifice is an old rite, as old as humanity, regardless of what modern western culture dictates about cannibalism." I got to my feet. It looked like I'd have to spoon-feed her, literally. "The goddesses give us a gift, allowing us to sample their feast as they impart their power to us."

Daphne moaned.

I reached back into the corpse. "Here." I pulled out something the color of pate and the size of a fifty-cent piece. Spleen maybe? I had never learned anatomy. "Try this."

Daphne stared at me, utterly stricken, and I pushed back a strand of her hair with the back of one blood-soaked hand and brought the organ to her lips.

"You must," I coaxed. "Think of your upcoming contest. Think of all that awaits you. You will be the strongest, the best."

With a pained look, she screwed her eyes shut and opened her mouth barely a sliver. I squeezed the dripping meat against her lips so some of the blood splattered against her teeth and onto her tongue. She cringed and shuddered, but then telltale flush crept along her neck. She cracked her mouth wider and I pushed the rest of the piece in, pleased as pie as I watched her slowly chew and finally swallow.

A second later, Daphne opened her eyes, all but nearly glowing. Her lips spread in a wide smile. I grasped her hand, hot now, and gave it a squeeze, blood oozing from between our palms. "You're goddess-imbued now. Congrats, new initiate!"

Daphne stared down at her hands. "I feel every part of me, every muscle. I feel..." She stepped over to a boulder as high as my waist and picked it up with a groan. It hovered an inch off the ground before she dropped it.

"So strong," I purred in approval. "Isn't it marvelous?"

"Can I have more?"

"That's enough for your first time. And we're only allowed a taste—the goddesses require the bulk of the sacrifice for their sustenance."

I cleaned off my hands as best I could and tossed down the used wipes onto the mess. The goddesses would dispose of the remains.

Daphne bounced on the balls of her feet. "Now what?"

"You're an official initiate." I gave her a hug. "You can meet up with any of the others now. Anything you need, they'll help you. There's some private Facebook groups, codenamed, naturally. Once in awhile the goddesses have us congregate together for the rites. That's pretty fun. Great networking, too." I dug out my compact and silk handkerchief to dab at my cheeks and lips before reapplying foundation.

"Thank you for helping me, I don't think I could have done it without you." Daphne looked teary-eyed. "This is like the sisterhood I never had."

"Aw, sweetie. I am truly touched. But the best is yet to come. Now, after the sacrifice, we are honored with one of their presences." I zipped up my purse and stretched, feeling more refreshed than a week at the spa. "We should be able to feel it any second."

Sure enough, the cave walls flared an ethereal luminescence, like a glowing pearl. A shiver ran across my skin and concentrated at the base of my spine and back of my neck.

"She's here."

My goddess—Venus, Aphrodite, Hathor, Xochiquetzal, Rati, Astghik—whatever you called her, tapped a primal instinct, twanging nerves deep in my groin and chest and filling me with a sweet, near orgasmic bliss. My head went light and buoyant with the nearness of the bringer of love and lust, words too superficial and inept to encompass the whole of her being. My goddess was not just of affection and sexuality but the ingrained animalistic instincts that make the world turn, which give birth and rise to generations, shaping the very wants and needs and whims of each culture. For a moment, I could almost *see* them all, the hordes of women that had worshipped before, and would worship after me. Their humbly devoted minds fanned out for all eternity, pinpoints of twinkling stars on the tapestry of the universe, lightly threaded together with her affection.

"Wow," Daphne breathed next to me. She looked as in awe as I felt.

Something moved out of the corner of my eye and I whirled around. "One of the goddesses reveals herself!"

A primal part of me always wanted to throw myself down in supplication in their presence but instead I knelt carefully, gracefully. Next to me, Daphne gave a half-strangled scream. I turned to look up to see the whites of her eyes all but bulging, a picture of perfect horror.

Once upon a time, some of our scholars speculated, the goddesses had looked human, circa 2000 BC. Slowly, with their immortality, they had morphed to look as they do now: gelatinous, greyish masses larger than refrigerators, with black eyes shining like beetles as they regarded us in their infinite wisdom. It was hard to look directly at them—something in the way the light bent around them, or perhaps emanated from them, made their gray forms indistinct, fuzzy and gave one a sense of vertigo after a few seconds. The air electrified around us, sending my own blood humming and cascades of pleasure along my spine.

"Be mindful," I murmured and nudged Daphne's knee. "You won't see one every time. To gaze upon them is an honor to be received with the utmost grace. And quickly— we must close our eyes when she takes her prey."

She swallowed. "Sorry, sorry." She followed suit.

We waited, eyes closed, listening to the goddess rustle forward to encompass the prey. Once the rustling retreated, I stood, nudging Daphne.

"Now what?"

"You're all done. The goddess power is in you forever if you serve them well, and you'll feel the calling for another marking soon. But before we go, follow me for an extra treat."

I hurried down the tunnel. The goddesses always left a temporary iridescent trail along the spaces they moved in, almost like a snail trail that sparkled against the stone like frozen stardust. We followed the glittering trace around the corner.

I grinned. "Sometimes we can watch her descend."

"Do they ever talk to us?"

"Silly girl, why would they need to talk when we feel them in our souls, our very cells?"

I liked to gaze upon them as long as possible before they descended back to whatever Olympus they inhabited. I had seen descents a few times before with some other initiatives, all of us giggling shyly like turn-of-the-century children marveling at their first glimpse of an automobile.

"Look," I whispered.

Together, we peeked from around a corner of a tunnel. Two—no three—enormous gray masses slid behind a piece of whitish film stretched across the tunnel like an enormous cobweb.

I elbowed Daphne. "Lucky us! Seeing all three is a rare sight. It only happens a few times."

"Um, Vanessa? There's way more than three."

I followed her gaze further down the tunnel and it took me a minute to register what I was seeing. Behind the giant cobweb-like film more gray figures, a dozen at least, stirred. My jaw dropped. How was that possible? Some trick of the light, a reflection?

"An M told me once that they suspect a more obscure god or goddess makes an appearance every hundred years or so," I said once I had picked my jaw up off the floor. "But this, this is unprecedented. The forums are going to go crazy."

As I craned to see better, the ground rumbled. Dust rained down around us and I yanked Daphne back. "This isn't part of the rite," I hissed as footsteps pattered behind us.

No, that wasn't possible.

Someone else was in the Shimmer Cave.

* * *

"Close it!" someone screamed and I turned to see—of all things—a man, dressed in black Kevlar. He rushed past us and hurled a small black orb toward the goddesses. It bounced off the film and flared a blinding light.

It was then that I heard a sound that sent every nerve in my body throbbing at once. The goddesses—our beautiful dear goddesses—squirmed and screeched as their film lit up.

The pain of their agony seared through my own temples for an instant and I cried out with them. The fire in my head receded to a more tolerable buzz, but the goddesses still writhed in pain.

"Stop, stop!" I cried.

I moved next to Daphne as six more men in armor streamed around us. I didn't know if they were military, private or what, but it didn't matter. I jumped in front of the soldier nearest us and he stopped, perhaps in surprise, peering at me through his visor. The others fanned out and propped up guns.

"Whatever contact you've had with these things is off-limits," he barked. "Go to the entrance of this tunnel and we'll debrief you then."

I crossed my arms. "You have no idea what you're messing with, little man." The injustice of it tore my heart. "The goddesses are meant to be *worshiped,* not hunted like animals. Do you get that through your toy solider brain?"

I let the full force of my charisma burst outward and directed it at him like a solar beam. The man grunted and grit his teeth, then grabbed my arm.

"If only that were the case, ma'am," he said. "But we gotta plug up the hole and stop the infestation. Step back before we force you to."

"What are you going to do to them?" Daphne shouted. Behind her, the goddesses were still wriggling behind the flashing white film. My eyes fell to the strange black device resting against the cave wall, pulsing its deadly electricity like bottled lightning toward the goddesses. Whatever it was, it was the source of their pain and distress, which I could still feel, buzzing at the back of my mind.

"Daphne!" I pointed and her eyes followed with a look of dawning.

She leapt up with a shout and shoved past two of the soldiers, sending their bodies and rifles slamming to the ground. With a screech that pierced my eardrums, she smashed her foot against the device, a soldier next to her staring in shock.

"Shoot her!" my soldier screamed, his grip on my arm loosening. With a smile worthy of Marilyn Monroe, I leaned forward to plant a kiss on his visor, just barely smearing a bit of gloss along the plastic to mark him for my goddess.

The flashing was gone now, and the goddesses swept forward through a flap in the milky membrane, their wondrous gray forms doubling in size, billowing gray creatures filling the entirety of the tunnel. Their black eyes grew as large as plates, fathomless depths whose gaze simultaneously felt like the scrutiny of a hundred wise women and the cold analysis of an ancient reptile.

"Don't look!" I yelled to Daphne and quickly fell into another kneel.

"Jeez—" one voice started to shout before cutting off.

A rustling sound moved around me, accompanied by more shouts and the thud of bodies hitting stone. The goddesses were furious and I wanted to look, to help them, but it was an unforgivable grievance to see them collect prey. Something warm sprayed against my leg and a strangled cry went silent. I heard Daphne panting but kept my gaze down.

When the sense of the goddesses' approval and relief finally ran through me in coded spinal shivers I opened my eyes. "*Look*," I gasped.

The men were gone and the film was completely transparent, as though it was an enormous soap bubble. A small crack ran down its length with a sound like muted thunder. I watched in amazement as goddesses began pouring out from the film, so many gray, squirming bodies that it brought tears to my eyes. Daphne and I pressed up against the cave wall as we watched them stream by. We'd find out later, but at that moment all of the greater Los Angeles area began to shake, great cracks rupturing downtown, toppling cars and upheaving buildings. We were protected from the quakes in the goddesses' proximity even though this was the "big one" people had speculated about for years—though no one had expected what would soon follow.

"A miracle," I whispered.

There were more than could ever be named, dozens and dozens of the gray figures, graceful and silent save for a few squelches. None of the goddesses looked at us as they slipped into the other tunnels. They were all here now. The forums would speak of this moment for centuries to come. I began to tear up even as my thoughts began to race. But how could the initiates sustain this many? We would need an M to calculate it, but we'd have to mark a thousand people, hundreds of thousands at least, depending on how many goddesses there were. Could the population sustain it?

I felt another shiver through the front of my chest as, from somewhere amidst the crowd, my goddess strummed my heart and pleasure hormones coursed through my brain. Of course, she would see to it that we would sustain. All of them would.

Appropriate, I thought, that such ethereal and otherworldly beings should chose the City of Angels as their entry point for what the rest of the world might see as the Biblical end of days. This new stage of humanity wouldn't be marked by rains of locusts, storms, or plagues after all, but simply more gods and goddesses—hungry, waiting, ready to be served. The delight flowed through me like a drug and I wondered how many goddesses one could worship at once, how far we could really go.

"We need more initiates," Daphne breathed, her eyes wide and shining with joy.

And more prey. Lots and lots of prey.

JUNE GLOOM

KEVIN WETMORE

Kevin Wetmore is the award-winning author of over three dozen short stories found in anthologies such as Midian Unmade and Whispers from the Abyss 2, as well as such periodicals as Cemetery Dance, Mothership Zeta, and Devolution Z. He is also the author of numerous non-fiction books such as Post-9/11 Horror in American Cinema. You can learn more about his work at www.SomethingWetmoreThisWayComes.com

THE SUN HAD ALREADY risen when Bryan woke up Memorial Day morning, although you would never know it from the lack of light coming in the East-facing bedroom window above their bed.

"Ugh," he groaned as he sat up on the bed. He peered down at the large gray and black lump taking up most of the foot of the bed. "Starting early this year, boy."

Seamus's tail thumped enthusiastically, but no other part of the Irish Wolfhound moved, unwilling to give up any of the queen-sized real estate.

A decade ago, his first year in Los Angeles, Bryan had been quite surprised. He had left Pittsburgh not just because Los Angeles offered more opportunities for actors and stunt men, but also because he was so tired of living under overcast skies. Like most people, he thought Southern California was all sun and warmth and shorts year-round. Then he experienced "June Gloom," the marine layer that made early summer mornings overcast and damp for much of the month.

"Didn't know I had moved to San Francisco," he joked more than once, to which his friends smiled as if they had never heard that one before. It wasn't that bad. Just early summer mornings were foggy and cold until midmorning. Once he moved to the Westside, living in Brentwood, there was even fog until about noon. Afternoons, of course, were still sunny and warm.

Bryan jumped out of bed and threw on sweatpants, an old Rusted Root concert t-shirt, and a baseball cap from some film he had worked on and long forgotten but still wore because he liked how it fit. Kissing Lisa on the head (she grunted something, maybe about love or morning, he couldn't tell), he walked out of the bedroom, Seamus following.

He used the bathroom, made sure the coffee maker was set to start in fifteen minutes, tied on his cross trainers, put the dog on the leash and went out the front door.

He followed his usual route— which led up Barrington to Sunset, along Sunset to Bundy, back down Bundy to home, the route so familiar they could do it with his eyes closed. About three miles. Good enough for Seamus and him to get going in the morning, for the dog to take care of his business and for Bryan to feel he was doing something in the war with the small tire forming around his abdomen.

They came down Bundy, passing the Simpson/Goldberg murder site. It was just a condo with a gated sidewalk; the numbers had been changed and the whole thing repainted so it didn't look like it did back when it was in the news for months. In fact, it looked very much like every other condo on the block—white with brown or black trimming. Nothing special, nothing different. But since something terrible had happened there once it acquired an aura of mystery. Sometimes there was a van full of tourists taking photos outside of it, but never this early in the morning (Bryan always thought since they changed the number you could park the van in front of any of the white, fancy, multi-unit buildings with the garage underneath and tell them it was the site and they would click away and tell their friends back home they saw exactly where IT happened with nobody the wiser). Bryan liked to joke to his friends he lived in a dangerous neighborhood because the "real killers" were still out there, unpunished, ready to strike again. They'd roll their eyes but then fall to talking about other famous L.A. murders.

Usually by the time they were home the sun was starting to peek through the gloom, which was his favorite time of day, like stepping out of a cold pool into a hot tub, just warming and wonderful, but not today. The layer of clouds seemed unusually thick and low.

"Gonna be a dark morning, big guy," he said aloud.

Seamus just panted.

Coming back in the apartment door, he turned on the lights in the kitchen. He drank most of a glass of water (again, a concession to fighting weight gain now that he was more sedentary), and dumping the rest into the dog's bowl, then poured a glass of orange juice. He filled the dog's bowl with kibble and the gentle giant bowed his head and began devouring the crunch pellets. Bryan knew the next time the dog looked up the bowl would be empty and licked clean well after all the food was gone.

He dropped bread in the toaster and peeled a banana while waiting for the toaster to pop. He grabbed his cell phone from where he set it to charge the night before (Lisa charged hers on the nightstand next to the bed. "You have to," he'd told her. "You're a nurse—someone may need you. Stunt men have no emergency calls and I need the sleep.") He saw that his agent had texted him.

He called Susan, who offered him some work that week. After being assured it did not involve any falls or other hard impact, only some driving and easy fights for some sort of cable technothriller pilot called *Reboot* that would be lucky to last more than one season, he accepted the job.

"Who was that?" Lisa asked as she trudged sleepily from the bedroom. Her eyes were half open, black hair sticking out in all directions. She wore gray, baggy sweatpants and Bryan's "I do my own stunts" t-shirt that fell almost all the way to her knees.

"Susan. Just got some work this week. Why are you up?"

"You're loud on the phone. Coffee smells good." She pushed him to one side of the small kitchen as she grabbed a mug and poured herself some coffee.

"Why not wait on that?" he coaxed. "Go back to bed. You've gotten, what, three hours sleep?"

"Mm hmm. Got stuff to do though." She trudged to the small table and sat down, nursing her cup of coffee like a feeble flame.

"You're on graveyard again tonight, right?"

"Yup," she pushed the hair out of her face and looked at him through bleary eyes. "All week."

He sighed. "Maybe you can nap before you go in tonight. Was last night rough?"

She took a sip and stretched. "Sunday nights are usually quiet, but we had two accidents and a kid who had eaten some cleaning supplies. I freakin' hate parents who don't watch the little ones and they get under the sink and start playing with the pretty bottles, you know?"

Bryan nodded. "Kid OK?"

"Most likely. We're keeping an eye on her. She was only fourteen months and the parents didn't know which thing she had put in her mouth. They're lucky it wasn't the drain cleaner or it would have been all over before she even got to the emergency room."

"Anything else?"

"Naw, just a couple of banged up people, including one drunk driver. So the cops were waiting for him until we got done with him. I guess it wasn't that rough, all things considered, but still, I hate seeing hurt kids."

"Part of the job when you signed up to be a nurse, babe," Bryan told her. He gave her a wink as he set his glass and plate in the sink.

"Cleaning up after you is not a job I signed up for. Dishwasher, Bry. Come on."

He sighed again and picked up the dishes again. "Sorry. I'm going to shower, run some errands and meet Mike for lunch at the Literati Cafe. Dinner before you leave for Saint Luke's?" He closed the dishwasher.

"Sure." She looked out the window. "Jesus, it's freaking gray out there."

He chuckled. "I know, right? 'Palm trees and warm sand,'" he sang.

"Maybe I will go back to bed." She got up, put her mug in the sink, kissed him on the cheek and shuffled back towards the bedroom. "I'll clean up later."

Seamus followed her.

Bryan grinned. "You're both horrible."

He headed to the bathroom, hoping a warm shower would go a long way to washing the gray damp and gloom from his mind.

Bryan glanced at the paper while waiting for Mike at the café on the corner of Bundy and Wilshire. It was something to keep his mind off until the fog had dissipated but it was almost one in the afternoon and the sun had yet to put in an appearance.

"Put that thing away," said a voice behind him. "It's all bad news and it's just designed to sell papers."

"I don't know that," he drawled, then waited as Mike took the seat across from him. "Murders are down in the City of Angels. In fact, last year there were the least number of homicides in thirty years. The economy is improving. Police rescued a dog trapped in a canyon in the valley. The only bad news is that you're late."

Mike grinned and looked at him over his glasses. "Don't believe everything you read. Were there really fewer murders last year?"

"Yup. And you are late."

"This is Los Angeles, baby. The city decides when you arrive somewhere. I'm fashionably late. I'm 405 late. Which is right on time. And why are you reading that mainstream rag? The independent papers are more reliable, more in-depth, and less dominated by their corporate masters."

The server came over and took their order—the same thing they always got here—and small talk followed. Mike was a friend from college back East; they met up again out here and renewed their friendship, lunching together once a month as their schedules allowed. Mike was a journalist for a small independent paper, which explained his dislike of what he called "mainstream rags."

"So good news all round, huh?" Mike joked as he shoveled another forkful of avocado from his salad into his mouth.

Bryan shrugged. "Just not all doom and gloom either."

"'cept for this weather. I'd swear we're back in Pittsburgh, dude."

"Hey, even the overcast sky isn't bad news. It's variety. A healthy change of pace."

Mike put his fork down and folded his fingers over his salad. "You know what your problem is? An unhealthy lack of cynicism. It'll get you killed in this town."

Bryan grinned. "Naw, man—I'm just feeling better. My back is better, I've got some work this week."

"Congrats! What are you doing?"

"Small pilot for a cable series. Nothing too strenuous. Some driving, throw some punches and can finally pay the rent again then."

"Can't let Lisa have you as a kept man forever," Mike agreed.

"She's been a rock, so I'm glad to be able to start contributing again. If we weren't together I don't know what I would have done."

He awoke the morning of the shoot two days later, put on his running clothes, threw Seamus on a leash and walked out the door, ready for a quick three miles to get him ready for work that day.

The cloud cover was thicker and lower than he had ever seen it. As they reached the sidewalk he looked up and realized he could not see above the tenth floor of any building on Wilshire. Bryan listened to the eerie quiet. Traffic down the street sounded subdued, as if the cars themselves wanted to maintain the peace and noiselessness of the clouds.

They ran and as they ran, nothing changed. The cloud cover did not burn off. The sun did not peek through. They pulled up back in front of the apartment building and Bryan noted the clouds were still in the same spot as when they left twenty minutes before.

He walked in to his cell phone buzzing on the counter. He picked it up with one hand while removing Seamus' leash with the other.

"Bryan? This is Chris Mattarazzo. I'm the first on *Reboot*. We need it to be sunny for the driving scenes today and the forecast is for this cloud cover to last for much of the day, so we're rescheduling your shoot. How's Friday look for you?"

"Oh, uh…fine. Yeah. Just text me the time."

"Yeah. Thanks."

They hung up without saying goodbye.

The cloud cover stayed the whole day and into the night. As she left for work that night Lisa said something about Los Angeles looking like London now. Bryan watched a movie on television and then went to close the blinds in the living room. Instead, he watched the foggy air circle the lights in the alley behind the apartment building, a shark preparing to have a feeding frenzy on the luminescence. Bryan could hear a narrator's voice in his head saying, *The little light is unaware of the danger just below the surface, sensing the predator only when it is too late,* before he laughed at himself. "Morbid and paranoid much? I mean it's water vapor, man. Calm the hell down." He went to bed around eleven and did not wake up when Lisa came home after the graveyard shift at St. Luke's and pushed Seamus to the foot of the bed so she could climb in and crash.

When he awoke that morning, however, before even rolling out of bed, he pulled back the curtains on the window above their pillows. The clock said seven but the sun was nowhere to be seen, hidden behind fields of grey that extended in all directions. He checked the clock one more time to make sure he had read it properly and that it wasn't still five.

As they ran, Seamus oddly fell behind, almost being dragged at some points of the run rather than his usual excited pulling. Bryan looked up at the palm trees lining Bundy, unable to see their wide fronds through the thick fog. Those things were about fifty feet tall, he realized. Today they were just poles going up into the mist. He heard but did not see any birds, and the spark of electricity running through the wires along the street crackled somewhere up above him. He heard a plane pass overhead to turn around over downtown and make its final approach to LAX (an instrument landing, no doubt). It was as if the fog was a wall separating the earth from a land immediately above, a land where very different things were now happening.

I wonder if something else is up in there, he began thinking. *There could be all sorts of monsters or ghosts or whatever and we'd never know.* Then he laughed. *Jesus,* he thought. *Last night I'm thinking the fog is out to eat light and now I'm imagining monsters just out of sight. I'm the freakin' definition of seasonal affective disorder right now. Stay positive, man.*

"How about you, Seamus?" He asked the dog. "Is a big guy like you worried about the fog? Naw. You're ready for monsters, boy!"

Seamus kept his head low, as if he might be thinking the same thing.

"It's water vapor, dude. It's nothing. It's cool air and warm water from the Pacific making fog. You think there might be monsters up there?" Mike was practically laughing, but Bryan noticed there was a bit of an edge to it.

Mike seemed louder than usual, and Bryan couldn't figure out if it was because Mike was on edge or if it was because the noise in the café also seemed subdued. Everyone carried out quiet conversations. The noises from the kitchen were much more audible than usual, but they were the noises of food being prepared, pots banging, not human voices. Bryant suddenly felt like he was at a wake.

Instead of mentioning that, he said, "I know. I mean I know it's just clouds or whatever, but this is LA. I'm not used to going this long without seeing the sun and so you kinda let your imagination go." Bryan picked up his burger and took a bite, smiling grimly.

"Are you listening to yourself? You think there might be ghost pirates or dinosaurs from another world thirty feet in the air above Santa Monica, just waiting to pounce?"

"You're missing my point, Mike. The overcast sky is making everyone uneasy. It's like the mountains that surround LA. You know they're there, but the smog means you don't see them most of the time. Then the Santa Anas blow, and you're like 'Holy shit, there are mountains there!'"

"That's because the mountains are actually there and we're surprised to see them because air quality here is so shitty."

"You know what I'm saying." Bryan leaned back in his seat and shook his head. "This weather is oppressive. It's like being a kind of blind. Plus, everybody in this town gets seasonal affective disorder if the sun goes behind a cloud. So, a few weeks of overcast skies is enough to drive everyone crazy."

"Everyone in this town is a moron. Next week when the sun is out all day again, they'll all be fine and talking about how heroic they were for surviving a week without sun. These morons would die in Seattle in a matter of days."

"I don't know, Mike. This seems different. Darker."

"Morons," Mike muttered again. He fell silent as he picked at the avocado in his salad.

As he rolled out of bed the next morning Bryan was determined to not let the weather affect his mood. He did not look out the window as he got ready for his run. He and Seamus walked out the door and he stopped. The fog was now at ground level. He could see about ten feet in front of him. He could barely make out the mailboxes on the side of the building. In the seeming distance, a streetlight could be seen as a glowing orb floating in the air. It winked out. At first, Bryan was startled, his heart suddenly pounding and he instinctively moved back toward the apartment door until he realized it was on a timer and scheduled to go off.

Seamus whined, pulling back towards the door. "I hear you, buddy. But it's just fog. We gotta run. So, let's go."

It took a moment of coaxing to get the dog down the walkway and onto the sidewalk.

They ran, slower than usual, following the route they had every day for months. There were few cars on the road, and those moved slowly with their high beams on, reflecting even more of the fog.

He was practically walking when they stepped off the curb to cross Gorham. Headlights, low to the ground and feral-looking, roared out of the gloom, the low hum of an electric engine giving way to the guttural purr as it switched to fossil fuel. The mist in the car's path fled in all directions as it leapt through the intersection, Seamus pulling back just in time, and Bryant felt rather than saw the car pass within an inch of him, dragging the fog with it in a rush of air and aggression, its rear lights savage eyes warning that next time he would not be so lucky.

The damn thing never even slowed.

Bryant stood there, heart pounding, breathing heavy. Seamus sat, unwilling to venture back out into the street. Bryan couldn't even bother giving the driver the finger— the jerk wouldn't have seen it even if he was looking.

After being coaxed into resuming their course, Seamus growled for much of the run, his ears back and hackles raised. Bryan tried to speak calming words and then forceful commands as they followed their usual route. Though to placate the dog or himself, he wasn't sure.

The terror of the near hit-and-run faded after breakfast, but Seamus was surly all day, staying in the bedroom and Bryan threw himself down on the couch and watched old movies only half paying attention. That afternoon, Lisa's shift switched again, so she was now off at four. They decided to go out to dinner at the bar they had met at down near the beach, figuring the happy memories might improve their mood, though the mood in the bar was anything but uplifting. They didn't talk to each other, but listened in to the other conversations as people argued in hushed voices.

"I bet it's some kind of terrorism," said a drunk guy in a Lakers hat.

"You think al Qaeda has a weather machine?" came the sarcastic response.

"Not external terrorism, *internal!*" said another voice in whispered tones. "Al Qaeda might not have a weather machine, but I'll bet the government does. Between HAARP and the black ops projects, I'm telling you guys...the government has been screwing with the ionosphere since 1993. HAARP is fully operational and can cause floods, earthquakes, droughts and hurricanes anywhere in the world."

Bryan took a sip of his drink as he listened to the man continue.

"You think they can't make Los Angeles foggy forever? It goes all the way back to secret a-bomb tests in the forties and fifties. We already have the technology, the government just is keeping knowledge of it from the public."

"You're even crazier than he is," returned sarcasm guy. "Why would the U.S. government create a permanent June Gloom?"

"I don't know. And that's the scary part. Somebody is profiting from it. Follow the money and you'll know who is doing this to us."

At another table, a guy with glasses and long hair held a stance on how the strange weather pattern was proof of global warming. "This is just another example of radical climate change happening sooner than we thought it would. You can't warm the planet, warm the oceans indefinitely without serious consequences. And we're just dealing with some fog. Imagine what this is doing to the fish and the animals!"

His friends nodded. "The irony," said another, "is that we are in the middle of the most serious drought in decades and yet the same heat doing that is now filling the air with this water vapor."

"Oil companies suck," chimed in a third.

Bryan stopped listening in. Nobody really knew what was going on. Everybody was edgy and had an opinion. Maybe Mike was right. Maybe everybody in Los Angeles was a moron. He looked across at Lisa, she was focused on her plate. She wasn't actually eating, just moving the nachos around the plate, dipping them in various things and setting them down on the plate.

"You okay?" he asked.

"Fine," she answered without looking up. "Just tired, I guess." She glanced up at him quickly and he saw the bags under her eyes. He realized he was tired as well. His head hurt and his body felt like he had run a 10K with all of the exhaustion but none of the exhilaration, He was going to mention it to her, maybe ask her medical opinion, but she didn't look like she wanted to talk and come to think of it, he didn't feel like it either.

They decided not to go out to dinner again. Instead, they walked to the supermarket the next day and stocked up on food and supplies. They filled the cart with bottled water, canned goods, dry foods, and things that did not require cooking. Bryan noticed others at Ralph's also filling carts with supplies. It was like there had been a moderate earthquake and so everyone finally decided maybe they *should* get ready for the Big One. There was no friendly camaraderie in the store. Everyone seemed anxious and afraid.

Bryan stopped running in the morning. He realized on the morning that began the third week of this phenomenon that he no longer felt safe outside. The production company had called back and said they would call him into film when the sun was back, so he was now just stuck at home all day. Lisa would drive to work and drive back, their only contact with the outside world, other than television and the Internet.

But Bryan had stopped going online by then. Didn't seem much point, anyway. Nobody knew what was going on or why and the rest of the nation seemed amused that Southern Californians were uncomfortable and even panicking at overcast skies. He just kept watching old movies on television. Though even that activity slowed to infrequent glances. He'd stare at the fog out the window and put the classic movie channel on just for background noise, so he knew he wasn't alone in the world. Lisa tried to put on the news once, to see if the rest of the nation was being affected by this weather pattern and what others in Southern California were doing to cope, but Bryan walked out of the room. As he left, he saw the news was not on when it was supposed to be. Instead, the channel was rerunning an old sitcom.

He woke up in a panic the next day, his heart pounding, sweat drenching the sheets. He wandered around the apartment from window to window, Seamus following. He stared at the gray and tried hard to slow his heartbeat. Nothing was wrong. Nothing. Yet he could not shake the feeling that something bad was about to happen. That feeling followed him for the next few days. At first he called Lisa a lot to check in. Then she stopped answering her phone. Mike, too.

The fourth of July came and went with little fanfare and no fireworks. It wasn't like total darkness, just an absence of any direct light. The whole world was gray.

Lisa came in from working the late shift on the fourth. When she did that she usually had stories of drunken idiots and missing fingers and burns. This time she came in, put down her bag, looked out the window into the alley and said quietly, "It seems as if Los Angeles is shutting down." Then she simply went into their bedroom and he heard the mattress creak under her weight.

He said nothing. He just stayed on the couch, staring at the gray.

A week later, cable cut out, but it no longer mattered as Bryan stopped listening to the television altogether. Some days he just did not get out of bed at all. One morning he woke up and smelled something terrible coming from the living room. The bedroom door was only open a crack but when he walked through it he was hit with the overwhelming smell of shit and piss. He saw that a corner of the living room away from the window had a pile of shit and a puddle and he realized he could not remember when the last time he had taken the dog out. In fact, he couldn't remember the last time he had been outside at all.

He also hadn't noticed immediately that Lisa hadn't come home one day. She left without saying a word in her nurse's scrubs. He waited and waited. It was hard to tell if it was day or night without looking at a clock, so he just slept. And he woke up and she was not there. He went out to the kitchen to look for her. Her keys were not on the table next to the door, and her purse was gone. He wandered into the kitchen and saw the sandwich he had made for her when she was leaving for work was still just sitting there, a mushy banana next to it. He went over and touched the bread. It was hard as a rock.

The power stopped working at some point, although he could not have sworn when. Then the water. It takes so little for society to crumble and the world to end, he thought. What's going on in the rest of the world? Are they now experiencing this, too? If not, why haven't they come to help? None of this made any sense and that made it even more terrifying, but he was too lost to actually feel terror anymore. Instead, it was a numbing sense that something bad was going to happen soon.

He had always thought it would be an earthquake to ruin LA. 8.0 or higher. Level the city and turn it into ruins. Or riots or fire or tsunami or terrorism or any one of a number of things. A lifetime of movie-going had helped his imagination. Hollywood loves to see itself destroyed. Aliens, quakes, fires, monsters, tsunami, meteors, terrorists, nuclear weapons— even a volcano or sharks in tornadoes—you name it and Los Angeles had been destroyed by it on film. But fog? In his more lucid moments, Bryan smiled grimly.

"Not with a bang, but a whimper," he told Seamus, who stared at him blankly.

The television wasn't working. It took him a minute or two to realize that was because he had smashed it. And there was no power, even if he hadn't. There was a smell. Rotting. It might be coming from him or maybe the kitchen or maybe both.

He looked in every cabinet. Empty. He held out as long as he could, until hunger finally overwhelmed sentiment. But by that point Seamus was mostly skin and bones himself and provided little in the way of nutrition or sustenance.

He finally pulled the chair up to the window. He figured it was day, because the landscape was light grey and the fog swirled. Through the glass he thought he heard a woman across the street screaming in her apartment. Later he heard a child crying somewhere down the alley. A dog howled. He wondered absent-mindedly if it was Seamus. As the gray grew darker, he heard a crash and more screaming from across the street. He wasn't certain, but he would have sworn he saw the same car that almost hit him prowling through the alley, its lights flaring, looking for him, needing to finish the job. Then there was nothing but the swirling mist and fog, aimlessly circling and drifting. No longer a shark, now just fish in an aquarium that he could stare at endlessly.

Bryan stared out the window, no sense of time or day. It didn't matter what the weather would be tomorrow. There was no tomorrow. Only fog and whatever was in it. He climbed into bed. Afraid, but he knew not of what.

HIDDEN DEPTHS

ALEXANDRA S. NEUMEISTER

Alexandra S. Neumeister was born and raised in California, and has been scuba certified since the age of thirteen. Her great uncle served as a radarman in the Navy, and went down with the TBM Avenger Bureau Number 53439 outside of San Diego Harbor on October 1st, 1952. Information about the wreck can be found at the UB88 Project website.

MIRA STARED DOWN AT the dingy green-brown rocks, trying to spot crabs in the murky black water. Half broken foam cups floated next to sickly looking patches of loose sea grass, but the only living thing she saw was a whitish shape scuttling across the gray concrete. It went under the surface and disappeared like a phantasm before she could get a good look. She tried to lean closer.

"Sweetie, don't climb on that."

Mira straightened up on the railing, caught fooling around. She hopped down and raced over to her waiting mother, who took her hand. Mira's mother always looked tired, but whenever they could get a day out of the house she looked a little brighter. She tipped her white, floppy brimmed hat against the mid-morning sun, her expression guarded as always but not stern enough to suggest Mira was in any real trouble. Mira clung to her dark blue sundress, the one her mother said she didn't care about getting dirty but was scratchy-stiff from too many washings, and they went down the docks.

Her parents had brought her down to San Diego Harbor, using one of her father's rare days off to rent a sailboat for a relaxing trip around the bay. It didn't seem that fun to Mira, though. She hated boats, and she hated the greasy smell of diesel and salt and gutted fish that suffused the air. Bringing her to a place with water so gross she didn't even want to jump in was the fastest way to ruin a day at the beach.

They approached Mira's father while he was talking to an old man in a green jacket. They were laughing at something, and wore wide grins.

"Is everything set?" Mira's mother asked.

"Just getting the keys," said her father.

When the old man noticed Mira clinging to her mother's sun dress, he leaned down and smiled. "Hello there, little lady."

Mira buried her face in the dress.

"She doesn't talk to strangers," her mother automatically.

"Well, a stranger's just someone you haven't met yet," the old man said, squatting and leaning around to get a better view of Mira. "Hey, wanna hear something interesting?"

She really didn't.

The old man continued, ignoring her discomfort. "Lots of old sunken wrecks are hiding deep underwater, right below where you'll be sailing. There's a place offshore called Wreck Alley, where they sink ships on purpose." He leaned in for a conspiratorial whisper. "But they got regular crashes out there, too. There's a naval base near here, and the boats and planes have to be tested. Sometimes they sink, and it's all left out there like a graveyard. In fact, in 1952—"

"Thank you," Mira's mother said, "but we should be heading out, right?"

The old man straightened himself up. "Right, almost forgot." He dug through the pockets on his jacket, one with the image of an anchor that had a pair of wings on it, and he pulled out a single, slightly corroded key attached to a bright orange floater. "Dock 5 A. Y'all have fun out there, and keep an eye out for planes and choppers taking off when you go by the base."

Mira's father smiled and took the keys. "Will do."

They set off down the dock, Mira running ahead to get out of starting another conversation.

She could hear her father talking behind her. "I'm sure he wouldn't have docked our time if we listened to a yarn or two."

"I just didn't want her hearing about that kind of thing," her mother answered.

"What, the military thing? I tell her my old army stories all the time."

"Not ones about wrecks and graveyards."

"Scary stories were never a big deal before," he said. "You let her watch *Night of the Living Dead* with me. How's this any different?"

"It…" Her mother paused. "It just is. It's one of *those* things."

Her father's voice grew serious. "Ah," he said. "Got it."

They did this sometimes, started talking about *those* things and then stopped when they noticed Mira close by. She didn't pay it much attention, since it seemed like one of those boring adult things she didn't have to worry about, like taxes or getting the car fixed. Mira would have been more curious about it, but it only seemed to come up when they talked about the trouble she had with the other kids at school, and she wanted to avoid that subject as much as possible.

They came to their assigned dock, where a sailboat waited for them. It was small, not even as big as their car, and bobbed high above the water line. Mira's father lifted her onboard, then set the icebox in the center of the boat. She tolerated her mother slopping sunscreen all over her face and arms while her father got the sail ready. After what felt like forever, they clipped on life vests, traveled slowly through the maze of docks and finally gained speed once they were properly out in the San Diego harbor, the stink of diesel giving way to the sweet briny smell of clean water and fresh kelp.

The sky was gray and foggy at first, but the mist quickly burned away under the mid-day sun. As it cleared up, Mira's skin started getting too hot, the oil from the sunscreen made it feel more like she was boiling than being protected, and her fingers were uncomfortably greasy. They passed a dock where people refueled fishing boats, then went beyond it to see a submarine suspended just above the water in a giant metal stall.

Her father slowed the boat as they neared the naval base. He pointed up on the hill and started talking about the Cabrillo cemetery, but her mother gave him a look that made him stop.

They crept closer to the chains separating the base from the rest of the harbor.

"Never approached by boat before," her father said, "but I had a few buddies—"

The PA system crackled to life, making Mira nearly jump out of her skin.

"*You are sailing into a restricted area,*" a scratchy voice said. "*Turn back now.*"

Mira's father glanced at her mother. "Guess we should probably leave before we're arrested," he said, nudging his wife.

She hit his arm and looked away, but the corners of her lips turned up in a rare smile.

Her father grinned. He moved them farther away toward the naval base, and continued. "So some buddies of mine were stationed—"

Mira barely paid any attention, though, wishing they hadn't bothered with the base in the first place if they were just going to get in trouble. She poked her head out to try and get a better look at a green buoy, where huge sea lions were piled on top of each other, napping in the sun. When they made their way back out into the middle of the bay and out into the open ocean, Mira kept one hand on the rail, and she stretched her other one out into the spray of the boat's wake, slapping against her skin like a hundred tiny needles. That was the only fun part of sailing, going somewhere fast and feeling that new crash of salty wetness every time they hit a wave.

After an hour or so, they went out past the tall rocky cliffs of Point Loma, like someone had cut a piece of the continent clean off, and they stopped near a rocky shore, shallow enough to anchor but still far enough that the waters were a dark and murky green. The sky above them was clear, and the surface of the ocean was a glassy green color, with a rare patch of golden kelp. Tiny wavelets smacked rhythmically against the hull of their boat with a small plop and gave off a little spray of water each time they hit. Once they'd settled, her mother went about making lunch. Mira stood near the back, straining her eyes to see a patch of soft sandy shore further up the coast.

"Can we get to Cabrillo beach from here?" she asked. "I wanna swim." She was tired of being stuck on the tiny boat and wearing the greasy life vest.

"You can swim here," her father said, standing close to her but keeping his hand on the tiller.

"No, I can't," Mira said, insistent. "It's too deep." Mira peered over the edge. She always swam from the beach, where her feet could touch the ground, or at the pool classes where the water was clear enough to see the bottom. Not that she was afraid of sharks or anything, she just didn't think it was as fun to float around aimlessly.

She turned around, just in time for her father's outstretched hand to hit her shoulder, and shove her off the boat.

Mira's stomach twisted as she plummeted down, and a thousand pricks of pain hit her back when she crashed onto the surface. Her eyes and mouth instinctively closed. She bobbed below the water for a moment, until the buoyancy of the life vest brought her back up.

She wiped the water away from her eyes and opened them, salt stinging. Her father laughed loudly above her, and she could even see her mother glancing down with a smile.

Mira didn't think it was so funny.

"Stop it!" she said. It sounded petulant even to herself, but she was not in the mood to be nice.

"I thought you wanted to go swimming?" her father said.

"I said not here!" she yelped. "Help me out!"

"You can get up yourself. You're a big girl."

But Mira knew he was wrong. The preserver made it awkward to move, her body sinking down while the scratchy vest bobbed up, constricting her throat and keeping her either on her back or her stomach instead of the freedom swimming usually gave her.

Finally, she twisted around and managed an embarrassing doggy paddle to the boat, but it had no ladder, and the sides of the boat were too round and smooth to get a purchase. She had never been strong enough to pull herself out, even from the pool, and now she couldn't even bring her legs up to help push.

Her small hands gripped the edge, and Mira felt tears stinging her eyes. It was just like PE, where she could barely lift herself up in a pushup and always got left behind in running. If she couldn't get out they might leave without her. Her parents were above her on the boat, still smiling, still watching her struggle.

She slipped again, her sunscreen-greasy fingers sliding off the rail, and splashed into the water, eliciting another round of laughter from her parents.

Her body bobbed up above the water once.

Then something yanked at her life vest, and pulled her down.

Her chest tightened as she sank deeper and deeper into the murky water. Though her eyes had instinctively closed, somehow, she could still see. A strange bulky shape floated above her, and beyond it the silhouettes of her parents, looking panicked before they disappeared. The pulling sensation came from the back of her life vest, dragging her down and down and down.

When the darkness became almost complete, the pulling slowed, until she finally stopped. She floated like a buoy, wobbling with the swell of the currents yet staying in place. It was cold, like sticking her hand in the freezer, but there was no sharp sticky feeling of ice. The temperature was steady, it was encompassing and almost comforting as she grew used to it. Mira knew enough that she should've run out of air by now, but hadn't. While she still felt on edge, her insides tensed up like tangled yarn, her limbs relaxed a bit. She twisted around. Below her, Mira saw the rocky bottom of the ocean, bits of kelp and fuzzy algae sticking up and small slithery shadows of fish going about their business.

Directly underneath her was a jagged metal shape, half buried in the sand with one flat rounded end sticking up. In the rusted wreckage, she recognized the familiar shape of a small airplane. Since she didn't seem to have to worry about breathing, Mira began to feel more curious than afraid. She willed herself to sink a little more, surprised when for once her body did as she told it to, and saw painted on the side of the plane was a star with red and white bands next to it. Her dad had taken her to museums, the boring kind without big dinosaur skeletons or models of space shuttles, so she recognized it but wasn't quite sure what it could be. She peered closer and barely made out the number on the tail. 53439.

Mira floated down until she came to eye level with the window of the plane where she saw a slight, greenish glow.

A skeletal hand wrapped in kelp and gristle rose up from the window, followed by a skull. Crabs skittered out of the empty eye sockets.

Mira's blood went colder than the water surrounding her. She wanted to scream, but she was afraid she would lose air.

The skeleton sat motionless for a moment, and she managed to get a good look at it. It wore a thick, poofy jacket, but the fleece on the collar had worn off, and the leather looked rotted. On top of the skull was a cap almost like a boy scout's, and a patch sewn onto the jacket's breast showed a winged anchor on a shield.

She struggled to push herself away in the water, her tiny limbs barely moving her, but when she realized nothing had happened, Mira's body relaxed. The skeleton's movement was just part of the ocean tides, nothing worse than the slithering fish nearby. She started to float up a bit.

Then the hand snapped out, grasping tight around her arm.

Mira did scream then, but no sound came out—just a burst of bubbles that warped the water in front of her. Her lungs squeezed, and her chest burned.

She tried to pull her arm away, but the other skeletal hand rose up and encased her fingers, curling over them. Mira pulled and pulled. It felt like being stuck in tar. The more she moved, the tighter the grip.

All of a sudden, she felt a yank.

Mira slid out of the skeleton's grasp, and the green glow faded to be replaced by darkness, then by the blue light of day through the water just above.

Ahead of her she could see the bulky shape from before, and she nearly panicked as she came at it faster and faster, until she was about to slam right into it.

* * *

Her eyes opened. Water stung them, and she realized they had been closed the whole time. The cold water enveloped her, but then something grabbed the front of her life vest and pulled her up. Her father's massive arms plucked her out of the ocean, hauling her back into the boat.

In the moments that followed, Mira was significantly calmer about the situation than her parents were.

"What happened?" her mother asked.

"Does anything hurt?" her father asked.

"I'm fine," Mira said, only feeling a little dizzy and for once happy to be on a boat instead of in the water.

"This is why we wear life vests," her father said. He sighed. "At least she only went under for a couple seconds."

Mira frowned. That couldn't be true. It had felt like she was down there much longer.

Her father gave her a concerned look. "Are you sure you're okay?"

"It wasn't so bad," she said. "I saw a plane down there."

Both her parents went still. Her father's grip on her tightened.

Mira's mother stared at her, getting that worried but angry look she had whenever Mira hurt herself. "We're going back."

Her father nodded, and went to pull up the anchor and get them going.

Mira laid down in the middle of the boat, leaning her head against the cabin on a cushion of spare life vests. Her lungs burned, and she appreciated the chance to just lie still.

Once her father had gotten them moving, she could hear him say something to her mother in a low voice. "Everything's fine," he said, "she must've had some sort of hallucination down there."

Hallucination, Mira thought, testing out the word in her mind. That was another word for dream, right? It felt sort of like the way dreams felt, a foggy memory now that she was back on the surface. Yeah, that must have been it.

Except, as the cold and tension left her body and the feeling started to return, Mira realized there was something in her hands, a pointed shape that dug into the meat of her palm.

Something that had been there since she was pulled from the water.

She uncurled her fingers. It seemed like a wad of wet, dirty cream-colored paper, but it was different somehow, almost plastic. The paper felt heavy in her hand, as if it had something wrapped inside, something sharp she could feel through the thin, damp material. She didn't have the energy to see what, though. Mira was just happy, once they sped up, that the cool breeze soothed the burning in her lungs.

They made it back to the dock without incident, and though Mira's limbs still shook, she stepped from the boat to the pier all on her own. Her mother kept a hand on her while her father, keys in hand, went back over to the boat rental shack.

The old man brightened when he saw them, and stepped out of the building. "How'd it go out there?"

"Not bad," her father said, smiling. "We had a bit of a slip into the water, but the trip itself was fantastic."

"That's why you wear life vests," the old man said, grinning as if he'd made a joke.

Mira was only half listening, though. She stared at the old man's jacket. It had a patch on the pocket, an anchor with a pair of wings, which seemed familiar somehow.

The old man noticed her staring, and turned his smile to her. "Hello again, little missy. How'd you enjoy the trip?"

Mira didn't answer for a moment, partly too tired to talk, partly thinking.

She looked up at the old man's cheerful face.

"53439?"

The old man's grin faded and his face drained of color. "Where did you hear that?"

Mira said nothing.

The old man stepped forward, practically growling now. "*Where did you hear that?*"

Her mother gripped Mira's shoulders and pulled her back, glowering at the old man. "Don't you dare speak to her like that."

Mira wriggled out of her mother's grip. The man watched her suspiciously as she approached, but Mira simply held out one hand and opened it, showing him the soggy crumpled package she had pulled out of the water.

"I think you might know what this is," she said.

The old man hesitated for just a second, then plucked it carefully out of her hand, making sure not to touch her. He unwrapped it, and when he saw what was inside his eyes widened.

A mechanical part, like some sort of screw, but it looked melted. The man stared at it lying on his open palm, mouth hanging open. His hands shook.

"It's warped," he said. "They put a warped one in."

Her father coughed. "I think we should be on our way."

He put his hand on her back and pushed her forward, but not before she noticed the uncrumpled paper in the old man's hand. On the other side it looked like a picture, of two men in uniform standing in front of a plane.

* * *

They got home without trouble, and Mira made no complaint about going to bed early. Her body felt drained, and she fell asleep not even a minute after the lights went out.

In the middle of the night, Mira stirred awake.

Slowly rising to consciousness, she felt a tightness in her chest, only relieved by shifting positions. After tossing and turning and waiting to see if she could fall back to sleep, Mira decided to at least get up and use the bathroom. She opened her eyes, expecting fuzzy gray darkness, but instead found the room bathed in a weird green light.

Mira sat up, and froze.

Beyond the foot of her bed, standing in the center of the room, was a green glowing mist in the shape of a skeleton, covered in a ragged uniform. It shimmered in the ethereal light, as if seeing it from underwater, and the kelp and scarf wrapped around its neck fluttered in an imperceptible current. Seeing she was awake, the skeleton stepped forward.

Mira wanted to scream, but her lungs went tight, almost like she was underwater again, like she would drown in the heavy air if she opened her mouth.

It drew closer, almost touching the foot of the bed, and the feeling intensified. Her vision went cloudy, melting into a green and black murk, and her body became lighter, like it was floating. If she didn't take a breath soon it would reach her and pull her away.

Mira used every ounce of energy she had to push the air out of her throat.

She screamed.

Almost as if on cue, her door burst open and her father came in. "Mira? What is it?"

Mira couldn't answer. Her lungs struggled just to take in air. Her vision cleared and she sat staring at the grisly, bony shape in front of her. The skeleton halted and stood motionless.

Her father crouched down next to her bed, placing a hand on her shoulder. He followed her gaze and frowned, then scanned the room, searching the darkness. Mira gripped his arm and prayed the skeleton didn't start moving again.

Her mother appeared in the doorway, rubbing the sleep out of her eyes.

"What's going—"

She froze, her gaze locked on the skeletal figure.

The skeleton didn't react. Its attention remained on Mira.

"I think she just had a nightmare," her father said, calm but almost dismissive. He turned to Mira. "Don't worry, sweetie. There's nothing to be scared of."

"Hank," Mira's mother said, "could you please go make a pot of jasmine tea?"

He frowned. "You sure, Bon? This late at night, might make it worse."

"Please." It didn't sound like a request.

Her father hesitated a moment, then he turned to Mira with a smile. "I'll be right back."

He stood up, taking a sense of warmth and stability from Mira. Her mother remained still, eyes never leaving the glowing shape, the green incandescence giving her a frightening complexion.

As soon as her father disappeared from the doorway, Mira's mother shot forward. Her arms wrapped around Mira's small form, and she scowled at the intruder at the foot of the bed.

"Momma?" Mira asked. "What's happening?"

She whispered into Mira's ear, urgent but calm, like she'd seen this before. "Just be still. Don't move until it does, and don't let it touch you." She raised her voice. "I don't know who you are," she said, "but get the hell away from my daughter."

The skeleton finally moved, lifting a hand, slowly like it was pushing through water.

Her mother tensed, as if ready to run, or to push Mira out of the way. The skeleton's hand stopped on its chest, resting on its breast pocket, and went still. A pocket, Mira realized belatedly, with a pair of wings on it.

She straightened up.

"53439?" she asked.

The skeleton dropped its arm, and nodded slowly.

"I gave it to him," Mira said. "That's what you wanted, right?"

Once again, the skeleton nodded. Then it reached out.

Her mother tensed and drew back, but the skeleton had stopped to hold perfectly still, its fingers curled around something in its outstretched hand.

Mira pulled away from her mother. She scooted forward on the bed until she could just about touch the skeleton, and held out her hands. The skeleton's hand slowly opened, and a weight dropped into her palm. Mira closed her fingers around it.

The skeleton stepped back, its scarf still waving. Its movements grew sluggish, and tendrils of green mist leaked away from its glowing form. Slowly, the skeleton brought one arm up, and pressed a flat hand against its head in salute.

It took Mira a moment to realize what it wanted, and she returned the gesture.

The skeleton let its hand fall, nodded once more, and finally turned. As it trudged away, the green color drained from it, leaking into the air and dissipating, until only a soft, blue glow remained, shimmering like the sky seen from below the surface of the ocean.

The skeleton walked to the window, and stepped through the wall like it was nothing. The room went dark, but Mira's vision adjusted quickly, as if the light had never really been there.

Mira's mother took a deep breath and shook her head. "Seven," she said. "I didn't get it until I was twelve. Even mom had been at least ten."

Mira twisted her head so she could look up at her mother. "What does that mean?"

"It means," her mother said, "that when you're older, you're going to be a very good spirit medium."

Mira thought for a moment, then nodded sagely, as if this made perfect sense to her on some level. "Can we go to Cabrillo beach tomorrow?" she said, already on to new subjects.

The kettle whistled from the downstairs kitchen.

Mira's mother blinked and looked down at her daughter in surprise. "Really?"

"Yeah," said Mira, "I want to go swimming."

Mira's mother was silent for a long time. Then she smiled. "Okay," she said. "Tomorrow."

She pulled Mira close, and Mira buried her face in her mother's shoulder, fingers wrapped tightly around a corroded metal pin, shaped like an anchor with a pair of wings.

FOR A MUSE OF FIRE

NICKOLAS FURR

Nickolas Furr is member of the San Diego HWA chapter and a resident of Imperial Beach, California, where he lives with his girlfriend, Liza, and their dogs, Adam and Liam. He loves writing, but he has no Muse and he doesn't really mind.

LIVING IN A SMALL beach town, new faces always surprised me. I don't mean tourists. I could spot a tourist at a quarter mile. Almost everyone carried a camera and most of them toted bags of cheap beach junk, purchased at one of our cheap beach junk stores. It was the ones who had relocated here and decided to make this piece of Southern California their home that surprised me. They had the same look of wonder and delight as the tourists, but there was a sense of pride and a bit of serenity about their faces—they had made the decision to come here, and as far as they knew, all was now right with the world.

Sometimes it was more than that. Standing on the beach that morning, the woman I saw *glowed*. It was no surprise that I spotted her, together with a man whose sense of pride was tempered with an air of smugness.

Hand in hand they stood, high up where the sand was soft and pulled at your feet with each step. I was enjoying late morning in the sun, walking several yards behind them when I first saw her. In a moment, I snapped a mental photograph and prayed that time refused to degrade the image.

They turned to watch the waves roll in. Had I never seen her face, I would still have called her stunning. Blonde hair cascaded down her back, dancing and blowing across her shoulders. A diaphanous white skirt blew against her legs in the sea breeze. A halter top of the same material left her arms, belly, and back bare. Her lightly tanned, gold skin shone in the sun.

I stopped and stumbled in the soft sand, enthralled by her cappuccino eyes, long straight nose, strong jaw, and utterly perfect mouth. She blinked and glanced toward me, warming me with a look and the slightest curve of her lips. Then...

She was inside me, warm and sweet, like clover honey flowing into my soul. I could taste her. Before I could get closer, they turned and walked hand-in-hand through the sand toward the street. Just before her features could blur with distance, she glanced back. A casual move, meant to be unnoticed by her companion. For only a second, she looked at me over the curve of her shoulder and smiled.

Hello, Nathan, I imagined her saying.

The sweet-honey taste bloomed; I swear my legs began to move of their own accord. I began to follow, but in my legs' semi-independent hurry, I staggered and nearly fell twice, like a damned tourist. A laugh pealed in the belfry of my imagination. I was certain that she would find this amusing. I forced myself to slow, so I was still a block away when they walked into one of the cafés that lined the boulevard.

Attempting to appear as a casual passerby, I strolled past the front window and looked inside. It was too dark and too crowded. I had lost her and wasn't brave enough to go inside and look.

Another time, I imagined her telling me. Then I felt her lips, flamelike yet feather-soft, on my cheek. Without even my lips being touched, I would have killed that man for her on the sidewalk. As it was, it took six more weeks before I did it.

* * *

For nearly a week, I walked to the beach two or three times a day then wandered past the café. I didn't see either the woman or her male companion, but during a casual conversation with one of the waitresses, whom I knew from a shared yoga class, I learned their names—Bodhi Reilly and Melanie Rhodes. Even though I didn't know him by sight, I'd heard Bodhi's name once or twice.

"Reilly is the guy who started buying up those little tech companies a few years ago," said Camilla, the waitress. "They all blew up and got huge. Microsoft or Google bought most of them. One of the guys from the Chamber said Reilly's considering putting in a bid to buy all the businesses for a couple of blocks along the coast."

But who was *she*?

"Probably a trophy wife," Camilla said. "She looks like one, and he's in his fifties. But I don't know. They might be here to stay. Reilly just bought that enormous place down at the end of Ocean Avenue. From what I hear, it's just him and her."

* * *

Though I'd only seen her once, Melanie Rhodes continued to bedevil me. Every few days, my mind would attune to her, like a radio that had suddenly found a new station.

A couple of weeks after I'd seen her, I woke with the lingering, fragmented memory of making love to her. I felt her tongue in my mouth, her lips on mine. Her hands clasped my neck and her legs clung to my hips. I vaguely recalled the feeling of being inside her, but I remembered the feel of my hand on her back and shoulders, and even the soft moan she made when she pressed her mouth to my cheek. I flung the sheet away and tried to roll over.

The pain surprised and shocked me. I glanced down and nearly laughed. At no point in my life had I ever been so aroused. I needed a shower.

* * *

Like everything else along the beach, my apartment was small and expensive. I was on the second floor, above a busy taco shop. Depending on the day of the week, and the special written on the sidewalk board downstairs, my apartment pretty much always smelled like *carne asada* or fish tacos. The bedroom was much too little in which to work, but I'd turned a piece of the living room into a workspace, with my computer, reference models and materials, and shelves of art supplies on display in the corner. Like a lot of graphic artists, I worked mostly on computer, but for some things, and for a few clients I still worked on paper. The feel of a pen or brush in my hand, the *skritch-skritch* of a pen nib or the nearly-silent hiss of paint on paper brought me back to when I was younger and couldn't afford the software—perhaps even more creative. I was currently on contract to deliver a logo for Elegance, a small chain of ladies' boutiques. I'd come up with the same five ideas I'd had for any similar logo. None of them made me happy, and that unhappiness translated directly into anxiety.

Being a freelancer in California was much harder than I thought it would be. When I moved to the sunny state from Iowa ten years ago, I had put together a stable of some of the biggest medical, financial, and retail clients in Des Moines. I now worked alone, drumming up my own business, doing all my own billing, and making all the creative decisions. I initially had big dreams, of a house on the beach, and a nice car with a soft top to drive along the coast... Though I'd realized quickly in Southern California, at least, it was almost impossible to make a living as a freelancer. Clients wanted large firms with large staffs and large offices charging large fees. Those of us unable to get a gig with a large firm hoarded our clients with almost paranoid fervor. Elegance wasn't my biggest client, but they were the second largest, and I couldn't afford to fail.

The anxiety scattered as I heard a laugh inside my head.

Nathan, I imagined her saying. *I'm here. I'm inside you.*

I stopped what I was doing, the tip of the camel-hair brush just touching the paper.

I'm inside you... like you want to be inside me.

I took a deep breath. "Where are you?" I asked, just barely audibly.

I'm the last place you saw me. You should come see me here—unless you want that to be the last time you see me...

"I want to see you," I whispered, the brush idly moving across the posterboard.

Then come.

"Now?"

Not now, I imagined her saying, *you have something to do first. I'll be here when you're ready... waiting for you.*

I blinked and looked down. I'd inked a simple line— a curve of a shoulder, the sharp inward swoop of a narrow waist, and a long-but-tight curve of a single buttock— *her* figure. I smiled and cocked my head when I saw the capital E.

I dabbed the brush into the ink and carefully drew an italicized, modified-cursive "l" followed by an "e" and then the rest of it.

Elegance. It was good.

* * *

I stepped inside the café and looked around. I wasn't surprised to see Melanie at a table at the back of the room, holding a small espresso cup in her hand.

She smiled.

I froze, unable to step any closer. Her smile fluttered, but reappeared. She set the cup down on the saucer and rested her elbows on the table with her chin on folded hands.

Well... come on.

I was quite certain that I didn't imagine that.

Nathan, come to me.

Or that.

I walked to the table, watching her. Her smile widened. Her light brown eyes enchanted.

"Hi," I finally said. "My name is Nathan."

"Hello, Nathan," she said in a voice exactly as I'd imagined it would be, "I think I saw you on the beach a couple of weeks ago."

I nodded. "You were with someone."

The smile crinkled but didn't go away. "I was." She unwound her arms and offered me a hand. "I'm Melanie."

I took her soft hand, shaking it lightly. "It's very nice to meet you, Melanie."

"Likewise. Please sit down."

I sat across from her, facing away from the door.

"Melanie!"

I turned in my seat. Bodhi stood in the doorway, tense and ready to attack, like a raptor looking down at a field mouse.

"Get away from her," the computer magnate said.

"I was just saying 'hi,'" I said.

"I know what you want." He rested a hand on my shoulder. "And I want you to leave."

"Bodhi, you're embarrassing yourself," Melanie said.

Still looking up at Bodhi, I couldn't see her expression.

"Take your hand off my shoulder," I said. "I haven't fought in years, but—"

"Nathan, don't."

Bodhi took his hand from my shoulder. Even though he was 10 or 15 years my senior, his gaze was primal; he was ready to go to war.

"Nathan, please."

I turned. Melanie frowned at us both. I apologized and stood up, glancing around the café as I left. The other patrons all watched in silence, as I expected. These were my neighbors, and I had known all of them a lot longer than her or Bodhi.

"My apologies, everyone," I said as I left.

I hadn't taken half a dozen steps on the sidewalk when I heard her voice in my head again:

Thank you, Nathan.

I now knew I wasn't imagining it.

* * *

Nathan!

I jerked awake, immediately forgetting a dream. Only her face remained.

"Melanie?"

You were dreaming.

"I guess so," I said out loud. "It's really you, isn't it?"

What do you want to believe?

"I think it's you. I don't know how. But it's either that, or I'm going crazy."

You're not crazy. Come for a walk.

"It's late... where?"

Wherever you want. I'll be there.

"Then you know where I'll be."

* * *

I found her where I'd first seen her, high up on the beach, sitting and facing the Pacific Ocean. The western sky was still dark, with only hints of light drifting over our heads from the east. Feeling bold, I sat next to her.

"It is you I hear, isn't it?"

Yes, she didn't say. *It's also me in your dreams.*

"I've dreamed about you a few times," I admitted.

You've dreamed about me a thousand times. In those dreams, we've been together. We've made love, I've pleasured you, and you've pleasured me, and sometimes...

"We've just fucked," she said, turning and resting on her hip, facing me. "A thousand times, at least."

"How are you doing this?"

"Do you really want to know?"

"Yes."

"Nathan, this is a door you have to choose to open. If you wish to know, I'll tell you, but I promise your life will change."

"What if I don't want to know?"

"Then we'll part as friends."

"And if I do?"

"Then, you can take me and I'll be yours."

"I... I... I..." It was as if a void had opened up inside me, and I was there, teetering on its edge, clinging to safety, but desperate to hurl myself into the dark.

"You want that."

Without another word, I leaped from the edge and plunged into the void.

"I want that very much," I finally said, gazing at her face. "Tell me. Tell me how you've done this."

"I'm a muse, Nathan, and now I'm your muse."

I thought about pooh-poohing the concept, but I didn't.

"Are you Bodhi's muse?"

"Yes, but I want to be yours. I can only have one artist at a time, and I want it to be you."

"I'm not that kind of artist."

"Of course you are." She reached out and took my hand.

Holding her hand was like holding something extremely warm, something that could ignite into flames in an instant.

"An artist is creative. Anyone who is creative can use a muse." She smiled. "Did the clients like 'Elegance'?"

I nodded. "They did. They want me to do an entire campaign for them."

"That was me," she said.

I thought about the curve of the drawn figure. "Yes, it was."

"This is what I do. I inspire. Ideas will come more quickly. Your talent will blossom. You'll find that things come into focus more quickly. You'll be much more successful at any anything you do. This is my gift to you."

"...And I get you?"

"This is your gift to me. Love and sex and passion are one to me. Gentleness and roughness, caresses and bruises, sweetness and filth; I desire it all. My appetites can be... amazing."

I caught my breath. My cock had been hard since I'd seen her sitting on the beach, but now it seemed to be even more swollen, radiating heat.

"Oh my God."

"I'm better than that," she said, smiling.

"What do I need to do?" I asked, trying not to let my greed appear.

"You need to take me from Bodhi," she said, leaning toward me. "You need to claim me as a man once claimed a woman. Like back from a long time ago, when I was much, much younger."

My voice broke. "What do I need to do... to Bodhi?"

She reached out and put her arms around my neck, brushing her lips against mine. After a bit, we slid down into the sand. It was... everything. Everything I wanted it to be. And it was better than that.

When we finally broke free and separated, the sun had climbed into the sky, banishing the dark over the horizon. She smiled as she stood, shaking sand from her clothes.

"I'll tell you soon," she said. She turned and ran up the sand, toward town.

I caught my breath and sat up. Exhausted and drained, I was barely able to move. It was like the aftereffects of the best sex I'd ever had and beyond it—and all that from only a kiss. It was a kiss that lasted half an hour, granted, but still only a kiss.

I had to have her.

* * *

There were either nine or three muses, depending on the source. I'd read they were the daughters of Zeus and Mnemosyne, the goddess of memory, or they were the daughters of Ouranos and Gaia, the mother goddess. They were called the embodiments of arts and sciences, or the personifications of aspects of the arts.

In no case were any of them named Melanie, and in no case were they known for their carnal natures.

I brought the mythology book with me into the café, hoping to see her. I hadn't heard her voice in my head since the morning on the beach, and I was desperate to hear it again.

She wasn't there, but Camilla was. She waved me to one of her tables.

"Did I hear that you hit on Ms. Rhodes?" she asked.

"I just spoke to her here a week ago."

"Someone said that Bodhi Reilly was pissed at you."

"He was," I said, "But I think he's just the jealous type."

"He might be," she said, glancing toward the door. "You should tell him."

I turned. Bodhi strode in and came straight toward me. Without invitation, he took the seat across from me. He glanced at the book then picked it up.

"You know," he said.

"I think I do."

"I want you to stay away from her," he said, *sotto voce*. "And I want you to stay away from me."

"Or?"

"I'll kill you," he said. "I'll shoot you in the head and leave your body for the crows to find." He stood and walked off.

I sat in sullen silence.

Taking her from him might be harder than I thought.

* * *

It took most of the day to take the freeway into Los Angeles to buy a pistol. I'd used one before for target shooting, so I knew what I was looking for. State law said it would be ten days before it would be released, but I could wait. In case things with Bodhi got difficult, I wanted to be able to defend myself.

Nathan.

I jumped. I hadn't heard her since that morning on the sand.

"Melanie."

I'm outside.

"Here?"

"Yes," she said, from outside.

I flung the door open.

"Can I come in?" she asked.

"Of course!" I motioned for her to step inside.

She grabbed my hand. I stand six feet and she was half a foot shorter than I, but I still felt as if I was looking up at her.

"Tell me," she said. "Tell me you want me."

"I do."

"Tell me you want to take me from him."

"I do."

"Then let me show you what I can do."

She pushed me backwards onto the couch. Before I could move, she'd straddled me and was kissing me. I don't recall actually seeing what she wore. What I remember is her hurling it away, and then her divine perfect figure pressed down on me. I told her I would do what I could.

When she slid her hand down the front of my pants, I told her I would do anything—anything she wanted.

* * *

We lay together on the couch, wrapped up in a handmade afghan that my grandmother had given me. Her soft, golden skin peeked through knitted holes in the pink, purple, and blue grandmotherly patterns. Her hair felt damp from sweat and her face shone from perspiration.

She was beautiful. And I, sweaty and wet and exhausted, almost certainly looked horrible. But she looked up at me with a gaze that said she either didn't care or didn't see it.

I needed this. I needed her. I wanted her more than anything else.

She glanced up at me and smiled. *I want that, too.*

"What do I need to do?" I asked.

"Take me."

"I did," I said, somewhat lightly.

"I'm not sure it was you that did the taking."

"Frankly, my muse, I'm not either."

Her smile became a grin and I could swear she began to purr when I called her 'my muse.'

"I *am* yours," she said, "but you have to kill Bodhi to keep me."

* * *

I brought us bottled water from the fridge. She was sitting up, the afghan not quite covering her breasts, looking a bit more serious and a little less disheveled than she had a few minutes ago. I'd cleared my head and was ready to hear what she had to say.

"A muse bonds with the artist," she said. "It's nothing I have control over. The bond is for life and ends at death—mine or his"

"I have to kill him?"

"I can't do it. The bond must be severed by someone else."

"And if I do this, I will get you?"

"You've already had me," Melanie said. "This is how you *keep* me."

"Do you really want that?"

"Of course. Do you want me to prove that again?"

"No—yes! Yes, but not… right this moment." I shook my head. "But why kill him? It's not right."

Melanie flung the afghan aside and swung a long, bare leg over me. She pulled herself up so she was nearly straddling again, but this time in a way that commanded my attention—literally. Exhausted, raw, and spent, with only an inch or so between us, my penis stirred and began to rise again.

"Listen to me, Nathan. You have the book. You should understand. I am a Muse. I'm not... human. In fact, by the time the Greeks had given us a name, I'd been alive for a very long time. This has nothing to do with morality. This has to do with forces more powerful and older than you can understand."

"Okay," I said, "But—"

Nathan, she tightened her grip on me, both mentally and physically. *If nothing else, this should prove that I'm not human as you know it.*

"Tell me something first. Did he kill someone else to win you over?"

"Like you, he won me over from afar. I sensed greatness in him—a spark of creativity in a relatively new field—much as I sense greatness in you. *That* is what 'wins me over.' And yes, he killed a man to take me."

"Who?"

"A South Korean poet—a fine man, a brilliant poet even before me, and a lively lover."

"You miss him?"

"Yes," she said. "I miss him like I'll miss Bodhi, and like I've missed the others that have gone before."

"How many?"

"I don't think this is a road you want to walk down, Nathan."

"What about... me?" I tried to swallow, but my mouth was dry.

"What about you? Nathan, it's *you* I desire! I sense greatness in you. I've already given myself to you, and I've opened myself up to you so you know what you're getting into!"

"Thank you, but... will you miss me?"

A bit of sadness crept into her smile.

"Of course, I will. Unless you give me reason to not miss you."

"Has that—?"

"Yes."

"How long would you be with me?" I asked.

"As long as I can be. As few as days, as long as years." She leaned forward and kissed me. "I'm thousands of years old, my Nathan. I stimulate, but must be stimulated." She kissed me again. "I am with you until I get bored."

* * *

I stood naked in the bathroom, steam from the shower rising around me. I faced the mirror again and again, too horrified to do more than glance at it. Twenty-two years was the longest, she'd said. The shortest had been under a week, back in the 9th century—her biggest mistake. On average, she was with someone three or four years. Bodhi had been with her just over three years.

Blood must be spilled, she'd said. That was the contract.

There was to be no poisoning, no slow deprivation of food or water, no abduction and abandonment. The pistol I'd purchased wouldn't even be good enough. It was too quick. The blood must flow from the wound an ancient might create—a blow, a slash, a gouge. That was the way of things.

But Bodhi had no such limitations. All he had to do was to stop me. If he did, then she remained with him until she met another.

He'd already done so once, she said.

"It's too late, my artist," she said. "I want you. I need to touch you. I want to feed your creativity, your soul. I want to feel you inside me while I am inside you. I want to *inspire* you!"

I wasn't sure this was something I could do. "And," she told me before she left, "I know you want that, too."

Goddamn it. I did want that.

* * *

Please don't do this.

I lay on the bed in a fetal position, a pillow over my head.

Nathan, I know you want me.

She wasn't always this insistent, but like any human, she had her moods. Today had been tougher than most, it being exactly two weeks after I'd last seen her. Two weeks of hearing her voice echo in my head, pleading for me to come take her. Two weeks since the beach had bloomed into summer numbers, and we found our streets crowded with noisy beachgoers and partiers. Two weeks that I had tossed and turned, sweated, sobbed, thrown up, fretted and wondered. Two weeks that I had obsessed on seeing her again, on touching her skin, kissing her lips, smelling her hair, and hearing her cry out as I entered her. Two weeks in which I had not had a single decent night's sleep, a peaceful shower, or created a single new image.

It was also two days since I had driven back into Los Angeles and picked up the pistol. Two days since I first shoved the barrel into my mouth and considered pulling the trigger. Two days since I begged for the strength to kill Bodhi, and even two days since I began considering the answer might be to kill Melanie instead.

But she knew when I thought those thoughts, and she invaded me with the vivid memories of being with her— memories intense and arousing enough to cause me to throw off the sweat-damp sheets and leap up in aching, single-minded mania. Seconds stretched into eternity before the rage of desire melted away to only longing and melancholy. There was no way I could see to hurt her. I'd shoot myself in the heart immediately after, because I couldn't imagine a future without her in it.

Please stop thinking things like that! It's not fair to you, and it's not fair to me.

"Why are you doing this to me?" I roared.

I don't mean to. I don't want to! She said. *I can't help it. This is who I am. This is how I was created. This is what I do.*

"I don't think I can do this anymore," I said. I staggered out of the bedroom and into the living room. The pistol lay on my desk. I picked it up and touched the barrel to my temple.

Don't! Please, don't!

"And why not?" I asked, my finger brushing against the trigger. "You'll simply find someone else to win you over, and you'll do this again." I rested the finger firmly on the trigger this time.

It's not easy for me, Nathan. I feel pain now as you feel pain.

"What?"

We are meant to be together. It is our time. And while you ignore me, you ignore the fact that I ache for you the same way you ache for me. Right now, I am... worthless. I'm an empty house, cavernous and silent, waiting for the right person to come inside. I am waiting for you!

"I didn't know that," I murmured.

Please... come take me. It's what must be.

"I need you to leave me alone. I need five minutes of silence."

With that, she was gone. I could hear the hum of my refrigerator, the buzz of the air conditioner, and the distant susurration of partygoers going out for the evening. The smell of fish tacos wafted up from the ground floor. I went into the bathroom and vomited again. Swigging Listerine from a nearly-empty bottle, I swished out the taste and spat into the sink.

She was in pain. I shook my head. It took two minutes to put on a loose pair of jeans and a t-shirt, another minute for shoes.

The knife I'd bought when I picked up the pistol lay on the kitchen counter, along with forgotten dishes and a broken coffee cup. I picked it up and slid it into my pocket. The pistol I tucked into my rear waistband, like a television thug. With a possibly-last glance around my apartment, I realized there was something I needed to do.

At some point in the past two weeks, I'd acquired a phone number. I punched the number into my phone and listened to it ring.

"Who's this?" Bodhi answered.

"You know who it is," I said. "I just want you to know that I'm coming for her tonight."

"You're going to die," he growled. "It won't be pleasant."

"I think we both know that's right," I said. "The question is simply when."

I disconnected and tossed the phone onto the couch. If I died, I might as well let the cops know who I'd spoken to last.

I slammed the door behind me and made my way down to the street.

* * *

There was no house further out on Ocean Avenue than Bodhi Reilly's. His entire yard was walled, with sand and sea grass on three sides. I spotted the cameras over the gate and went around toward the back. Sure enough, he had another gate that allowed access to the beach. I climbed the gate and dropped into the backyard, within sight of the house. Only a few seconds' soft padding brought me to the edge of the back patio. I stayed at the corner of the house, partially concealed by a bird-of-paradise.

"I heard you coming," Bodhi's voice rose from somewhere inside the shadows of his patio.

"I figured you might," I said, pulling the pistol out of my waistband.

I knelt and moved a couple of steps toward the house. The shadows on one of his wrought-iron chairs were darker than the others. I took another step closer to the house and raised the pistol.

"You know that gun won't do," he said. He moved. Metal glinted off moonlight. "Mine will."

"You seem awful calm for someone about to die," I said.

"And you apparently never asked her what happened if you don't follow the ceremony. You'll be the one who dies."

"I'm not afraid of threats."

"It's not a threat. It's a fact—*she* does it. Try to kill me with that, and *she* will tear you limb from limb."

"You don't know that."

"I do." Bodhi began to stand and raise the pistol. "You just haven't seen it yet."

"Well, for the record, I don't plan to kill you with this."

"Okay—"

Bodhi!

Melanie's voice echoed in my mind, but I can only imagine what it felt like to Bodhi. He staggered, reaching for his head. I knelt against the house and jammed the pistol into the gap between the wall and rows of plants and fired several times into the shadows.

Bodhi jerked and lurched into the light, a howl erupting from somewhere in the back of his throat. He dropped the gun and frantically reached for the damaged leg. I flung my pistol aside and pulled the knife from my pocket. I snapped it open and he staggered toward the back door to get inside.

I bolted after him, tackling him just as he crossed the threshold. We both fell to the floor, crashing hard on the ceramic tile. Bodhi cried out again as he hit, landing with his weight on damaged legs.

There was nothing else left to do.

I plunged the knife into his back. He roared, slamming his elbow back into my face. Something popped or something broke, and I was thrown mostly off him. He tried to scuttle away. I grabbed the knife again and yanked it from the wound. Surprising me, he spun and kicked at me with the grazed leg, hitting me in the face again. On hands and knees, I lunged at him, pinning his legs below my chest and slamming the knife into his chest for the first time.

He was stronger than I thought and grabbed my knife hand with one hand and the side of my head with the other. He began to dig a finger into my cheek. I wrestled the knife away and plunged it into his chest a second time. This time he released my head and tried to grab the knife with both hands. But then...

With a spitting, explosive hiss, Melanie leaped out of the darkness, fully nude, and grabbed his hands with fingers longer than I remembered. With feline grace, she threw herself up and over his head, yanking his arms up and out of the way. Muscles played under her tawny skin as she threw her weight on his fists.

Bodhi roared for help. Melanie's head snapped around to glare at me, all wide eyes and snarling teeth. I clamped one hand over his mouth and slammed the knife into his chest again. His back arched. He tried again to scream. My grip on his mouth tightened. I plunged the knife into him again, and again, and again.

Unable to speak or move, his eyes met mine—pleading mingled with anger, pain, and fear. He knew how this was going to end. He'd already been where I was, and done this same thing to someone else.

I pictured a small Asian man dying beneath Bodhi's strong hands, and stabbed him again.

Only when he'd quit moving did I stand. Melanie climbed to her feet, her powerful body spattered and speckled with the same blood that covered me from eyes to groin. I took a deep breath and spent a few seconds clenching and unclenching my fists.

"We're going to need to get this place cleaned up," I told her. "We have to get rid of the knife and the pistol, and we have to get rid of the body. We need to do it tonight."

"I don't think the police will come," she said.

"I don't either. We're out here by ourselves, and the people on the beach are always setting off firecrackers. The deputies are going to be in town, and they'll probably stay there, but someone will eventually come— Fed Ex, a neighbor, maybe a client. This place needs to look normal."

Melanie nodded.

"Take off your clothes," she said. "Take the knife, both pistols and the clothes, and throw them into the ocean. No one will look for them there."

"Are you sure?" I asked, pulling the shirt over my head.

"I've done this before," she responded. "Many times. I've often lived near oceans."

"What about him?"

"I'll take care of him." She stood there, tanned and gold, her hair blowing in the breeze coming in through the door, her cappuccino-colored eyes watching me, her utterly perfect mouth set tight. "I'll be done before you're back."

"...How?"

"Don't ask me that, Nathan. Just remember... I'm not human, and my appetites are not normal."

By the time I'd waded back in from the surf, the body was gone, the blood was missing, and she had dressed in only a thin nightdress.

She took me there in the living room, only feet from where I'd killed her former lover, and from where, I am certain, she disposed of him.

Inside her, where she always said she wanted us to be.

* * *

That was eleven years ago. I stayed in town; California and the beach was too much a part of me. As it was, after Bodhi Reilly had disappeared and abandoned his wife, she and I got together. We purchased a house at the far end of town, away from Ocean Avenue, but with several hundred feet of private beach of our own. I ended up starting my own ad agency, frequently hiring people from out of state, and last year, my share of income was nicely into eight figures— all for creating logos, fonts, simple images, things like that. It's a good life.

She never leaves my side. Though every morning I go out on the beach before dawn as the darkness slips down below the horizon to watch the early morning ships ply the coastline and listen to the seabirds circling above. This I do alone. It is my quiet time. She comes with the sun.

She inspires me, and she says I inspire her, too. Physically, she remains as beautiful, if not more so than ever before, and the sex... the sex is transformative. There are things she knows how to do that no humans know. It has been amazing. It has the greatest time of my life. And, if it wasn't for the fact that last year she told me she was starting to feel bored, it would be perfect.

It's not her fault she gets bored. It's who she is, and what she was created to be. I do what I can to alleviate it. I avoid patterns. There are no date nights, no weekly trips to a farmer's market or a movie. Instead I stagger them: an amethyst necklace here, wildflowers there, a handwritten letter, a trip to Santorini, gymnastic back-seat sex alongside the highway in Big Sur; but there is only so much I can do. She tells me she has only been with two other men as long as she has been with me—a fact that seems to make her oddly proud. It makes me happy, too.

Above me, I hear a step in the sand, high up, where the sand is soft and pulls at your feet with every step. It's the third time I've heard it this year. In the pre-dawn light, I glance down to my lap, where I have hidden a pistol. I touch my finger to the trigger. I plan to be with her a lot longer.

No matter how many people I have to kill.

After all, it keeps her from getting bored.

IN THE RIVER

JEAN GRAHAM

Jean Graham's short fiction has appeared in the anthologies "Memento Mori," "Misunderstood," "Dying to Live." and "Time of the Vampires," among others, and in the magazines "Mythic" and "Renard's Menagerie." She lives in the Serra Mesa area of San Diego with six cats, 5,000 books, one husband, and innumerable dust bunnies.

"SON OF A BITCH is late."

From across the service center's round concrete table, I watched Dix scratch his beard and squirm on the curved concrete bench. He hated being out here in the open, away from our river bed encampment. So did I. But we had good reasons.

"Relax, okay?" I told him, though I could see it wasn't likely. "If it happens, it happens. Besides, helping me sell Angel's bill of goods to Goff isn't the only thing I asked you to come up here for."

He just looked at me and waited, not bothering to ask. So, I didn't bother with any more chit chat and just pulled the rolled-up bit of white cloth from my jacket pocket and laid it on the mosaic table top in front of him.

Dix looked down quizzically, probably, I thought, not daring to hope. Finally, he unrolled the little bundle and exposed the limp, brown seedling inside.

His blue eyes glistened with excitement. "Damn!" He breathed the word like some sort of invocation. "She really let you have one— for *me?*"

"Yeah, well, it took a bit of persuading. So, it's for you to take with you to Fresno, bro." I smiled at my inadvertent rhyme. "You got your San Diego-to-Fresno bus ticket yet?"

Never taking his eyes off the open bundle, Dix patted his own pocket. "Yeah. Took four solid months of panhandling to raise the cash, but I got it. Leaving tomorrow." He stroked the seedling with an index finger. "Just never thought Angel would let me take along one of these. *Damn.*"

At his touch, the seedling rallied and began to move. Like a tiny brown hand, it flexed and stretched its tendrils upward toward the sun.

I never got tired of watching them do that.

Dix looked delighted, but then hesitated with what I could only assume was a sudden attack of doubt. "Jesus, Sturge, how do I plant it once I get there?"

"That's easy. Any body of water will do, even the ocean. They do like rivers best, though. Put it in a bit of mud and it'll grow just fine. Angel's sent them to Sacramento, Berkeley, 'Frisco, Malibu, a dozen other places in the good old Golden State. And so far, she says, they're all thriving just fine. I'm not sure how she knows that, but she does. Senses them, I guess."

As though reacting to this news, the seedling writhed and wriggled in what I figured was a sort of tentacled happy dance. I reached across the table and hastily re-wrapped it. Wouldn't do to let anyone else see it. Not yet, anyway.

"Keep it in your pocket along with your ticket," I said. "It'll sleep until it sees the sun again."

Dix did as I said and then turned his still-nervous gaze back to the center's parking lot. "Now the son of a bitch is even later," he said.

I looked around. Still no Goff in sight. The surly teenage clerk behind Body Beautiful's double-plex security window had been giving us the evil eye for half an hour now. This fancy-tiled table we were holding down was meant for the gas station/car wash/convenience store customers. Customers who might easily be scared off by the sight— or the smell — of two homeless guys sitting ten feet from the front door. A bath in the river's no substitute for a hot shower, and for most of us, laundromats are nothing but a distant memory.

"Just give him time," I told Dix, and eyed the giant wood-block clock face over the car wash entrance. Ten after six. "I know his kind of slime. He'll show."

On my least-favorite-vermin list, three names pretty much say it all. There's Fatso, the chihuahua-sized rat who's damned and determined to share my bedroll most nights. Then there's cockroaches— well, all roaches in general, really. They're the hardiest species on the planet, it's said, but you don't want to share beds with them, either. And at the top of the heap sits the worst piece of crap of them all, a certain self-proclaimed "independent film producer" who calls himself Marcus Bantam Goff.

"Can't say as I ever saw any of the shit he cranks out." Dix tapped an impatient finger on the heavy table's turquoise tile. He hadn't lived long enough to learn much about patience, I figured. He was twenty-four, though his blond beard and scruff of dirty hair made him look older. He sighed and hiked his grubby overcoat higher on his shoulders. (When you sleep outdoors, even sunny San Diego can get chilly on Autumn nights.) "Even before the old lady locked me out," he said, "I never had a computer, never had the Internet. But I've heard say that's where all the porn is these days."

"Most of it," I agreed. Hard to believe a kid Dix's age had never had the chance to experience web porn. "Of course, I can't access his crap from the library's free computers 'cause that sort of stuff is blocked. But I can sure as hell read his ads for it. The bastard has his claws into more than just porn. You ever hear of *Bum Bashing? Dead Chix Snuff Flix? Queer Killers?*" Dix shook his head. "All his," I said. "Or all yours if you've got an online account and the all-important credit card."

"So, this Goff is the creep who got Eddie Lantz killed doing the bum fight video? The one that they say went viral?"

"Yeah. Some sickos get off on watching down-and-outers like Eddie get their brains bashed in. And assholes like Goff never seem to get any comeuppance. But this is going to be different. This is our chance."

Dix subconsciously stroked the pocket he'd slipped the seedling into and glanced nervously at the stand of trees behind the car wash. The trees hid our river camp site from the rest of the world.

"All that happened before I got here," he said. "How'd you get him to say he'd meet up with you, anyway?"

"I hit the lottery, sorta kinda. Found Goff's business card in Eddie's bedroll and called him up, that's how. Had to panhandle a bit myself to scrounge up the two bits for a pay phone. Can you believe that? Fifty cents for one lousy phone call? For over forty years Ma Bell only charged a dime. Now, anyone still willing to host a pay phone can charge whatever they please."

"So, you called the creep and invited him to... what? Tea?"

"Nope. Invited him to meet Angel. Told him she'd make a hot addition to any of his skin flicks, especially the ones with the naked mud wrestling."

Dix laughed. "Angel? Oh, sure, like she'd..."

"No, wait." I held up a hand. "He's a greedy leech, see, and I'm a *very* good salesman. I talked her up, gave him a really graphic description, the whole nine yards, y'know? Had him dying to meet her ASAP."

"Uh-huh. Don't suppose you mentioned that she lives in the river, in a homeless camp?"

"Oh, hell no. He'd never have shown up."

"He ain't showin' up now, either." Dix made a face at Body Beautiful's beige vinyl siding and its trendy cobalt blue and fuchsia pink trim.

A well-dressed man and woman waiting for the cadre of red-and-white uniformed valets to finish detailing their Lexus had just given us a wide berth and headed off to the next-door strip mall's Chinese take-out. Bad for business. I glanced over. More glares from the gas station pay window. Much longer, and Kid Surly in there was likely to call the Gestapo and have us hauled in for vagrancy.

"Let's get out of here," Dix pleaded. "Angel won't want to see this sleazeball anyway."

I shook my head. "Oh, she wants to see him. Angel was very fond of Eddie."

"Yeah, well…" Dix slid off the curved bench and stood up. "I'm goin' back."

I couldn't blame him, really. I hated waiting out here in the open, too. I hate waiting, period. Always have. In grade school, in high school, in 'Nam, and in the forty years I've spent since 'Nam (my choice) on San Diego's streets, everybody's always made me wait.

Dix didn't leave after all, though. He sat abruptly back down and inclined his head toward the strip mall's parking lot. "That him?"

I had to twist clear around to see. A neon yellow Fiat roared into the lot and pulled into a handicapped space in front of the strip mall's Starbucks.

"Wouldn't be surprised," I said. "He'd be just the sort of jerk to park in a blue space and dare a cop to cite him." I puffed out my chest and waved my arms around. "'Go ahead, give me a three-hundred-dollar ticket. Think I'll pay it? Screw you!'"

Dix harrumphed. "Well, he doesn't look like much."

And he didn't. The man climbing out of the Fiat (hell, I'd half expected him to show up with some goon of a bodyguard, but he was alone) looked nothing like

I'd imagined the all-important Goff. On the phone, he'd sounded…. well, taller somehow. The guy ambling toward our table was boyishly slight, freckled and sort of mousy looking, a nerd in a pricey designer suit. He reached the table and gave us a rather disappointed once over. Obviously, we weren't what he'd expected, either.

"You Sturgis?" he asked me.

I nodded. "Yeah. And this is Dix."

He made no offer to shake hands. Probably just as well. I'd have needed to wash afterward. I gestured at the third, unoccupied bench, but he just stood there as though trying to assess which position might be upwind. He gave up after a few moments and finally sat down, twitching one scrawny shoulder in defeat and extracting an Apple iPad from an inside pocket.

"Okay," he said. "I'm here." Perfunctory, with an undisguised air of contempt. "So, where's the bitch?"

Dix started to say something, but closed his mouth when I shook my head at him.

"She's right over there," I told Goff, and used my chin to indicate the stand of trees.

You couldn't see the water from here: the river bank is too overgrown. Then too, there's very little actual water in the river because of the drought. We don't call it "the San Diego trickle" for nothing.

Goff squinted at the trees and huffed, "Right over *where?*"

"Angel lives in the river," I said.

"Somewhere around a thousand of us live along the river," Dix added. "Guess most people don't know that. It's twenty miles of tree-covered shelter."

Goff ignored him. "Angel, huh?" he said to me. "I thought you said this broad was from Vietnam? Aren't they all named Ni-goo-yen, or something like that?"

"Nguyen." I gave the name its proper "win" pronunciation. "But not Angel. Her Vietnamese name is Thân hô Mênh."

He tapped something into the iPad, but carefully kept it close to his chest so that we couldn't see the screen. "So that translates to Angel, does it?"

I nodded. "Part of it does."

He didn't ask what the rest translated to, so I didn't elaborate.

More screen taps. "And you think she's a good bet for my *Broad Brawls* videos, huh? Good in a scrap, is she?"

I gave him my very best brown-nosing smile. "She's never lost a bout yet."

"Uh-huh." Goff's freckled face pinched itself into a nonplused sneer. "So, why isn't she here?"

I kept on smiling. "Angel prefers to meet clients on her own turf."

"Clients?"

"Uh-huh."

He gave each of us a disgusted look, the sneer growing wider and uglier. "All right, what the hell is this? Some sort of a con? Are you her pimp, or something? I'm not looking to hire some whore for a lay here, you know." He slapped the top edge of the iPad twice. "You bring her up here. *My* clients come to *me*."

"Not this one."

Dix squirmed some more, and I let a lengthy silence go by while the *swish-clunk-whoosh* of the car wash droned on behind us.

"It's not a con," I said, my voice dripping sincerity. "But if you want to see her in the nude, in her element and at her mud-wrestling best, you have to go down there." I motioned toward Kid Surly. "It's not as if the car wash here would allow such a meeting unless you wanna involve the cops."

My sweeping gesture toward the tree-shrouded river sent Goff's eyebrows climbing.

"You're serious?" he squeaked. "She's down in the goddamned river bed somewhere?" He stood up, powered off the tablet and slipped it back into its silk-lined hiding place inside his coat. "Screw that, Sturgis. I have subordinates for that kind of crap. If you think I'm hiking through some fricking, trash-infested swamp…"

"Fine," I interrupted, and Dix and I stood, too. I figured it was time to give the fishing line a little slack. "I told her you wouldn't be worth her time. She can get a hell of a lot better deal out of Jack Trimble down in Miami. The guy's a jerk-off, but he's been putting out some killer naked mud-wrestling videos. They're shot in a giant glass tank. With alligators."

The look he gave me could have melted another six feet off the polar ice cap. But I could see just a flicker of indecision lingering under the indignant facade.

He was mine in that moment. Mine, and Angel's.

"How far?" Goff's tone clearly implied that his eight-hundred-dollar shoes weren't going to do any long-distance hiking through our river bed.

"Five minutes," I said. "Just down the slope over here."

"Yeah," Dix chimed in. "There's even a foot path."

Goff just stood there, glaring at us, waiting.

I turned to give the scowling kid behind the plex pay window a parting smile, then joined Dix to head for the river. There was a gap in the chain link fence where a small, natural rock shelf had stopped its two ends from meeting. Once we squeezed through that, we were on the south bank, though we still couldn't see any water. We turned west onto the path, letting Dix take the lead.

Down here, you didn't have to go far to be reminded that the river housed a sizeable homeless community. Goff's nose started wrinkling before we'd gone twenty paces. He fumbled a monogrammed handkerchief out of his suit pocket and pressed it over his nostrils. It only slightly muffled his string of scatological obscenities.

I didn't even notice the smell any more. Hadn't for years. Like everything else down here, you just got used to it. Given a thousand camped-out homeless people living on a swampy river bank, an overgrowth of weeds, trees and thick brush, and an algae-blooming river with water that doesn't move much, and well... calling it "pungent" would be an understatement, big time.

Goff didn't look any happier, presumably because his nose was still objecting, when the river's residents began emerging from cover all around us. None of them spoke, but then, they didn't need to. Like most outsiders who strayed into the river bed (or who encountered us on any street, for that matter), Goff tensed up briefly and then simply convinced himself that all those grizzled faces just weren't really there. You could almost see the shutters go down. The homeless, from time immemorial, have always been invisible to the homed.

We passed Carl, sitting with his terrier, Bitsy; Jonesy, watching us through Coke bottle eyeglasses taped together over his nose; Mona, our oldest resident; Ed, a new arrival who mostly kept to himself; Biker, who'd once been one; and Morrey, our chess master. But they weren't there. Next came Tweaker, one of our many substance abusers; Bud, a big, gray grizzly of a man; Merv and his lady friend Dinah, all non-existent. Each of them smiled and nodded at Dix and me as we passed. All of them had names, lives, a past, maybe even family somewhere who cared about them but couldn't care *for* them. To Goff, though, they had just become invisible.

Shutters closed.

We pressed through a narrow gap in the overgrowth. And though more than a few of the river's residents quickly moved in to follow us, Goff pretended that they hadn't.

"So..." he said, and his voice betrayed the barest hint of a nervous quaver. "What's this Angel broad look like, anyhow?"

"Like most of her kind," I answered, and almost added that this wasn't the racist comment it might sound like. "She came from the 'Kong."

Goff's baffled look said clearly that he had no clue what I meant by that. I guess 'Nam was just too, too long ago.

"The Mekong Delta," I explained, but there still weren't any light bulbs coming on. So, I fed him a little more fishing line. "She was a tiny baby when I found her. But I could tell she was already something special, even then."

That stopped him. He tugged on my jacket to stop me then wiped his hand on his used-to-be spotless coat sleeve.

"What kind of bullshit is this, Sturgis? I didn't come down here to see some middle-aged bitch you supposedly smuggled out of Viet Nam forty-five years ago!"

"Actually…" I made it a bit of a point to dust off the place on my jacket that he'd touched. "…You did."

On the path ahead, Dix had turned back to wait for us, one hand still covering the seedling's pocket protectively. The camp members who'd been following us had stopped to wait, too. So many faces: expressions that were curious, anxious, fearful, suspicious, and combinations of them all.

"Smuggling her out was the easy part," I said. "Growing her once she got here took a little more effort. But she did fine. Took to our river just as if it were the 'Kong back home. You'll see. We're almost there."

Goff's monogrammed handkerchief had vanished back into his coat, and the iPad had re-emerged. He began tapping more virtual keys, mumbling obscenities all the while, then held the thing up in front of him, presumably taking video of my back when I started off once more. Just a few steps farther on, our entourage reached the footpath junction, one fork of which led down to the river. When Dix turned off onto it, Goff balked again.

"Oh, come on! I've seen this river from up on the freeway overpass. It's wet, green and goddamned slimy down there. You go in and bring the bitch out here!"

Dix shook his head. "Angel doesn't take well to being ordered around," he said. "Be nice to her, and she might meet you halfway. Maybe."

It looked for a moment as though Goff might bolt. But he took one look at the growing crowd of homeless onlookers he'd have to charge through and obviously thought better of it.

Guess they weren't completely invisible after all.

"She's right through here." Dix pulled back a leafy, overhanging branch and gestured for our guest to take the lead.

With a snarl, he did, roughly shouldering through the brush to the water's edge. We all trooped after him.

He didn't see her at first.

No one ever did.

She's hard to see most of the time, unless you knew how and where to look for her. The San Diego River is overgrown with brush and scrub trees along its entire length. No buildings face the water, so many city residents never see the water in its entirety. All that makes it a perfect haven for us— and for Angel. She'd planted herself thirty feet out in the water, surrounded by rushes, floating debris, a few ducks, and the ever-present green algae. She was, when we got closer, very easy to spot. Most likely because I'd told her who was coming, she'd assumed a *very* pleasing shape.

Goff gawked.

From here, it looked for all the world like a brown-skinned, big-breasted woman was standing buck naked out there in the water. Long arms, long legs, long hair all flowed together into an idealized human form, a female shape that would set most males, and one particular porn peddler, drooling. Goff's iPad zeroed in to take video. When Angel moved, though, it took an abrupt dive from Goff's hands and *thocked* into the weeds.

"What the hell...?"

Angel began to morph as she moved toward us, green water slapping at her thighs, the mud making loud, sucking sounds beneath her "feet." I never tire of watching Angel morph. No matter what she becomes, the return to her true shape is, at least to me, a beautiful thing to behold. As were all her seedlings, soon to grace every waterway in California.

With a sound like hot oil bubbling, the voluptuous nude began to stretch skyward. The disturbance made the water ripple, startling three squawking ducks into flight and sending dank-smelling patches of algae bobbing up onto the shore at our feet. Angel's round, brown thighs grew taller and thinner. Head, shoulders, arms reached up and out until, no longer resembling anything human, they became the gnarled and twisted branches of what most people would assume to be a tree.

A dead tree.

Except, of course, that Angel was neither.

When she reached the river bank, her tentacled "feet" came slithering up out of the water to wrap themselves around Goff's expensive designer shoes. Goff made a frantic effort to back away, but Angel's needle-sharp branches, cracking like dry bones in a bonfire, had already reached down to embrace him.

Goff's eyes went wide, and his mouth fell open in a silent scream as writhing, snapping tendrils continued to envelop him. No one moved to stop it. Couldn't if we'd wanted to. We stood in silence and watched as Thân hô Mênh slowly drew a feebly struggling Marcus Goff into herself. Her brown trunk grew around his legs first, then gradually cradled the rest of him in soft, undulating tissue, until nothing but one clenching hand remained. Then that, too, was gone.

I took a deep breath and smiled.

Thân hô Mênh. Half of her name means "angel."

The other half means "guardian."

And she was very fond of Eddie Lantz.

* * *

SDPD towed the yellow Fiat from the strip mall's parking lot eight days later. Then they spent three more days dragging the river for a body that wasn't there. We stayed out of sight in the undergrowth and watched.

I found it more than a little ironic that the "body" they were looking for watched, too.

Yes, he's still alive and breathing. Angel's embrace can kill, but it can also nurture, transfigure, redeem.

The redeemed Marcus Goff has now traded his iPad for a bedroll, and camps every night on the river bank, within view of his redeemer and her budding offspring. Several of Angel's seedlings are sprouting on her island, ready soon to be carried to new homes elsewhere in sunny California. Their matriarch stands out there in the algae-green water and watches over them, over Goff, over us all.

Angel takes care of her own.

EYES OF THE SALTON SEA

SARAH READ

Sarah Read writes and reads in a house full of boys near Lake Michigan, with several short stories appearing in numerous magazines. You can follow her on her website www.inkwellmonster.wordpress.com

---

WE NEVER EXPECTED ANYONE to come back. Tourists won't eat fish that might have eaten other tourists, nor bathe on beaches where the sand is bone and the water dark. They don't sip drinks on a shore that comes and goes, rises and falls in floods and droughts, and every time it leaves behind a fresh blanket of dead fish. But the scavengers came. First, birds—for the fish. Then, men—for the wrecks that poked out of the fishbone sand like grave markers.

From the presidential suite of the abandoned resort, our balcony was a crow's nest where we watched for the treasure hunters and filmmakers who came in investor's SUVs towing rented boats. They brought their cameras and robots, their hired divers and diggers, and enough money for the few of us who had stayed behind to make a living. It was a new kind of tourist. Not rich, but wild. Dreamers, like Alden, all after gold and tragic stories. The Salton Sea had both.

We housed them on the first floor of the resort and I'd cook the fish they didn't think twice about—sometimes fish they'd bring in themselves. Their grins big—addicted to finding things, if only dinner.

And they'd ask Alden questions—interview him with their wide cameras. He'd show them his gold and pearl crucifix. But he never spoke of the ship in the inlet.

It was the sort of secret we didn't even tell each other. Because someday the water might clear again, or recede even farther, and all that would be left is gold and pearls. A treasure beach. When the shore shifts again.

I didn't like the big cameras or the questions or the way they stepped across the dry fish bones as if it was any other dirt beneath their feet. I encouraged the sunflowers and yucca claiming the old golf course, read the books left forgotten in the bedside drawers. Sewed the ballroom linens into new sundresses. I fed stale crumbs of ice cream cones to the swarms of birds who seemed to be the only ones who understood what it meant to belong here.

The treasure hunters asked Alden to guide them and he'd decline, on account of his feet—and they'd think he meant that it hurt or that he wasn't a strong hiker or swimmer. But I knew he was afraid that the curse would take another piece of him. Like it was waiting for the rest of him.

* * *

When we were young, the water was clear and fresh. My brother and I would swim in the shallows where a rainbow of polished round stones shone up at us like a thousand eyes. We'd watch the yachts bob across the sparkling water and listen to the music carrying over the waves. Alden celebrated the popularization of the bikini while I cupped my hands in the water, knowing that somewhere along the shore, The Beach Boys were swimming. While our mother cleaned resort rooms, we spent our days in an endless vacation.

We thought the sea was clear because it was young—unmarked by the wear of anxiety that had weathered our mother's face. We thought it was beautiful. But a young sea has a childlike temper, and one night it swallowed the towns and the desert around it. It had rained for a week straight and the swollen farm canals flushed their *agua negra* into the Salton Sea and the sea heaved. Some tourists ran for the boats and some ran for the surrounding hills. Alden and I perched on the roof of the resort. Mother stayed below, going from room to room—cleaning, as if in competition with the scouring wave.

When the water withdrew back into its bed—then lower and lower still till it shrank back to a fraction of its former self—the people withdrew as well. Each drifting farther from the other till nothing was left but the broken bits of resort towns and those of us willing to stay, and those who had died in the water. Like mother, her apron a shroud, a duster bouquet of wet feathers in her stiff fingers. The receding water had pulled her from the hotel, as if calling her to the beach to play. Her hair had caught on the wrought iron fence and tied her there. I spent hours untying those dark, wet knots. I would not let Alden cut them.

When the tourists left, the workers followed—their white service jackets the same no matter where they went. And then the fishermen left—back to the ocean coast, to happier shores where the fish didn't tie your gut in knots. To ancient oceans with mature tides and not the fickle temper of this inland sea.

The town was nearly deserted. The big hotels sat like empty seashells, still stinking of the life that used to be there, pieces beginning to break off around the edges. The news declared that the pleasure towns had turned to ghost towns.

We supposed, then, that we were ghosts. And we haunted our old resort, stretching across luxury linens in the presidential suite. We needed that familiar shore, needed to be near the cluster of concrete crosses set back from the water in the tall, dry grass. Near where mother lay safe under the desert. I dug my roots deep into the rocks.

The beach, now extending hundreds of meters from the resort doorway, shone white with crushed fish bones. Their desiccated bodies plated the bone sand like scaled armor. The sharp jaws and jagged ribs of wrecked yachts poked out of the slick mud.

As everything dried, baked under the desert sun, the toxins that had stripped that water to glass clarity concentrated in the remaining sea so that at high noon the water was the color of a sunset and a chalky residue clung to anything that had been wet.

When the wind blew, that powdered bone carried the poisons right between our teeth, into the corners of our eyes. It flavored the back of our throats like a bitter pill. If you squinted and held your nose, it was paradise.

We turned to the beach looking for whatever might be left of our lives—or anything we might use to forge new ones. We ran past the old shoreline out onto the mud flat that had once been seabed and across the rainbow eye stones that had watched as our world fell apart.

The new shoreline rose and fell as if the earth beneath it rocked. It carved out twisting inlets and hidden lagoons. We followed it, hiking the topography of old seafloor, near the hills where the stones betrayed an ancient high-water mark that promised a future of nothing but sea. We came to a stretch of choppy shallow water surrounding the battered hull of a ship. It was larger than the yachts of rich musicians that had dotted the water before the flood. It had a round hull and two tall masts that trailed tattered sails like funnel webs. A third mast lay beside it, half-buried in sand. The wood was crusted with an armor of sprawling arthropods.

Alden waded out into the water toward the wreck. He crawled around the hull in search of gold and silver, but instead we found bodies—staring up out of the water, eyes like a thousand polished stones.

I stepped lightly into the water. I was scared to see my brother splashing, leaving a foaming wake that disturbed the surface. He bent and dragged his fingers through the rocks, looking for coins. I nervously filled my sundress pockets with pretty stones, my own small treasures. I paced the shallows and sat in the stones and twisted my hair, tasting that new chemical tang that hung suspended in the still air on the back of my tongue.

The way the water nudged the bodies, they looked as if they slept, and might wake and grab my ankle. Small brown birds with feathers as fine as hair bobbed their heads in the water and nibbled at the corners of their mouths.

Alden pulled his hands from the water, cupping them below his face and smiling for the first time since the flood. His fingers—wrinkled and stinking from the water— clutched a gold and pearl crucifix.

He wanted to stay and find more. He wanted to move the bodies, comb the wreckage, pick it all apart like a bird on a fish. But the sky was growing dark, threatening rain. I backed away from the water, afraid of the fickle shore and storm-fed tides. Alden was forced to follow. He held his hands to the sky and marked the spot in his memory, tracing the old shoreline pattern on the hill above.

As we walked back to the resort, the bright white beach began to snap under our feet. The water turned red as rust, and the rainbow of stones was buried under stiff, dried fish.

He tried to go back the next day, but the skin of his feet had turned the color of the dry tilapia shore, the whites of his eyes the color of the rusted-out campers in the surrounding desert. Whether it was poison from the toxic water, a corpse virus, or a ghost ship curse, he didn't care. He limped, feet dragging through the fish, till the fever slowed him, then stopped him, and he knelt in the crackling granules of beach.

"Bones," Alden said, running his hands through the splinters. "Some are fish, some are birds, bet some are from the yachts we never found."

I knew he said it to scare me.

It worked.

* * *

The scavengers paid for their rooms at the resort, sometimes in food, sometimes in doubloons, or, when Alden wasn't looking, with pretty stones or sea glass. They tied their boats at the water's edge—a long walk, now, from the resort's door, and getting longer every year. They hiked across the bone beach, inspecting destroyed structures, tiptoeing around the bulbs and fins of unexploded dummy bombs from the naval base on the north shore. They followed old train tracks that lead straight into the water, and tied rags around their faces to keep from breathing in the dust cloud of evaporated pesticides and fertilizers. They dug in the sand and trawled from their boats, and—if they were brave or foolish enough—dove in the water.

They found artifacts of the Salton Sea's heyday. Speed boat parts, depression glass shards, even a flask engraved with F.S. that the diver swore was Sinatra's.

Some would ask about the lost Spanish galleon. Others would laugh, and the night would be spent telling tall tales of tall ships.

The diver with pale brown eyes the color of sand drying in the sun was the first to ever ask about a curse. He'd met a fisherman, now working far from here, who spoke of his old seaside town and its flood wrecks and the riches no local would touch and that no diver could find.

Alden just laughed and shook his head. *Don't scare away the business* is the motto of every haunted shore. Stories sell but paradise sells better.

"I'm going to find that wreck," the golden-eyed diver promised.

Every season there is at least one treasure hunter who wants to buy more than room and board from me. If I feel like it, I say yes. If he has nice eyes.

The golden-eyed diver had scars like he'd been at war with the sea. The snaking lightning of jellyfish whips. The dotted crescent of a small shark's appetite. The starburst of a rogue harpoon.

I traced them with my fingertips and gathered his stories. And then he asked for mine.

"I can tell you know about the wreck," he said, smiling with half his face, scolding with the other half.

"It's just an old wives' tale," I said.

"Tell me anyway. What do the wives say?"

"There's a ship, somewhere out there. Too big and too old for the Salton Sea and no one remembers it. There are bodies aboard—rich people with nice jewelry. Gold. Pearls. They must have gone down in a flood, or when the water receded."

"But no one has ever been there, to see what's left?"

"The water changes. Sometimes it's sea, sometimes it's sand. Bone. It might have been re-submerged in toxic water, or buried in a sandstorm. There are people who say they've seen it, but no one has ever seen it twice."

"Ah. Well, not much point then. How far have you been out onto the sea bed?"

His probing fingertips and thick red wine made me sleepy, dizzy. I wanted to lay my head on his sun-hot chest and sleep.

"A half day, no more. I could never sleep on those bones."

* * *

In the morning, he was gone, as adventurers often are—but this was the first time I felt sad for it. Alden noticed.

"You wanted that one to stay?"

"Wouldn't have minded. Best he left, though. He only wanted the wreck."

"They all want the wreck, even the ones who don't know it. You didn't tell him where, did you?"

"No. Told him it was probably long buried. Or never existed." I toyed with the stones in my pocket.

Alden nodded approval and handed me coffee. "Maybe he'll come back for you after he's made his fortune."

"Ass."

Some did come back, but not for me. They came for treasure.

I licked my lips, tasting him still. "I hope he does come back, though. He had good stories."

I stretched my sore back and made the climb to the roof to clean the day's fish. The birds had learned to catch the strings of offal I threw over the side. I named them by the way their pinions pivoted on the wind—after fish, the way they dove for each scrap. Marlin was the largest. He'd eat till the breeze couldn't carry him, then he'd drift into the sunflowers below.

The rooftop was a mess of fish guts and bird shit, awaiting a long overdue rain. The horizon promised a storm. Black clouds bubbled up above the dark strip of distant water studded with the bright jewels of treasure divers' boats. The rain would come and the shore would creep closer. The water would get deeper and bury her secrets.

Far to the north of the gathered boats, closer to the brewing storm and the distant hills, the water seemed rougher. The white gauze of chopped waves laced its surface.

A red boat bobbed on the inlet.

I dropped the pail of fish. I heard the frantic beat of descending wings behind me as I raced back down the concrete stairs, around and around, back to the lobby.

"Alden! Alden, he's at the inlet! He's in the water!"

Alden paled. "I don't know what to do about that."

"You have to stop him. We have to save him!"

"How? Dive in after him? Set a net? Bait a hook with your pussy?"

"Fuck you, Alden; we have to go."

"Go to the beach. I'll meet you there." He limped out from behind the desk.

I didn't wait to ask his plan. I ran.

My feet found their way across the bone beach, each footstep snapping down, sinking beneath the small skulls, their empty sockets folding shut under my toes. Raising a fine dust of chemical calcium. I dodged bubbling mud pools and slid over polished eye stones. I grazed my shins on young yucca growing up from the new beach, until my knees hit the bone grit of the hidden inlet. The water was deeper than it had been years ago. Only the tip of a mast was visible above the water, its scrap of sail like a grey flag.

The red boat rocked offshore, anchor dropped into the dark water, her deck bare, her winch line taut.

I advanced as far as I dared, my toes right up against where the sand turned wet.

"Robb!"

I knew he couldn't hear me. There was no one else on the boat. His whole life was strung on that winch line. I twisted my hair into fisherman's knots. The sky had begun to growl.

Alden came stumbling up behind me, a large package under his arm, his pack slung over his shoulder. He let it fall to the sand and pulled the ripcord, and a small inflatable raft expanded at our feet.

"Is it safe?" I stared at the dark water and the thin rubber bottom of the raft.

"No. Doesn't matter—we have to do this."

We dragged the raft to the chopping waves. I flinched as the water brushed my feet. Alden didn't touch the water. He hopped over the side and pulled me in after.

We cast off and paddled to the idling boat. I climbed over the rail and ran to the winch, slammed the lever, and anxiously watched as the line coiled slowly around the bobbin.

Alden tied the raft to the boat and stumbled to my side, pulling a pair of loppers from his pack. He reached out and clipped the line.

The sprung end whipped across my face. I cried out and fell back against the railing.

"Alden!" I cupped a hand over my bleeding cheek as my vision cleared. "What are you doing?"

He had moved to the side where he sawed at the anchor line.

"He knows where the wreck is. He'll lead a hundred other divers here. They won't wait for another quake wave or a drought to clear this dark water. They'll have it stripped clean in a day. And everything we've waited for will be gone."

"I wasn't waiting for anything. Is this the only reason you stayed?"

"We'll power the boat out of the inlet and set it adrift."

"What about Robb? He could die down there. Without his line—"

"Just another diving accident."

"You heartless fuck."

"Happens all the time. You think this is the first time a diver's found the wreck? I ought to throw you in, too. Blabbing secrets to a scavenger."

"*You're* a scavenger. No better than them. Worse. How many divers have you left down there? How many?"

Alden threw the boat in gear and angled it toward open water. He steered against the tide as we wound toward the broad horizon, our raft bouncing along the side.

I watched the black water behind us. It had gone perfectly still. Even the wake of the boat calmed too quickly.

There was no sign of the diver.

* * *

The other divers noticed Robb's absence. Their competitive nature didn't follow them ashore.

They assumed he'd run out of funding, or hope—or that he'd hit a honey spot and camped out. No one would think the worst for hours.

Maybe not till his boat was found.

If it was found.

I tried to remember how many times I'd heard this conversation. How many divers had been reported lost. I wondered how many I never even knew about.

Alden laughed with the crews, his twisted feet twitching under the table.

They were still gathered in the lobby, increasingly drunk, riding out the storm with an endless supply of stories on their tongues, when the report came in that Robb's boat had been found drifting. Al at the West Shore Casino had spotted it. The police were on their way—a courtesy call.

Alden took the phone from my hand. "No. We haven't seen him since last night. Or was it this morning? Sis, was he there when you got up?"

The divers stared into their drinks, cheeks red and ears straining.

I scowled back as the report continued. The boat's line had been cut. Anchor gone. They suspected something— foul play, perhaps by another diver. But they could prove nothing. Gulls make bad witnesses. So do the eyes under the water.

The divers drank more—to Robb, and all the others that came before, to all the souls claimed by the sea.

The ones they would plunder.

Come morning, the divers were strewn about the lobby as if they themselves had been wrecked there, tossed around as if by the storm. Outside, rain hammered the corrugated steel that patched our roof. Steady dripping echoed through the resort halls. The sea had crept closer. Boats that had been anchored to shore now bobbed a hundred meters out. Our raft had been tossed halfway up the shore.

I put rum in the orange juice. Extra grease for the eggs. I knew they'd dive anyway.

I had just set the steaming pots of black coffee on the table when I felt the weight of eyes on my neck and a hand on my waist.

I turned and met a pair of golden eyes, bright like beach agates, shining round like ancient coins.

"Robb!" I threw my arms around his neck. His wet hair dripped cold water over my arms. His neck against my lips tasted like oil and aspirin.

The divers began to groan and pull themselves upright. They rose scowling at the sound of my shriek, but soon switched to cheering as they saw Robb, whole and hale, in my arms.

The commotion brought Alden out of the office. His smile split his face, but his eyes stayed cold.

Breakfast ran long as Robb recounted his survival story—his voice rough, throat salt-water chapped.

He'd felt his line snap. Watched it sink around him in coils, tugged by swift currents. Instead of surfacing, he said, he'd followed the line, followed the current, hoping he might find a treasure trove—a deposit of flotsam.

"Did you?"

"What did you find?"

"The ship," he said.

Every mug slowly lowered. Full forks sank back to plates.

"Did you go in?"

Robb smiled. He reached into a bag at his wetsuit belt and pulled out a fistful of treasure. Some gold, some silver, some black with oxidization, some glittered with cut stones, bright with pearls.

Nervous laughter circled the table.

"You didn't... You wouldn't disturb the remains, though. Must have just been... Maybe a box of treasure, right?"

Robb's grin widened. His eyes did not dialate, but remained fixed discs of gold. "Must have been a chest," he said. "Big pile of goods all in one place."

The nervous laugh circled again. Alden's smile slipped.

"You register your find yet?" a diver asked.

The hangovers were gone. Sobered with gold lust. Filled up with need.

Robb's round eyes bored into the man who'd asked. "'Course. Sorry if I kept you waiting. Made you worry. But when I saw my boat was gone, I swam to one of yours. Radioed it in while you were down."

No laughter, then.

"Now, about my boat..." He slipped the treasure back into his bag, precious metal rattling like chains.

"I'll give you a share in mine till your insurance—"

"You're welcome to come with—"

"I can draw up a contract right now—"

Robb held up his hands for silence. "I only want one partner in this, and it's the man who knows these waters best."

Every diver smiled, sure Robb meant them. Alden looked ill. Robb looked at Alden.

"It's not your feet that stop you from diving. It's what's down there. That ends now. I know you've been waiting a long time. Suit up." Robb tossed a mask at Alden and rose from his chair. He kissed me and took my hand, leading me back to his room.

The divers sat silent behind us like a flock of greedy birds.

* * *

"You shouldn't have gone into that water," I said. "You shouldn't have taken that gold." I twisted my hair as he buzzed around the room packing his bags.

"I didn't."

"What?"

"I was never in the water. Not there."

My heart dropped like a cut anchor. "But, your boat—"

"I was watching from the shore. By the hill."

I sat on the bed, my hands shaking. Every secret I had now lay naked under his bright eyes, like exposed seafloor under a hot sun.

He knelt before me, ran his fingers over the scab on my cheek. "I saw what he did. I saw you try to stop him." He squeezed my hands between his and leaned in to kiss me again. I pulled back.

"But those coins?"

"From older dives, other shores. I keep them in a jar on my dash, as a reminder."

"Of what?"

"Time. Death. That the sea controls both." He let go of my hands and zipped up his duffel bag.

"Where are you going? What are you going to do?"

"I'm going to put your brother in the water."

My gut heaved and I felt the sea at the back of my throat. "Robb, no. That beach… I know you don't believe the stories. Yes, there are bodies under there. And yes, probably treasure, too, but it's not worth it…"

"You're right, it's not. Not to me. But it is to your brother—worth lying for, worth killing for. Worth hanging around this ghost town. Must be worth dying for, right?"

"Please, Robb. He did an awful thing. But please don't hurt him."

"I'm not going to. He's going to hurt himself."

I shook my head. "It'll be harder than you think to get him in that water."

"No, it won't."

* * *

Most of the boats waited near the shore, hoping Robb would come to them, waiting for him to pass, so they could follow. Other boats swept up and down the water line, looking for him. None had seen him lead Alden north, darting from ruin to ruin, across the bone beach to the deep inlet.

Robb had warned me to stay at the hotel. I watched from the roof, from the center of a cloud of birds angry that I hadn't brought fish. I twisted my hair till the ends broke off in my fists.

I waited till they appeared on the far side of the mud flats before I followed.

Robb had no need of a boat, not in the calm black water that followed the storm. He used the same inflatable raft we'd used to sneak onto his boat. The water didn't ripple under their paddles.

They moved toward the spot where the grey flag had been as I crept across the round stones. I watched as Alden slipped a snorkel over his face. Not even a tank. He was still shaking his head, still reluctant. But Robb held out something shiny in his hand. Alden froze.

The gold? A gun? It didn't seem to matter which. Alden slid his legs over the rounded side of the raft. His withered feet dipped into the dark water and his back arched. He dropped into the sea.

The water rippled away from him, the circles widening, growing—till they were a ring of waves cresting back toward open water and shooting up onto the beach, tossing limp tilapia at my feet. I danced away as the water chased me and sheltered in a mound of yucca and cactus at the base of the hill. Over and over, each ring curled into another wave, like a wild tide climbing the shore as if to make the resort waterfront property again.

Robb steered the raft over the unnatural swells, surfing their crests back toward the beach. A wave slid the raft over the sand and deposited it on a pile of drying fish.

There was no sign of Alden.

Robb climbed from the raft and pulled me from my hiding spot, leading me back across the beach toward the resort as tendrils of water spilled across the mud behind us.

"We need to go back for him, Robb." I pulled against his grasp, wanting to turn around. "He'll drown in that tide. Christ, you didn't even give him a tank."

"Would have been a waste of a tank. The thing is done."

"What are you talking about?"

"They have the gold back. Their treasure is returned and they've caught their thief. The curse is broken."

"There's no goddam curse! We need to get him out of the water—he can't swim—"

"He can swim fine. He knows what the water wanted; knew what it would cost him. He didn't steal that gold, he bought it. Now he's paid for it."

He pulled me off the bone beach and into a copse of tall sunflowers.

Behind me came the sound of lapping water. Of music. The Beach Boys playing from a yacht that cruised past the resort. The arcing waves dragged at the beach, pulling dried fish back into the water, leaving fine white powder sand in their wake. I squeezed my eyes shut and swore I could hear laughter, the buzz of neon. The smell of fish frying, not baking on the shore.

I looked out at the sea, waiting to see if the water foamed with hunger, if it would surge right through the front doors and fill the rooms with bones and the dead. But the water had stopped, just kissing the beach. The music continued. Robb hummed along. The people on the yacht danced and waved.

"They can't stop here now—there's nowhere nice enough to stay. But they'll be back. A whole fleet of them. Crowds." Robb reached down and pulled up a fistful of weeds, the small beginnings of my sunflowers. "Better get to work. Let's get this place ready. Clear out the trash and trailers, fill the pool. Clean the rooms."

"What are you doing?" I grabbed the seedling flowers from him and pressed them back into the dirt.

"Treasure hunting." He shook the sticky soil from his hand.

I shook my head. The birds above us, circling, made me even dizzier. Robb placed his scarred hands on my shoulders. They felt like anchors, like heavy stones pressing me in place.

"I'm not the guy who takes treasure out of the sea," he said. "I'm the guy who puts it back. But if I found a billion dollars in treasure, I'd use it to live in a beachfront palace with a beautiful woman. So, I don't much see the need to sail off again. I'm staying."

I tore myself out of his grip, spat in his golden eyes, and ran back to the beach, north across the powdered bone to the edge of the water, as close to the hill as I could get.

The water was clear. Fresh as a young sea with a temper. I could see straight to the bottom. There was no Alden. No wreck. There were a thousand smooth stones, round and bright as eyes.

ABOUT THE EDITOR

A founding co-chair of the Horror Writers Association (HWA) San Diego chapter, Danielle Kaheaku is an active member of the HWA, Science Fiction & Fantasy Writers of America, and Romance Writers of America Professional Authors Network. With a BA in English from UHM and MA in English and Creative Writing from SNHU, she is a multi-published author and produced screenwriter.

Many of her projects have won literary and screenwriting awards, including Gold at the California Film Awards, Silver in the International Independent Film Awards, an Award of Merit at the New Renaissance Film Festival in London, and Foreword Book of the Year Awards. You can follow her online at www.TheWordWraith.com

CPSIA information can be obtained
at www.ICGtesting.com
Printed in the USA
FSHW010714040421
80139FS

9 780999 449509